NO ONE WILL HEAR YOUR SCREAMS

By
Thomas
O'Callaghan

WILDBLUE
PRESS

WildBluePress.com

NO ONE WILL HEAR YOUR SCREAMS published by:
WILDBLUE PRESS
P.O. Box 102440
Denver, Colorado 80250

WILDBLUE PRESS is registered at the U.S. Patent and Trademark Offices.

ISBN 978-1-952225-14-7 Trade Paperback

ISBN 978-1-952225-13-0 eBook

Cover design © 2020 WildBlue Press. All rights reserved.

Interior Formatting/Book Cover Design by Elijah Toten
www.totencreative.com

NO ONE WILL HEAR YOUR SCREAMS

For my beautiful granddaughter, Kristin

Into this wild abyss, the womb of
nature and perhaps her grave.

—John Milton

ACKNOWLEDGMENTS

I owe a very special round of gratitude to:

Eileen O'Callaghan, my loving and supportive wife, who shares life in so many wonderful ways, Kelliann Green, for her ongoing encouragement and support, Stephen Ohayon, Ph.D., a true gentleman, who inspired me tirelessly from the conception of my writing career, Noreen Nolan Patrone, who kept me on track, Matt Bialer, a trusted friend, Dick Marek, a man from whom I've learned much, and my dear friends Christine Charles, Marla Feder, Kathy Lord Nicolosi and Priscilla Winkler who listened, considered and advised.

Phil Adaszewski, NYPD, Margaret Timlin Johnsen, NYPD, (retired), and Doctor Susan Sachs, DACM, FASEMIP, L.Ac for their expert technical advice and skillful guidance.

And to my loving granddaughter, Kristin, who calls me PaPa and watches me melt.

CHAPTER ONE

"Hello? Is anyone there?"

The echo of the woman's voice was her only reply.

Where the hell am I? she wondered, as frenzy riddled her brain. "Hello?"

She attempted to move. But couldn't. Her head was restrained. As were her wrists and ankles. *Something smooth,* she thought. *And strong. Cloth?* "Oh, my God! It's rope!"

Heart racing, she caught sight of a shadowy figure that appeared to be moving above. "Hey you! You! Up there. Please help me!"

Silence.

It felt as though she were lying on moist sand. Cold moist sand. A glimpse of her left nipple fueled her growing hysteria.

Why am I naked? Her adrenalin surged. *Jesus Christ! . . . What's happening to me?*

The figure above was still moving.

As stomach acid refluxed into her throat, something slimy slithered across her abdomen before sliding down between her legs. She opened wide her eyes, willing herself to awaken from her nightmare only to have panic fill her for her gaze climbed walls of clay that formed a rectangle open at its top. She at its base.

She let loose a bestial scream. Blinked rapidly, and screamed again.

Willows, visible through the aperture of the grave, swayed against a cloudless sky, deaf to her howling. Indifferent to her plight.

CHAPTER TWO

Inside the shed Tilden put down the rubber tubing he'd been toying with and checked his watch. Reaching for his notebook he wrote: 'sodium thiopental, 100 mg. – ninety-seven minutes'. Tapping on the pad with his pencil, he narrowed his eyes, lost to thought. *Allowing for the difference in doses, between the sodium thiopental, a barbiturate, and the Isofluane, an ether, this filly had recovered slower than he'd anticipated. He raised an eyebrow. Maybe an interaction between the two drugs? A clash of anesthetics? That might do it.*

Putting an ear to the door, Tilden smiled. The bitch had finally stopped screaming. He made note of the time, reached for the device he had fitted with an adequate extension for the cleansing then stepped out of the shed and approached the grave. Embalming corpses inside the mortuary was rudimentary. It was important he be proficient in irrigating the living. Especially this one as she lies six feet below the surface of the ground.

Her adrenaline had stopped surging. Replaced by the flow of hopelessness. Resigned to her fate, she believed she was hallucinating when someone, or something, darted past the opening above.

"Is anyone there?" she hollered.

There was no reply.

"Anybody? Is anybody up there?" Her voice was coarse, her throat chafed.

Still no reply.

"Please! If you're up there . . ."

Someone's head emerged, partially blocking the blistering sunlight. After lingering for a second, maybe two, the head retreated. It was impossible to make out who it was.

Within seconds, the figure returned. He was holding an apparatus that resembled an elongated harpoon which he extended into the grave. As adrenalin surged and her heart pounded, she felt a searing sensation on the right side of her neck just before the embalming fluid gushed through the orifice he had made.

"Prostitutes," Tilden muttered eyeing the dying woman. *"When I'm done, every one of these vile sluts will be tracked down, cleansed, and obliterated."*

CHAPTER THREE

Silence filled the Manhattan courtroom as the jurors returned to their seats, fatigue and trepidation marking their faces.

"Madam Foreperson, I'm told you've reached a verdict?" It was the voice of State Supreme Court Justice Everett Hathaway.

"We have your honor."

Hathaway instructed his bailiff to retrieve the folded sheet of paper from the woman's hand. Receiving it, he read what had been decided after three days of deliberation. "You're all in agreement?"

The twelve jurors nodded.

The judge asked the defendant to stand then cautioned all in attendance to maintain silence and decorum while the verdicts were read before turning his attention to the sallow-faced woman who had agreed to act as the jury's voice.

"To the charge of unlawful imprisonment in the first degree, how do you find?"

"Guilty, your honor," she whispered, prompting the court reporter to ask her to speak up. "Guilty," she exclaimed.

"To the charge of predatory sexual assault against a child?"

"Guilty," she said, ignoring the defendant's glare.

"And to the charge of murder in the first degree? How do you find?"

"Guilty."

The defendant shot up out of his seat, pushed the defense table to the side, and bolted toward the jury box. Within inches of the foreperson he was tackled by a court officer who slammed his face into the floorboards.

Judge Hathaway pounded his gavel. "They'll be order in this courtroom!"

The lead juror screamed. Two of her cojurors quickly stood and huddled around her in an attempt to console her. But their efforts did little to remove the look of pure terror that marked her face. This same woman, who, only moments ago, had mustered the courage to stare down the coldhearted killer was trembling. Judge Hathaway hadn't missed the transformation. "You, ma'am, deserve the keys to the city," he said before thanking the jurors and dismissing them. After setting a date for sentencing, he brought the session to a close.

From his seat near the back of the room, Lieutenant John W. Driscoll nodded, pleased to see justice rendered. Reaching for his Burberry, he was about to leave when he was approached by a familiar couple.

"Mr. and Mrs. Keating, I thought I saw you leave."

Mrs. Keating smiled. "Not without saying goodbye."

"That's nice of you. These past few days must have been hell for you."

Mr. and Mrs. Keating exchanged looks. And as they did moisture coated their eyes. "I know justice was done but our grief may never end, Lieutenant," Mr. Keating said. "Thankfully, what has ended with the delivery of this verdict is our frustration, our impatience and a litany of sleepness nights."

"We know how hard you worked on this case, Lieutenant and to see you in the courtroom day after day truly warmed our hearts. Your presence helped lighten the burden of our emotions," his wife added. The Keatings were the parents of twelve-year-old Lori Keating, a blue-eyed innocent who had been abducted, sexually assaulted, and brutally murdered by the monster they had just seen convicted of his crimes. Driscoll, as Commanding Officer of the NYPD's Manhattan Homicide Squad, had led a task force of thirty dedicated professionals in the apprehension of the newly convicted felon, Arthur Covens.

Mrs. Keating opened her purse, withdrew a small envelope, and pressed it into Driscoll's palm. She took hold of her husband's arm, and headed for the exit.

Driscoll eyed the envelope upon which someone had etched 'Lt Driscol' in green crayon.

Inside was an unevenly folded sheet of loose-leaf.

Dear Lt Driscol -

Lori was my friend. She helped me with my
homework and stuff. If I did somthin bad she
would'nt tell on me. She was the bestest big sister
in the world. I know somthin bad happened to her.
Mom and dad told me she is in heven. Anyways.
Now I know shel'l be there when I pray. Thanks
for catching the bad guy. Your friend. Tammy ☺

A soft smile formed on the Lieutenant's face. Mindful of his ten-year-old daughter Nicole's 'Welcom Home Dady' Post-its his eyes glistened with tears.

John Driscoll was an 'everyman', of sorts, whose heart had been shaped by the happenings of his present and the hauntings of his past. His father, a machinist for the Long Island Railroad's Port Washington line, had provided for the physical needs of his family, but came up short in filling their emotional needs. Spending much of his time in what his mother sarcastically called 'the beer garden', John, Sr. may have outrun his own demons, but his absence at home scarred the souls of his wife and two children. At the age of eight, young John suffered the loss of his mother, who, despondent and dejected after the death of her father and tired of her husband telling her he avoided coming home because she had the face of someone who'd been hit by a train made it real by leaping in front of one. So, just days shy of his ninth birthday, John Driscoll found himself motherless. Shortly after, a suffocating cough wrenched him out of sleep. His tiny room was filled with smoke. Panicking, he rushed to save his dad. But his bed was on fire. His father's screams were horrifying and the stench of his burning flesh made John want to vomit. He raced to the kitchen and pulled out the Naugahyde chair. Climbing it, he reached for the phone and dialed 911. Trembling, he hid inside the cabinet under the sink and waited. "Is there someone in the house?" a loud manly voice hollered. John cracked open his cubbyhole's door. The policeman scooped him up with his burly arms and rushed him out of the burning house. He then went back in and rescued his sister. John knew that he owed his life to Officer Patrick Donahue of the 72nd Precinct. Angels were real, after all, as his mother had told him. After the fire, John was raised by his mother's sister, Aunt Lorraine, a baker at Silvercup Bread in Long Island City. Not only did John Driscoll choose the name 'Patrick' at his confirmation, later in life, he applied to John Jay College of Criminal Justice as a salute to his blue-clad savior.

Enter Colette, a landscape artist who'd come to the precinct to lodge a complaint against vagrants and homeless men who'd scrawled obscenities in a culture garden she had designed for a park in Flushing. Driscoll, after accompanying her to the scene of the crime, took several photographs of the defiled abstract sculptures. She talked about her love of art and asked the young policeman if he was a fan. He told her he was which prompted her to invite him to the Museum of Modern Art where they were exhibiting the new works of Alexander Calder. It was a truly magical afternoon for the young sergeant from the 110th Precinct. Falling in love with her was wonder-filled. She was fond of surprising the uniformed Irishman by greeting him at the end of his shift with tickets she'd secured for a movie at The Dekalb, an

RKO theater a few blocks from the precinct. One evening she had arranged for a limousine driver to chauffer Driscoll from the Queens police station to One If By Land, Two if By Sea, a romantic restaurant on Barrow Street in lower Manhattan. Upon his arrival the restaurant's pianist played *Danny Boy,* Driscoll's favorite Irish ballad. A smile creased his face as he hummed the tune while walking toward Colette who was seated at a corner table. Before they met, Driscoll's entire wardrobe had consisted of polyester suits. It was Colette who educated him on English tailoring on sale. She convinced him it was better to own one exquisite suit, than to have five mediocre ones. Shopping with him at Barneys Warehouse, she had introduced him to names like Dior, Ferragamo, Kenneth Cole, Giorgio Armani, and Ralph Lauren. To please her, his wardrobe became his indulgence. He dressed for Colette, not for the distinction of being New York City's best dressed cop, nor for the moniker 'Dapper John', that his well-cut suits had earned him.

Driscoll, at 6'2, exhibited a forceful and intimidating stride. There was a swagger to his walk, not unlike that of Gary Cooper in *High Noon.* Women found the blue-eyed Irishman charming but his heart belonged to fashion consultant, Colette.

Together, he and she set up a home, raised their daughter, Nicole, and looked joyously ahead. But on a bright and cloudless May afternoon, fifteen years into a blissful marriage, the family van was broadsided by an eighteen-wheeler, robbing Driscoll of Nicole, and catapulting his wife into an endless coma.

Smiling, the Lieutenant thanked Tammy who pointed to a small card that had been clipped to her note. Opening it, he discovered it contained another message. The handwriting was clearly not that of a little girl.

Dear Lieutenant Driscoll,

We know you also lost a daughter to tragedy.
We've asked Tammy to have Lori watch over your
little girl in heaven. Considering she was your
daughter, we're certain that's where she'll be. God
bless you, Lieutenant. This world's a better place
with you in it.

~ J & R Keating

Tears coated Driscoll's eyes. He thought of his daughter.
Looking up, he smiled at the unseen heavens and disappeared
out the door.

CHAPTER FOUR

Tilden was satisfied that the body of the harlot who had violently assaulted him was going through the early stages of putrefaction a stone's throw from where he lay his head at night. Thankful for her demise, which enabled him to perfect his method of murder by arterial embalming, he turned his attention to his new sinner. She'd been restrained. To what, she wasn't sure. Something cold. Something hard. A pool table, perhaps. In her line of work, this was sometimes the norm, but she wasn't sure she was "at work". Last night was a blur. She vaguely remembered having seen the man before. This man who was hovering over her now wearing rubber gloves, medical scrubs and a polyethylene apron. That was new. She'd never seen anyone come to the swinger's club dressed like that.

"Doctor?" she moaned.

Ignoring her, Tilden scoped her naked body with lifeless eyes before probing the right side of her neck with his finger.

"Doctor, please. You're scaring me," she pleaded, as adrenalin rocketed through her.

He looked at her. Seeing the face of his first victim, he cocked his head to the side, and just as she thought he was about to speak, he produced a glass carafe, uncorked it and doused her from head to toe with liquid. *The guy's a doctor, could that be some sort of antiseptic? Am I in an operating room?* The thought terrified her.

Indifferent to her dilemma, Tilden moved to the opposite side of the cold air ice casket where he checked that her body was level, and that the back of her head rested squarely on the casket's headrest. After making certain her right arm was tightly secured by the Gleason support and that her chin was firmly clasped in its leather strap, he turned his attention to the Barnes' nickel-finished Kant slip plate ensuring that it was snug around her triceps where it met her deltoid muscle. Nodding in satisfaction, he attached a stretch of tubing to the slip plate and forcefully inserted the arterial inlet nozzle into her right common carotid artery. Deaf to her wailing, he used the Jonathan Crookes scalpel to open her right jugular vein and inserted the drainage tube. He glanced at his watch, then to the gravity fluid injector suspended ten feet above her head where its clear glass jar was filled with his special blend of embalming fluid. Removing the stainless steel clamp from the tubing, he watched as the purifying liquid cleansed her circulatory system of all transgressions.

The casket, originally designed to hold ice, was filling with her drainage. Poaching in her own blood would slow down her body's putrefaction. He imagined the last time she was similarly soaking was when her untainted body was sustained only by the amniotic fluid inside her mother's womb. Long before she chose a life of immorality.

CHAPTER FIVE

During his much heralded career as Chief Medical Examiner for the City of New York, Larry Pearsol thought he'd seen it all. Cadavers void of bones, bodies burned so intensely the fillings inside their teeth had melted, and unspeakable mutilation. In his 'city that never sleeps', homicidal maniacs regularly displayed a host of imaginative skills.

What fulfilled Pearsol's sense of duty was uncovering murder disguised as accidental death or death by natural causes. And that's what he believed he had before him now with the Jane Doe who'd been pulled from the East River.

A tugboat operator, navigating the waterway, had spotted what appeared to be white flotsam. Upon approach, he discovered it was the naked body of a woman. After fishing her out, he called 911. Harbor Patrol then brought her to the Chief Medical Examiner office where at first glance it looked like a drowning.

Upon beginning his Y incision a fluid seeped out, staining Pearsol's scalpel. It wasn't blood. He brought the blade to his nose and instantly detected a familiar scent. He then cut open the femoral artery which oozed profusely. Why was the body of his subject filled with embalming fluid? Pearsol had never encountered such an enigma. Someone had injected a copious amount of formaldehyde and phenol into her bloodstream. Had this body been stolen from a funeral parlor and dumped in the river? Who would do such a thing?

Bringing the blade to his nose a second time, he detected the hint of something else. Something odd. Sidestepping administrative protocol, he called One Police Plaza, and asked to speak to Lieutenant Driscoll.

CHAPTER SIX

The Lieutenant pulled the unmarked cruiser to the curb in front of 520 1st Avenue, tossed the NYPD Vehicle ID placard on the dash, and got out. Ducking inside the vertical depository of secrets, he rode the elevator to the sixth floor and made his way toward the double glass doors marked 'City Morgue'. The spacious room was tiled floor to ceiling in white. While six halogen bulbs provided an alabaster sheen to four cadavers lying atop their gurneys a pair of coroner's assistants worked in silence, dissecting and weighing the individual organs from one of them.

Pearsol appeared and extended his hand to Driscoll. "Holding up OK, Lieutenant?"

Driscoll smiled at the M.E. Although a drunk driver had robbed him of his wife and only daughter, the Lieutenant never considered himself alone in the world. "Because of friends like you, I am," he said.

"What brings Homicide's top gun to our ethereal halls?" asked Jasper Eliot, the M.E.'s assistant, who'd popped his head out from behind a stainless steel scale.

"Top gun, Jasper? An oldie but a goodie. Nice to know Tom Cruise still has a fan."

"Honestly, I thought his star would have faded by now but he's still "the man" in those never ending *Mission Impossible* flicks. I'd have figured he'd never land another gig after jumping up and down on Oprah's couch over Katie Holmes only to have her bail because of Scientology? This is the same guy who'd made room for Holmes by tossing a hot Australian redhead out of the casbah. Who does that?"

"Last time I looked, Nicole Kidman was a blonde," Driscoll said with a smile before turning his attention back to the M.E. "Wha'd'ya got, Larry?"

Pearsol opened the mortuary cooler and pulled out the stainless steel tray supporting the victim. "Lieutenant, meet Jane Doe," he said sliding the woman's bloated body under Driscoll's gaze. "Harbor Patrol fished her out of the muck. I'd say she was a feast for the gulls for a day. Maybe two."

"What's that smell? Paint thinner?"

"Phenol."

"She was doused in phenol?"

"Injected."

Driscoll's eyes narrowed.

"The complete autopsy will fill in the blanks, but I'd bet my pension I already know what killed her. The who, and the why, I'll leave to you." Pearsol handed the preliminary lab report to Driscoll. It identifies a mixture of substances inside her vascular system.

"Phenol, formaldehyde, and Chloride of Zinc?" Driscoll looked perplexed. "The same Chloride of Zinc they put in dry cell batteries?"

Pearsol nodded. "There's three more."

"Myrrh, aloe, and cassia," Driscoll read aloud. "That's a strange mix." He glanced at Pearsol, who nodded. "Says here you drained 851 milliliters from her circulatory system. What's that? About two pints?"

"Just under."

"A body contains five to six quarts of blood. So the rest of this mixture?"

"Still in her."

Using his finger, Driscoll pushed back a lock of the victim's hair. "What could you have done to warrant this?" he whispered, eyes on the corpse.

"Right now the unofficial cause of death is phenol poisoning by arterial injection. Familiar with the German word, 'abgespritzt', Lieutenant?"

"No."

"Abgespritzt was a method of genocide favored by the Nazis in the early 1940s. Hitler's henchmen delivered instantaneous death by injecting 15 milliliters of phenol directly into the heart."

"What kind of syringe injects six quarts?"

"More than likely he used a centrifugal pump. And he knew what he was doing." Pearsol pointed to the side of the victim's neck, where a semi-translucent latex adhesive covered a two inch stretch of rippled flesh between the carotid artery and the jugular vein. "An extreme method of murder, Lieutenant. He arterially embalmed her."

Driscoll winced.

"There's more." The M.E. produced a transparent evidence bag containing a locket. It was an inch in diameter and featured Saint Vitalis of Gaza; his name etched in a half circle below his likeness. "I found it under her tongue. Someone apparently placed it there before suturing the tongue to the floor of her mouth."

"What's that about?" Driscoll wondered aloud.

"Good question. I'm not familiar with that saint. You?"

"She's the patron saint of prostitutes."

"Well, there's a lead. Oh, and there's one other bit of information you're sure to find intriguing. The myrrh, aloe, and cassia injected with the embalming fluid were once embalming solutions on their own. Sort of."

"Sort of?"

"They were the purifying fragrances applied to the linens that wrapped the crucified Christ before he was laid in his tomb."

CHAPTER SEVEN

Tilden was kneeling. Waiting. At forty, his thin, unblemished face with eyes the color of the sky made him look younger. He rolled his tongue around a Vicks VapoDrop that was melting in his mouth. That morning he had woken up with a sore throat and a cough. Three spoonfuls of Robitussin helped but had made him dizzy. He hoped it wasn't the onset of something serious. The hard oak of the kneeler pained him. *Why does a confessional booth have to be so uncomfortable?* He was not very good at kneeling. Bending the knee was not a favorite position. But he understood the purpose behind the design. Anyone who entered that constricted narrow chamber must genuflect, assume the choreography of penance, acknowledge his transgressions, and be open to repentance. And that's what he intended to do.

The claustrophobic feel of the confessional booth made him recall an image buried deep in the sands of memory. It was his recollection of one of the nights he hid inside the closet of his mother's bedroom waiting for the wall clock to chime 10 p.m. That's when Hank, his mother's favorite client, would barge in with an open pint of Wild Turkey in his hand. He was eyeing the man through the closet's slatted door when his mother came out of the bathroom wearing lingerie she'd shoplifted from Macy's. Tilden watched as she turned on the transistor radio which was set to a country music station. Johnny Cash began to wail that he'd walk the line. His mother loved that Johnny Cash. Grabbing the bottle from Hank's hand, she chugged a mouthful.

"How do you like my new bra and panties?" his mother asked Hank. "You're into black lace, right?"

"Yeah. I like black undies. Now take them off, bitch."

"That's your job, Daddio."

"Come here you little whore."

The sound of movement in the priest's cubicle dispelled Tilden's memory. As the metal screen slid open, a faintly lit silhouette of the cleric's face appeared.

"Are you here for confession?" the priest asked.

"I guess so," Tilden muttered.

"How long has it been since your last confession, son?"

"I don't remember."

The strong smell of burnt tobacco filled the priest's sinuses. It was nauseating.

"You're not smoking in there, are you?"

"No. But, I smoked a few on my way over here. I'm trying a new brand. The ad says it's natural tobacco. But, I miss those chemicals. They kick ass, ya' know? Here, Father, try one." Tilden pinched out a cigarette from his green pack of American Spirit and forced it through one of the small holes in the screen.

"You know son, I start every day with the Lord's prayer and there's a line that fits right now: lead us not into temptation. But, you know what? I'll save this one for later."

"Okey dokee."

"So, son, what brings you here?"

"My soul, Father, it's getting darker."

"Well, Jesus said 'I am the light', so you're in the right place. Let's make the darkness visible."

Tilden kneeling before the priest felt a sudden rise in temperature. The heat started in his lower back and moved up his spine towards the center of his neck making him feel flushed. He unbuttoned his shirt and was tempted to rip it off. "Father, all of a sudden it's hot as hell in here. I think I'm gonna pass out," he groaned.

This wasn't the first time someone felt sick inside his confessional booth. He knew it had to do with the sinner's realization that someone was about to see inside their troubled conscience. "Hang in there. Just breathe deeply."

Tilden did as he was instructed.

"What's your name?" the priest asked.

"Tilden."

"Well, Tilden, anything that's said here is in confidence, you know."

"Even if I hurt someone?" Tilden's eyes were down, his lips tight.

"Did you hurt someone?"

"Well, yeah." Tilden searched his pocket for his packet of Trident Splash. "OK if I chew gum?"

"Sure, suit yourself," he said. "Who is it you hurt?"

Tilden's eyes glazed as he stared at the silhouette of the priest through the screen.

"Someone very close to you?" the cleric asked.

"Yes," Tilden muttered.

"Are we talking about a relative?"

"Now you sound like a cop."

"I'm not a cop, I'm a priest. And like I said before, the sins you tell me you've committed are held in strict confidence. And you know, Tilden, speaking the truth cleanses your heart."

"I have no heart."

"God gives a heart to every newborn."

"Father, I was never born."

"Well, you're inside a Catholic church, the perfect place to be reborn."

Silence was the reply to his encouragement.

"You said you hurt someone very close to you. We often do, son. I sense it's weighing heavily on your heart," the priest coaxed.

"Like I said a minute ago, I have no heart." Tilden replied angrily, his voice growing louder.

Tilden caught the immediate hitch in the cleric's breathing pattern. He had become adept at reading a person's temperament by taking note of their non verbal responses.

"I'm not here to judge you, Tilden. I'm here to help you. Who is it you hurt?" the priest asked in another attempt to get Tilden to open up about what he'd done.

Why does he keep asking me who I hurt? What difference would it make? Tilden wondered, becoming angry and increasingly suspicious of the man's motives.

"I killed my hooker mother and her live in john," Tilden said, flatly. "The guy raped me. Jammed it right up my ass. Called me a peeping Tom 'cause I got off watching the two of them screw. You happy now?"

"I'm glad that you told me. That's why you're here, right? To confess your sins?"

"I thought I was. You're not curious to hear more of the lurid details?" Tilden asked.

"No. You confessed to me and to God that you've committed murder," the priest said, a tremor in his voice.

"So, what now?" Tilden asked, an unseen sneer filling his face, having rattled the man he was certain he shouldn't trust.

"I absolve you, Tilden. I absolve you of your sins. Go, now, and sin no more," the priest said, his words of absolution delivered in rapid fire fashion.

Saying nothing, Tilden opened the door and left.

CHAPTER EIGHT

Tilden had been putting off his confession of matricide for years. Since he also confessed to having killed Hank, he'd felt he'd been cleansed of all sin. The fact that he hadn't talked about the purification of the embalmed hooker who now occupied the grave behind his house wasn't his fault. Afterall, it was the priest who'd rushed him out of the confessional. The mere thought of that squirrelly hooker brought their first encounter back to consciousness.

It wasn't long before a knock sounded on the door of Room 423 at the Esmeralda Hotel, a short-stay joint that catered to the middle management engineers at the Northeast Electric plant off Route 13 in Camden. Tilden approached the door, a tight knot in his chest. He always felt that tautness when he was about to hook up with Angela. She was the working girl he'd been paying for an afternoon of nastiness every Wednesday for the past two months. After unlatching the security chain, he unlocked and opened the door. The hooker entered, the heels of her stiletto pumps pitting the industrial carpeting in the room.

"Who the hell are you?" Tilden asked, scoping the stranger.

She was a tall woman, lanky, bony. There was an absence of femininity in both her face and demeanor. Her walk was brisk and awkward. She wore a tight black leather skirt and an off-white blouse. A brass necklace adorned her emaciated neck. She'd been around the block a few times and it was visable in the circles that circumnavigated her eyes. Those eyes had a grayness to them, much like the ones on bottom feeding sea creatures. Tilden knew this go 'round was not going to be fun. Everything about her was unappealing. She was not his Angela. Far from it.

"I'm Valerie, Angela's sister," the woman said, cracking her Doublemint gum.

The quizzical look on Tilden's face said he wasn't buying it.

"She didn't tell you she had a sister?" the hooker asked.

"No."

"Well, now you know."

"You can't be her sister."

"Why, because I'm not chubby?"

"You look like a ghost."

Valerie's eyes flared. "Screw you, pal. I'm outa here," she growled. Grabbing her purse, she headed for the door.

"No, no, no. Don't go. Who am I to talk? I'mm a ghost, too. Hell, I look homeless."

"You're a wise ass, aren't you?" Valerie pried open her purse and scrounged around for her cigarettes and a BIC lighter.

"Can't you read?" Tilden pointed to the 'NO SMOKING' sign on the door.

"Go ahead, call the fucking manager." She blew a cloud of smoke in his face. "You look like a smoker to me." You're craving one, ain't ya?" she said, spewing out a second billow.

Tilden gagged on the smoke. Coughing repeatedly, he raced toward the window and forced it open.

Valerie sashayed toward the mirrored armoire and unbuttoned her blouse.

"Do you like tits?" she asked, unclasping her bra.

"Where the hell is Angela?" Tilden hollered.

"Don't know. Don't care."

"What the fuck? I paid her in advance," he moaned.

Valerie shimmied out of her leather skirt. "What's your guess? Hairy or shaved?" she asked, massaging her mons pubis through her panties.

Tilden's brow creased. He bit down on his lip. "Angela's supposed to be here. Not you. What happened to brand loyalty?" he grumbled.

"Hey, I'm not Customer Service. Just pay me and let's get on with it."

"The trick's been paid for I told ya'."

"That's not what Angie said."

Tilden stared at the woman, undecidedly.

"You want me or not?"

"Oh, what the hell," he groaned. Reaching for his jacket which was wrapped around the bedpost, he snatched his wallet. "How much?" he grumbled

"A hundred and a half."

"No first time discount?"

"This ain't Walmart."

Tilden crumpled the bills and tossed them on the bed.

Scooping them up, Valerie slipped them inside her Jimmy Choo knock offs.

"I know your routine. You're a closet peeper. Go ahead Rover, get inside your dog house."

Tilden stripped off his clothes and crawled inside the closet.

Unpocketing a humongous strap-on from her Tory Burch imitation bag, Valerie called for Tilden to come out.

"That's not part of the routine!" Tilden hollered, watching her through the slatted door.

"Now you're pissing me off," the hooker seethed, hostility etching her face.

"That's not part of the routine!" Tilden yelled again.

"Me and my compadre say it is." She pulled a Bersa Thunder pistol out of her purse and aimed it at his hidey-hole.

"Whoa! Ease up, honey," Tilden stammered, crawling out of the closet.

"Face down on the bed, Pal."

Tilden complied.

"Spread those legs," she ordered, standing naked beside him. When Tilden rolled his head to look at her, Valerie slipped on a twelve inch strap-on.

"This ain't part of the routine. How many times do I gotta tell ya'?" he spluttered, his heart racing.

"I don't like peeping Toms. My grandfather was like you. The bastard watched me every night for years. And when I was ten he'd put his worm up my butt. Felt like a branding iron. I cried to my mother, but the witch didn't believe me. Her dad was a saint."

After climbing on top of Tilden she whispered in his ear: "If you know what's good for you, don't clench."

"Please don't," Tilden pleaded.

The screaming echoed throughout the fourth floor. Tilden faded into unconsciousness. When his eyelids eventually fluttered open, the steamy air gushing in from the open window gagged him. He was hauntingly alone in the cheap room. His attempt to get up produced a throbbing in his rectum so intense he froze. Motionless, he yelled, despairingly, for help again and again and again. A strident pain radiated from his rear end. "Holy mother of God, please help me!" he cried out. *When is the cleaning lady coming?* he panted. He had rented the room for a full twenty four hours. He was screwed.

CHAPTER NINE

The room was white, bleached, colorless. The mattress on the bed, hard. "I must be in hell," Tilden groaned. *What's with the plastic tube taped to my hand? Is that Juicy Juice in the hanging bag attached to the tube?* As a child, his mother only bought Juicy Juice, fake orange juice. Tilden felt a wave of nausea. *Who was this Asian man approaching?* "Who are you?" he asked.

"I am Doctor Yang Lee, trauma surgeon. How are you feeling?" the physician asked, palpating his Tilden's hand.

Doctor Lee was a thin man. Ralph Lauren glasses framed his artificially tanned face, accented by a thin mustache. Fastened to his avocado green tie was a Tiffany gold crucifix.

"Where am I?" Tilden stuttered.

"Saint Clara's Hospital. You feeling any pain?"

"Who are you?" Tilden asked again. He glared suspiciously at the crucifix on his tie.

"I'm Doctor Yang Lee," he repeated, checking the medication chart clipped to Tilden's bed frame. Turning to the man standing beside him wearing an oversized cotton cap to cover his mane of braided hair, he said: "Robinson, we're going to increase the anodyne."

"What's that?" Tilden asked, anguish in his eyes.

"It'll help with the pain," the man explained.

"And who are you?" Tilden asked, sizing up the lanky black man who looked like Bob Marley.

"I'm your nurse."

"If you say so," Tilden replied.

"Did they bring you breakfast this morning, Mr. Quinn?" the nurse asked, revealing a Jamaican accent.

"No. And I'm hungry as hell."

"I'll check with the nutritionist and see what she can come up with," he said before leaving the room.

"Do you know where you are?" Doctor Lee asked Tilden.

Tilden panoramically scanned the room. "It looks like a hospital room to me."

"Do you know why you're here?"

"No."

"An EMT crew brought you in yesterday morning."

"What happened to me? Was I in a car accident?"

"No. They found you in a hotel room."

Tilden shot the physician a look of disbelief. "No way," he muttered.

"Looks like you were mistreated."

Tilden studied the doctor's face. *Was this reality or was he dreaming?* he wondered. "Mistreated how?" he asked.

"You were hurt pretty badly."

A look of skepticism filled Tilden's face.

"How about we talk about it after you've had something to eat," the surgeon suggested.

"No, I gotta know now."

"You were… violated."

"What?"

The doctor paused. "You were sodomized," he told him.

The color drained from Tilden's face.

"And, like I said a moment ago, you were hurt pretty badly."

"But I don't feel any pain," Tilden said.

"That's because of all the analgesics you're on." He pointed to the hanging IV bag.

"Who did that to me?"

"I don't know. The police are reviewing the hotel's security cameras."

"I don't remember a thing."

Doctor Lee hesitated, growing silent as was his custom before delivering the news no patient wanted to hear. "You'll be needing surgery, Mr. Quinn."

"Surgery? For what?"

"You were severely ripped up."

"Please tell me you're kidding." Tilden's chin quivered as he began to sob.

"I'm a damn good surgeon. You'll be in good care." Doctor Lee placed his hand over Tilden's. "I have a few more questions. Ok to ask them now?

Tilden nodded as he wiped tears from his face.

"What do you do for a living?" the surgeon asked.

"I'm retired from the funeral business. You're gonna cut me up, right?" Tilden asked, his face awash with fright.

"Well, your large intestine's been torn. In fact, it's in tatters. It will require repair and many sutures. You'll likely be wearing a colostomy bag for awhile."

"Oh, my God! I'll be a walking toilet."

"I won't know for sure until I perform the surgery."

"Oh, my God!" Tilden repeated, his eyes widening.

CHAPTER TEN

When Tilden opened his eyes it felt as though he was looking through a thin layer of gauze. There were undefined shapes creeping across the ceiling. He heard voices, garbled cries. He felt numb and listless. Darkness soon seeped back in and he vanished into a void.

Time was out of joint.

At some point, he felt his arm being poked and a woman's voice ringing out. "How're you?" the voice reverberated. When his eyes flickered open and the shadows were more defined, a Hispanic woman was holding his hand.

"How am I? Lousy," he stuttered, through parched lips.

"You're recovering nicely, sir. And they'll be no need for a colostomy bag," the perianesthesia nurse said, checking his vital signs on the CO_2 monitor. "But, I know how you're feeling, dearie, you're still in that post surgical fog."

"I feel rotten. I don't remember a thing."

"Your memory will return. I see you haven't listed any relatives to call in case of emergency. Maybe, you'd like to talk to a social worker?"

"No."

"A priest?"

"Why? Am I dying?"

"No, I just thought you might like to talk with someone."

"I just want to go back to sleep."

"OK, dearie, I'll be back later with some juice. Would you like apple or cranberry?"

"Tequila," Tilden managed to mutter as he faded back into oblivion.

CHAPTER ELEVEN

The scream reverberated through the ICU unit on the Sixth Floor. The night nurse sprang to her feet and rushed to Room 608. She turned on the fluorescent lights flooding the space with a milky white luminescence. Tilden's awakening from his sedated sleep had been abrupt. Consciousness, which had been up until now muddled, suddenly emerged.

"It's ok. You're alright. You're alright," the night nurse repeated.

"I'm not alright," Tilden shouted. "It hurts like hell."

"From one to ten, how bad is the pain?"

"30! It feels like got a harpoon up my ass."

"The doctor prescribed a painkiller. You'll need more. I'll get it."

"It hurts like hell. Hurry! Hurry!" he hollered as the nurse rushed out of the room.

When she returned she was pushing a Harloff medication cart. Unsealing a sterile syringe, she loaded it with Fentanyl and injected it into the IV's port. "You'll feel a lot better in a jiffy," she said.

"Oh dear fucking mother of God," Tilden shouted as the recollection of what that prostitute had done to him came racing back to consciousness. He vividly remembered the bondage, the assault, and the rape. "You're a dead bitch walking, Valerie!

The nurse paid little attention to her patient's ranting.

CHAPTER TWELVE

Armed with his hospital discharge papers, Tilden walked toward the vast parking lot. Searching for his black Econoline van, he patrolled the endless aisles flanked by row after row of cars. He had no memory of where he had parked it. Exasperated, he returned to the hospital, approached the administrative attendant who had just discharged him and demanded to speak to Security.

"Why do you need to speak to Security, sir?" the attendant asked.

"My van. It just vanished from the parking lot. Someone must have stolen it," Tilden said, his voice weak.

"Why would you think that?"

The quizzical look on the desk clerk's face confused Tilden. "You think I'm making this up?" he groaned, confused and exasperated.

"Not at all, sir, it's just that your chart says you were brought here by ambulance." She showed him the entry on the computer screen.

Tilden blinked rapidly. "By ambulance?"

"Yes, sir. On June 14th at 11:25 am," she added, pointed to the time stamp on the
scanned document.

"I don't remember that at all."

"It's not uncommon, sir, to be forgetful after a long stay in a hospital.

Especially after having surgery. Is there a relative or a friend you can call to pick you up?"

"There's nobody." he muttered.

"I see," she said, sympathetically. "You might want to call for an Uber. Are you registered with them?"

Tilden shook his head.

The woman checked his chart again, taking note of Tilden's address. "You live locally, sir, I'll be happy to arrange for a hospitality van to drive you home."

"That'd be great," Tilden replied.

"I'll do it right now," she said, reaching for the desk phone's handset. "Have a seat in the waiting room. I'll let you know when the van arrives."

Tilden headed toward a set of Naugahyde chairs and gingerly sat on one of them. His butt still hurt and he felt tired and disoriented.

At the sound of an automobile horn, he looked over at the woman who'd been kind to him. Her nod told him his ride had arrived. He thanked her, ventured outside and stepped inside the minibus.

"Where to?" the bearded driver singsonged.

"To hell and step on it," Tilden muttered.

"Any particular street in hell?"

"Your guess is as good as mine. I'm looking for a woman."

"Aren't we all. But why search hell?"

"That's where she belongs."

"So, she's not there yet?"

"No. But she will be soon. You can count on it."

"If you say so. In the meantime, you got another address I can take you to?"

After rattling off his home address, Tilden sighed, closed his eyes, and rested his noggin against the van's head rest.

Arriving home, Tilden thanked the driver, got out, and ambled up the steps of the Victorian structure. Instinctively, he put his hand in his pocket for his key, but it wasn't there. That's when he remembered Valerie had taken his wallet, his keys, his iPhone, and all his cash. *"That bitch,"* he muttered, heading up the side of the house. Using his elbow as a battering ram, he shattered the glass in one of the cellar's windows. Retrieving a fallen branch, he cleared away the shards of glass, reached in and unlatched the window's lock and pushed it open. After managing to climb in, he staggered up the stairs to the living room and threw himself on the couch.

Was that a police siren he heard? It sounded like it was getting closer. He groaned when he heard the sound of vehicles coming to a stop outside the house, their emergency lights still flashing. "Jesus Christ, what's that all about?" he griped, still confused and disoriented.

A voice bellowed through a bull horn. "You, inside the house, come out through the front door with your hands in the air. Do it now!"

"Son of a fucking bitch," Tilden muttered, pulling himself off the couch. Waddling toward the front door, he pried it open.

Three police cars where blockading the street. He eyed four uniformed officers, their guns drawn. One of them ordered Tilden to get on his knees.

"Don't shoot. For Chrissake don't shoot," Tilden pleaded as he followed the officer's instructions.

"Tilden? Is that you?" the sergeant with the bull horn cried out. "We got a call someone broke in."

"I broke in."

"Why the hell would you do that?"

"I didn't have my key. It's a long story."

"Holster your guns, boys," the sergeant ordered. "I know him. That's his house."

The crackling sound of the police cruiser's radios alerted the officers that a jack-knifed tractor trailer had caused a multi-car pileup on Route 13.

After the police cars skittered away, Tilden went back inside the house and returned to the couch. For hours he slept, marooned in that murky space filled with darkness. When he woke up, his mouth was dry and his butt stung. Dragging himself to the kitchen, he unpocketed the vial of oxycodone he'd been discharged with, popped two in his mouth and washed them down with tap water right from the faucet. Heading out of the kitchen his eyes caught sight of a framed photo hanging on the dining room wall. He removed it and glared at the portrait of his mother and her lover on one of their trips to Disney's Magic Kingdom. For reasons he couldn't quite grasp the sight of his mother cozying up to Hank made him angry. Studying the photo, he reasoned he might be angry simply because he wasn't in the picture. *Damn these drugs. I can't think straight, he muttered under his breath as he returned to the couch.*

CHAPTER THIRTEEN

"God damn it, who the hell is knocking on my door?" Tilden grumbled, pressing a couch throw pillow against his ear to muffle the sound. "Go away!" he hollered.

The knocking stopped for a moment and then continued.

"Please, mister. Don't you wanna support the Girl Scouts of Oneida County?" the girl's voice echoed.

"Go to hell! I don't need no goddamn cookies."

"Please, sir…"

Slipping off one of his shoes, he flung it at the door. The knocking ceased.

As Tilden closed his eyes, sleep soon followed making him a dead man to his surroundings once again.

Waking, he dragged his body off the couch, stripped off the clothes he'd slept in and made his way upstairs to grab a shower. The blast of hot water startled him. "Jesus H. Christ!" he wailed as the torrent of water pelted the taped gauze that shielded his surgical stitches. Moistened by the water, the bandage peeled off. He washed himself from head to toe. Staring at his gaunt face in the wall-mounted mirror, he shaved his head and face. Stepping out of the shower, he felt a waive a dizziness. Fighting the urge to vomit, he toweled down. Applying Neosporin to one of the sterile gauge pads they'd given him upon discharge from the hospital, he attempted to cover the wound. The task wasn't easy with the room spinning. Closing the lid on the toilet, he placed the gauge pad on its flat surface and sat down. "God, I feel like I'm an old man," he groaned.

After taking his time slipping into a pair of jeans, he reached for his Grateful Dead tee shirt, the quintessential casual attire for an embalmer. There was much to be done but his strength had been sapped by the entire ordeal. His sluggish post-surgical recovery wasn't helping.

Tilden was sure Home Depot would have what he needed for the task he'd planned but wondered if he could handle the stress of the errand. *Hell, it'd only be an eight mile drive there and back,* he reasoned.

Having retrieved the vehicle's spare key that had hung on a hook inside the cabinet over the kitchen sink since the day he'd acquired the van, he headed out of the house and climbed behind the wheel of the Ford Econoline. As soon as he started the engine he felt a sharp pain; like a sliver of glass had sliced through his gluteus maximus. "God damn it, why didn't I remember to take the pain meds?"

Turning off the ignition, he slowly climbed out of the van and ambled back to the house. "Where the hell did I put those pills?" he muttered, before finding them near the kitchen sink. The surgeon had prescribed two tablets every six hours. *Have I taken any?* he asked himself. Shrugging, he popped a handful in his mouth and washed them down with water. Driving was out of the question for the time being. He'd shop online and ask for a delivery, certain the hardware giant wouldn't turn down a guy just released from the hospital.

Grabbing his laptop, he gingerly sat, and turned it on. Waiting for his apps to populate the computer's home screen, dizziness set in. "God damn it, it's gotta be those fucking pills," he griped, as his hands began to shake. "Oh my God? Have I overdosed," he moaned, feeling a rush of nausea. His legs, refusing to obey his command, wobbled as he stood. Bracing himself against the wall, he made his way to the kitchen. Grabbing the Keurig thermal carafe, he sucked down a full container of week old coffee. *Should I be calling 911,* he asked himself feeling like he was about to faint. "Hell no! I'm not going to that hospital again," he groaned. Getting on his hands and knees, he crawled to the couch.

But sleep didn't come. The caffeine had prevented his escape, freezing him in that zone between the living and the dead.

CHAPTER FOURTEEN

After finally feeling well enough to place his online order, it took five hours for Home Depot Rentals to deliver the machine. But Tilden didn't mind. He had taken advantage of a discount and rented it for a week as he needed time for his wound to heal before using it. He dreaded the noise the contraption would emit and would need a way to muffle it. The last thing he wanted was for one of his neighbors to call the police again, this time to complain about the racket. He turned on the machine to make sure it worked and then quickly turned it off. Covering it with the tarp he'd secured from the shed, he returned to the house. If he couldn't find a way to curb the noise he'd simply run it and hope for the best. What he had planned for Mother and Hank wouldn't take long. But, if he were to power it up, he'd need one of those sound muffling headsets those guys at the airport use when they're waving batons around to assist in the taxiing of jets. *Where the hell would he find one of those?* he wondered. His pondering was interrupted by a knock on the door. Opening it, he was surprised to see a utility worker with a yellow hard hat holding a clip board.

"Are you Mr. Quinn?" the man asked.

"I am," Tilden replied.

"We'll be starting the upgrade of your water service next week."

"What upgrade?"

The man sighed giving Tilden the impression he wasn't in the mood for questions.

"We sent you a letter telling you all about it," the man said to Tilden, his voice a bit coarser.

"I got no letter."

"Well, it said we'd be digging a trench to lay pipes down your entire block."

His body language suggested he wanted to wrap up his visit and leave.

"What's wrong with the water I'm using?"

"It's well water."

"And what's wrong with that?"

The visitor's eyes narrowed making Tilden feel threatened. The guy had a good six inches on him.

"Tests show it contains contaminants that may pose a health risk," he explained.

"I've been drinking it for years. I'm healthy."

"In the 20's this neighborhood was all grape farms. They dumped a ton of pesticides to kill the phylloxera bugs that ate the grapes. Those pesticides ended up in the wells, sir."

"You're making this up."

"Why would I do that?"

Whoa. He really looks pissed now, Tilden's inner voice cautioned. "Well, maybe not you, but the County is. That water they'll be pumping through ain't gonna be free."

"There's not much I can do about that."

"When's this work supposed to start?

"Next week. We'll open the street and begin laying the pipes on Monday. So starting then, it's important that all homeowners pull their cars into their driveways."

"That sounds all well and good, but did you take note of the road sign at the intersection of Maple and Elm?"

"No, what's it say?"

"There's a number to call in case of noise pollution and you'll be making a ruckus. We like it quiet up here."

"Well, sir, I hate to break the news to you, but we'll be bringing in earth moving equipment."

"There's no muffler on those. That phone at the Noise Pollution Center is gonna be ringing off the hook."

"That may be so," his visitor groaned. "But, in the long run, water from the Oneida City Reservoir will be brought right to your kitchen, sir."

"How long are we going to have to put up with the noise?"

"Give or take, three months," he said, looking like he was pleased to tell that to Tilden.

"Three months? To lay pipe?"

"There's a lot involved, sir. We'll be bringing in cranes."

"There goes the neighborhood."

"The county records lists your residence as a funeral parlor."

Tilden stared at him wondering what that had to do with anything. "Where ya' going with that?" he asked, suspiciously.

"Well, sir, with all due respect, the dead don't hear."

"What do you know about the dead?"

"Only what I see on TV. *The Walking Dead*. You a fan?"

"I don't watch the dead. They watch me."

"That's spooky."

"I gut them. And pump them with formaldehyde so they're ready for their next life," Tilden said.

After an awkward pause, he handed Tilden the clipboard. "I'll just need you to sign here." He pointed to the 'X' next to his name.

"What happens if I don't sign?" Tilden asked.

"You own the house, but the County owns the street and they can do whatever the hell they want whether you sign or not."

"Then I won't sign."

"Have it your way, sir. Your signature simply means you've been made aware of the County's plans."

Tilden grunted.

"And yes, they're gonna bill you monthly for the water."

"Water I don't want," Tilden griped.

"What can I tell ya' sir? Progress has its price."

Closing the door, a sly grin formed on Tilden's face. "I'll have all the noise I'll need in just a few days," he muttered to an empty room.

At 9:15 on Monday morning the clatter of earth moving equipment woke Tilden from a dreamless sleep. He dressed in a hurry and slipped on a pair of crocs. A rush of adrenalin carried him to the rear of the kitchen and down the small set of steps that lead to the yard. Swinging open the door to the shed, he retrieved the shovel. Standing over the creeping charlie that blanketed their graves, he began to dig.

After their exhumation, Tilden cleared the clutter from the shed's work table and laid out Mother and Hank to inspect their petrified remains. After he had slit their throats, he'd buried them without the benefit of embalming, nor coffin. He was pleased the earth wasn't kind to their rotting flesh, leaving only bone.

Pressing his new Decibel Defense Safety Muffs against his ears he yanked on the pull-cord of the Briggs & Stratton gasoline powered appliance and smiled as its tumultuous racket was drowned out by the humongous jack hammers pulverizing the asphalt on the street.

Grabbing his mother's skull, and Hank's tibia, he fed them into the 19 inch hopper of the steel reinforced wood chipper. Their powdered bones would be a tasty treat for the feral cats that roamed his yard at night.

CHAPTER FIFTEEN

Tilden cut the headlights as he pulled into the parking lot of the seedy hotel, sideswiping a black Jeep Cherokee with a bumper sticker which read: **Marriage is Grand...Divorce is 100 Grand**. He turned off the ignition but the Grateful Dead's *Friend of the Devil* continued to play. Checking the 'Find My Phone' feature on his iPad again, he grinned. It indicated his iPhone, the one Valerie had stolen, was fifty feet away. "She's probably screwing over some other sucker inside this rundown dump," he muttered. Though Tilden was thrilled to have tracked her down, he was surprised she'd left his iPhone on. But, then she wasn't the sharpest knife in the drawer. He checked his watch. It was 9:45 p.m. Tilden slumped down in the Econoline's seat and staked out the motel's entrance.

He didn't know how long he'd waited, but there she was, that skinny bitch, stumbling down the steps with a burly stevedore on her arm. He fucked her hard. She was stumbling on her twiggy legs. She stopped and asked for something. The John slid a cigarette in her mouth and lit it. She snatched his lighter and slipped it in her pocketed. The guy looked like he was asking for it back, she laughed and walked away. A click on her key fob triggered the flashing lights of a car in the distance. Tilden exited the van and fell in behind her, a shadow in the dimly lit parking lot under a moonless sky.

Valerie flailed her arms as Tilden jammed the rag soaked with Isoflurane over her face. In less than 15 seconds she was unconscious. Lifting the lanky hooker over his shoulder he returned to the van, opened its rear door and tossed her limp body inside. Climbing in behind her, he closed the door. Wrapping duct tape around her face, he secured the rag he'd doused with the powerful halogenated ether to insure she'd remain unconscious for the ride back to his house where he'd settle the score with her and eventually, others like her.

CHAPTER SIXTEEN

Fresh from her shower, NYPD Sergeant Margaret Aligante was seated at an oak table in her living room dressed in a blue robe. A white towel covered locks of chestnut hair. At 5'7 she was stunningly beautiful. Her caramel eyes were set above a sleek nose that sloped downward toward her lips. Throughout high school, she had run with the Pagano Persuaders, a New York street gang, that intimidated ten city blocks. That ended when Victor, the self proclaimed leader of the pack of thugs, was arrested for threatening the life of a ten-year-old girl. Wanting to put as much distance as possible from Victor, and others like him, she decided to turn her life around. She thought about pursuing a career in social work, but when a trusted friend suggested she could do more to shield children at risk on the streets of New York by walking a beat while wearing a badge she decided to become a cop. At John Jay College Of Criminal Justice she excelled, completing the four-year curriculum with a 3.96 grade point average, while studying Criminal Behavioral Science, Forensic Psychology, Profiling Methodology, and the martial arts of Aikido and Tae Kwon Do. After graduating from the Police Academy in 1991, she took on her first assignment as a patrolman monitoring the arteries of the 72nd Precinct in Brooklyn. In six years she had earned her gold shield, and had passed the Sergeant's exam. After a stint undercover with Vice, she transferred to Homicide where she reported to Lieutenant Driscoll.

Phone to her ear, Margaret was tolerating the patronizing prattle of one Mr. Miller, Public Relations Manager at Ricketts, a home appliance manufacturer who had called in response to a complaint she'd lodged with their corporate office. He was at a disadvantage. His customer service department had yet to respond to five messages she'd left on voicemail.

Something he'd said set her off. "And that's another thing, Mr. Miller, you keep referring to this lame excuse for a dishwasher as my problem. I didn't make the machine. You did. And since day one your problem has failed to wash anything. The pans come out more grime ridden then before I put them in."

Margaret was asked to stay on the line so Miller could discuss the situation with his superior.

"Yes, I'll hold," she griped. "But if your boss doesn't have an immediate remedy, he'll be looking for a new job… No, Mr. Miller, that's not a threat. I don't make threats. Only predictions."

Margaret tugged at the blue bath towel to better contain what a brazen member of the Pagano Persuaders once called her dukkys. He had borrowed the reference from King Henry VIII who used it when referring to the breasts of his second wife, Anne Boleyn. Margaret wondered whose dukkys he was ogling three years into the marriage, when he had Anne beheaded on trumped up charges of adultery, incest and plotting to murder the King. It annoyed Margaret that royalty, like politicians, claimed immunity when it involved their sexual misconduct.

The NYPD strictly forbids sexual harassment in the work place. Every cop knows that. Does every cop abide by it? Margaret felt most did. However she was a woman on a job where eighty percent of her fellow officers were men. She had a unique take on the male species. A deep rooted distrust. Why? Because her father was an adulterous bastard and an incestuous pig. Long before she'd reached puberty, she'd been the victim of his repulsive proclivity. She wished the terrifying ordeal would have ended with his death. Physically, it had. But years of repeated molestation had left her emotionally traumatized. Some of that wreckage she was conscious of, some not, but, like the lint that lined her pockets, it accompanied her everywhere.

Margaret's cell phone chimed. It was Driscoll. As she was about to answer, Miller's voice sounded in her ear.

"Ms. Aligante, I'll just be a few more minutes."

"Mr. Miller, I've got my boss on the other line. You've been granted an extension. We'll take this up tomorrow."

Getting a call from the Lieutenant an hour before her scheduled tour usually meant he had something significant to share. But after hearing what Driscoll had to say, she didn't feel a floating corpse containing embalming fluid was out of the ordinary for New York City and told him so.

That's when Driscoll told her about the myrrh, aloe, and cassia.

"Whoa! I'll be there in twenty."

Margaret hurried to her bedroom to dress. She'd apply her makeup at the red traffic lights she'd encounter on her way in. After zipping up her Gap cargos and checking her reflection in the mirror, she darted for the door.

CHAPTER SEVENTEEN

The rain that had pelted the city for two days showed no signs of letting up, adding to the gloom that filled the Community Room of Saint Edwin's Church.

Detective Second Grade Cedric Thomlinson had been attending weekly AA meetings here for the past three months. Sutton Street near Eighth Avenue, was miles from One Police Plaza and two boroughs from his residence in St. Albans, Queens, yet Thomlinson wished he was wearing a mask. This was New York City, and some friends of Bill wore police blue. Relating well to the first "A" in Alcoholics Anonymous, Thomlinson knew he belonged here. But not all attendees heeded the anonymous part. Pulling down the brim on his Cleveland Indians baseball cap, he nodded to the sandy-haired gentleman who'd just arrived. The newcomer knew Thomlinson as Roy.

George, a fixture at Saint Edwin's, had the floor. His opening was a beaut: "I was born in 1962, having begun my drinking career in the Fall of '61."

Many non-alcoholics think it's all about putting a cap on it. That's part of it. The trick is to keep the cap on while focusing on the disease, not just the symptom. Alcoholism is incurable. Everyone in the room knew that. Twenty eight days in a treatment facility, whether it be Betty Ford's or Jacamar Rutherby's, will not rid you of the sickness. At best, you'll be armed with the tools needed to fight off the urge to drink, and learn how a change in the 'people, places, and things' aspect of your world could bring about healthier living. Thomlinson knew what every alcoholic knew. That the disease, like a sleeping tiger, was insidious and cunning. Laying in wait, ready to pounce in a millisecond. It didn't matter if you were three feet from an open bar when a sudden thunderstorm delivered buckets of rain, or sitting in the first pew of St. Patrick's Cathedral on Christmas morning, your guard need always be up.

Thomlinson had already done two stints at the police department's rehab facility, colloquially known as "the farm". He wasn't about to do three. To ensure that, he'd turned to Alcoholics Anonymous to enlist the aid of a higher power.

Or, so it seemed.

AA encourages you to arrive at meetings early and to stay late. 'Become part of the dynamic of the room. Don't just take a seat,' was the battle cry at St. Edwin's. And that's what Cedric was doing. He was arriving early and staying late.

But, was the tiger at play for this Trinidadian born Casanova? Delivering a new trigger of compulsion right inside the Serenity on Sutton chapter of Alcoholics Anonymous? Many addicts stop a habit by starting a new one. Was that the case for Thomlinson who'd just slipped Giselle, a buxom blonde, his phone number? The same Gisele he'd been chatting up for the past three weeks. She had to know she was the real reason he was here. Would Cedric pick up again? Not a drink, but something as dangerously intoxicating for this insatiable man. Eighty proof lust.

These questions would remain unanswered, for now, as his cell phone was ringing. Answering it was a major faux pas at an AA meeting. But it was Driscoll, and Thomlinson knew the Lieutenant needed to speak with his lead detective.

Smiling at Giselle, Thomlinson headed for the door, regretting he had lied to Driscoll about his whereabouts.

CHAPTER EIGHTEEN

Driscoll was puzzled as to why the demon who'd murdered their Jane Doe had injected myrrh, aloe, and cassia into her circulatory system. While he awaited the arrival of his team, he was doing a bit of online research on the subject of embalming.

One particular site, *Embalming101.com,* intrigued him for it featured a place where visitors could post a comment or submit a question. In the archives, Driscoll found the following: "It's a cold night in 1958 and my girlfriend, a minister's daughter, suffered a fatal coronary while she and I were getting it on. If her father finds out I stole her virginity, he might kill me. Do I sprinkle her with myrrh, aloe, and cassia and dig a grave?" The question remained unanswered. Though the Lieutenant doubted there was any connection to the case, he felt the reference to the biblical anointing oils required he have someone look into it.

Peering over the Dell desktop, he spotted Margaret and Thomlinson approaching his office. As they filed in and took their seats, he logged off the computer.

"Margaret tells me we may have an embalmer to thank for polluting the East River," said Thomlinson.

"It looks that way," Driscoll said, answering his phone.

After a chorus of ah-huhs, he thanked his caller, hung up, and looked to his two assistants. "What can you tell me about Saint Vitalis of Gaza?"

"Not much," said Thomlinson. "He's not a suspect, is he?"

"I'm pretty sure we can rule him out," Margaret said. "He's the patron saint of prostitutes."

"That's right. And our embalmer has invoked his name," said Driscoll.

"Invoked?" Margaret asked, looking puzzled.

"That was Larry Pearsol on the phone. When I was there earlier, he showed me a piece of jewelry, a locket featuring a photographer's depiction of Saint Vitalis. It had been imbedded in the floor of our victim's mouth. Held in place by a sutured tongue."

"Charming."

"It gets better. Pearsol found an inscription written in ink on the flip side of the photograph inside the locket."

"What'd it say?"

"Go into hell, into the fire that never shall be quenched."

Thomlinson and Margaret exchanged glances.

"It's from the Book of Matthew," Driscoll said.

"The first book of the New Testament, Matthew?" Margaret asked, looking astonished.

"That'd be the one."

CHAPTER NINETEEN

"Our Jane Doe has a name," Driscoll said to Margaret when she answered his phone call. "Sinthia Loomis. Philadelphia PD has a rap sheet on her for prostitution. She's been missing for two months."

"A prostitute calling herself Sinthia? Why am I not surprised? Her pimp report her missing?" Margaret asked.

"Not unless his name is Geraldine Hankins."

"Probably another hooker."

"Or her sister. Where are you now?"

"Behind the wheel. Heading in."

"Change of plans. I'll need you to drive down to Philly to speak with this Geraldine. Find out if there's a pimp in the picture. Two months without his cut might give a guy motive."

"Will do," Margaret said exiting the Brooklyn Bridge where she bypassed One Police Plaza and headed for the Holland Tunnel. "Philly PD come up with anything useful in their Missing Person inquiry?"

"It appears this Sinthia Loomis dabbled in low budget porn. Billed herself as Lolita Love. Favored latex. The spray-on kind."

Margaret was no stranger to latex, nor to porn, having spent two years with the Vice Squad.

"Didn't think you'd be wearing your Vice cap in Homicide, did you?" Driscoll asked.

"Don't have a Vice cap. I turned it in when I was asked to decoy wearing just the cap."'"Knowing Lieutenant Sparks, I wouldn't be surprised if that were true."

The Lieutenant was aware of Margaret's frightful past. There was history between them. While working a major homicide they realized they had feelings for each other. And on more than one occasion, had expressed those feelings.

"You still working things out in therapy?" he asked.

"Yep."

"Good."

"OK, I'm about to enter the tunnel so I'll need to end the call. I'll check in again when I get to Philly."

"Travel safely, Margaret."

"Will do."

CHAPTER TWENTY

Traffic crawled along the New Jersey Turnpike. Margaret was approaching Exit 4, where she hoped a less congested Route 73 would take her into Philadelphia, when the car ahead of hers, a late model Volkswagen Beetle, began swerving. A sandy-haired male was behind the wheel. His head, pressed against the headrest, rolled from side to side. Had he fallen asleep?

Margaret hit the siren and placed the red flashing light atop the Chevy's roof. It prompted an immediate reaction. Not only did the driver's head bolt upright, but the head of his female passenger popped up like a jack-in-the-box. After pulling together a mop of errant hair, and fussing with her blouse, she slid to the right.

Lovely, thought Margaret. Going at a snail's pace, smack dab in the middle of a three lane interstate, and he's getting road head.

As Margaret turned off the siren and retrieved the flashing light the sexual display she'd just witnessed made her mind wander to long ago when her drunken father had his way with her. As memories of her sexual abuse filled her head the man's voice echoed in he ear.

"You're daddy's little girl, Margaret. Show daddy how much you love him. Just like I taught you."

At the age of nine, Margaret's goal was survival. She knew not to upset the man. He'd only drink more and things would get uglier.

"You're daddy's little girl. Daddy's pretty little girl...."
The blaring of a truck's horn brought Margaret back to the present. Narrowing her eyes, she closed the distance between the nose of her Chevy and the rear of the Volkswagen Beetle. "Go ahead, pal. Swerve again and I'll ram ya'."

CHAPTER TWENTY-ONE

It was after one when Margaret crossed the border into Philly. By 1:35 she was sharing a rickety booth with Geraldine Hankins inside Cassirer's Café on Spruce Street, a once thriving mercantile thoroughfare in Center City, Philadelphia.

Not wanting to add to the woman's misery, Margaret had explained that she was assisting her Philadelphia counterparts in their Missing Persons investigation and that she wasn't from Vice. The mid-twenties prostitute, who bore an uncanny resemblance to Natalie Wood, seemed to accept that explanation.

"Sinthia Loomis. I take it she was a friend of yours?" Margaret asked.

"Still is. And I'm praying to God the police find her before he does."

The woman nervously toyed with the assortment of sweeteners that filled a small plastic packet holder on the glass-topped table.

"Before he does? Who's he?" Margaret asked.

"Dagwood. He's got a posse of freakin' reptiles tracking her ass."

"I take it he's her pimp."

Geraldine studied Margaret's face and then nodded.

"Yours, too?"

"Fraid so."

A waitress appeared sporting a wide streak of ice blue dye through jet black hair. Margaret ordered coffee. After telling her the NYPD would be picking up the tab, Geraldine asked for two scrambled eggs, rye toast, and a grape Snapple. When their server disappeared into the kitchen, Margaret continued the interrogation. "Dagwood. That's quite a name."

The woman grinned, showcasing a haphazard assembly of teeth. "Yep. And Sinthia was his Blondie."

Margaret wondered if Blondie had stepped out of line. "Tell me about Sinthia."

"She's the sister I never had. Tough stuff, that girl. Me? I fold like a pretzel. Sinthia doesn't take shit from nobody."

"Not even Dagwood?"

"'specially, Dagwood. He was scared of her. I'm not sayin' she out-muscled him. He was twice her size. But it made him edgy that he couldn't control her from having a say in her life."

During Margaret's years in Vice she'd witnessed that uneasiness in many pimps. Total control. That's what drives men like that.

"That doesn't sound like something a pimp would put up with. Not having a complete say in her comings and goings. Maybe why she disappeared?"

"Could be. But, Dag's got the bloodhounds after her ass. If he had any part in her going missing, he wouldn't be shellin' out big bucks."

"Does he know it was you who called the police?"

Geraldine's eyes widened.

"I sure hope not," she said as her eyes strayed.

Margaret studied the woman. "What is it you're not telling me?"

"Whadya mean?"

"I think there's more to the story."

"There ain't."

"What are you leaving out?"

Anger erupted on the woman's face. "Why you doin' this to me? I'm the one who called it in. You're making it sound like I tossed her off a cliff!"

"Did you?"

"Hell, no!"

Margaret watched the woman squirm in her seat like a schoolgirl caught cheating on an exam. A moment later, Geraldine caved.

"This has gotta stay between us."

"Depends on what 'this' is," Margaret said.

Geraldine leaned in and lowered her voice. "Me and Sinthia don't do much hustling for Dagwood any more. We're part of another one of his enterprises." After a quick scan of the eatery assured her no one was eavesdropping, she said, "Dag's into porn."

"Into?"

"He films it."

"Does he sell it?" Margaret detected fear in Geraldine's eyes. "Look, like I explained before, I'm not from Vice." Margaret hoped she wouldn't need to reveal she worked Homicide as instinct told her this woman wouldn't handle the news of her friend's brutal demise well.

"You sound like Vice. If you ain't, what kinda cop are you?"

"A New York cop. We believe that's where she disappeared to. And the more you tell me about Dagwood Studios, the more help you'll be."

"You swear you're not from Vice?"

"Not from Vice."

Geraldine studied Margaret's face. "He's into fake snuff," she said.

"Snuff? He's making snuff films?"

"He's got no Academy Awards to brag about buthe shoots some mind blowing snuff. You heard me say fake, right? All hocus-pocus. Ain't nobody gets killed."

"I heard what you said. Who plays the victim?"

"Usually Sinthia. Sometimes me."

"Where's Dag while you're performing?"

"Usually behind the camera. If he ain't, I wouldn't know where's he's at. I get paid to fuck, get knifed, and die. Not keep track of him."

A second waitress, a young redhead wearing her ginger tresses in a bun, sashayed over with Margaret's coffee and Geraldine's scrambled eggs and toast along with the woman's Snapple.

After Margaret thanked the youthful waitress she smiled revealing a full set of dental braces. Turning on her heels, she headed for the kitchen.

"Is it ok if I resume my questioning while you eat?" Margaret asked.

"Sure," Geraldine replied, buttering her toast.

"Is it always murder by stabbing?" Margaret asked.

"Fake, remember?" the woman replied, twisting the top off her Snapple.

"All fake. I got it."

"Not always a stabbing. Sometimes Sinthia or I will get shot if we're running low on chocolate syrup. That's what they use for blood, by the way. Don't ask me how, but on camera it looks like the real thing."

"They ever use syringes or medical supplies?"

Geraldine stopped chewing and stared at Margaret with a blank look on her face saying nothing.

"You ok?" Margaret asked.

"Yeah, sorry. I just thought of a great scene. Damn, I always wanted to play a nurse!"

"So, any syringes or medical supplies get used?"

"Nope. But, I'll run that by Dagwood. I'd make a good nurse. Thanks for the suggestion."

"You're welcome," Margaret said, feeling a bit odd having inadvertently supplied a snuff enthusiast with a new scene. "Any machines ever used in a fake snuff scene? Ones that would be extreme or out of the ordinary?"

"Nah. Extreme? That sounds more like S & M."

"Does Dag shoot S & M?"

"Doubt it. If he did, I'd hear about it."

The young waitress reappeared and topped off Margaret's coffee.

Margaret smiled at her and resumed her line of questioning.

"Anything really bizarre?"

"Like what?"

"Oh, I don't know. Hoses, let's say, for forced water, or forced air. Pumps. Something you might see in an operating room. Anything like that?"

"This is porn, not New Amsterdam, though I wouldn't mind getting it on with Jocko Sims."

"What would be Dag at his kinkiest?"

"In snuff?"

"Yeah."

"Me getting' hanged. In one film I was gang banged while tied up in bed sheets draped over a light fixture. Slow suffocation with each thrust. All fake, as you can see, 'cause I'm still here. Jeez, I had a helluva time swallowing after that."

"And Sinthia? Anything kinkier?"

"Nope."

"You said she was Dagwood's Blondie. Was she serving up more than a moan and groan?"

"No way! If he was slippin' her the dipstick, I'd know."

Margaret stifled a laugh. Geraldine's delivery was entertaining. "Sinthia have family?" she asked.

"You're lookin' at it."

"Anyone else notice her missing?"

"Only the entire crew! Men. Big fans of tit. Though Sinthia was thin, she had one helluva rack. All natural, too." Geraldine glanced down at her modest bosom. "Unlike me, that girl was blessed."

"Where'd the filming take place?"

"What's with the rapid fire questioning?" Geraldine's face showed signs of fear. She tightened her lips and scoped Margaret. "You're beginning to scare the shit outa' me. Tell me again you're not from Vice."

"I swear I'm not from Vice."

The woman took a sip of her Snapple, eyes still fixed on the inquisitive cop.

"Dagwood have a particular set he likes to shoot on?" Margaret asked.

"Yeah, he's got a set. A set of balls. Big ones!" Geraldine replied.

"And Dagwood's favorite set for filming porn?"

"No favorites. Any roach motel will do."

"You're not a big fan of the boss man. Considering how you make a living, that's no surprise. But you scowl at the mention of his name. Why's that?"

"He tells me I'm his super star. Feeds Sinthia the same line. Says he treats us special 'cause of that. Look around. You see any swimming pools? Any playmates playing Marco Polo? Nope. Hugh Hefner reincarnated, he ain't. There ain't no mansion in Phila-friggen-delphia. No bunny ears. No cotton-tailed tushie. Just seedy motels, sheets spattered with fake blood, and a crew with hard-ons. Me and Sinthia? We might as well really get killed 'cause Dagwood's got little use for us after the camera stops rolling."

"How do I meet Mr. Bumstead?"

"Who?"

She knows of Dagwood and Blondie. Does she know they're comic book characters? "Dagwood Bumstead. Ring a bell?"

"Should it?"

Yep. She thinks they're legit names. "Dagwood. How do I meet this charmer?"

"Nobody meets Dag. Dag meets you."

"The guy's a pimp, remember? Philly PD wouldn't have a problem delivering him."

"I wouldn't bet on it. He's got this big shot cop in his pocket. Clarence Pembrook. Prefers redheads. Unwaxed. Dagwood's his go-to guy."

"Quite the provider."

"Besides, you'd get more out of Dagwood if he thought you were auditioning for a role."

She might be right. "OK. Let's say I go along with your suggestion. How would I arrange for Dagwood to meet me?"

"It'd depend on how good are you at hiding those brown curls under a blond wig. Dag insists his stars resemble Marilyn Monroe. Says a well funded group of kinky Turks love platinum bombshells. That makes them his triple B cash cows. Blondes, boobs, and bozmak."

"What the hell is bozmak?"

"Turkish for murder. Now let's get down to business. I'm guessing you're a 38C. Right?"

"You forget you're talking to a cop?"

"That ain't easy to forget. But, trust me, if it's info you want from Dag, go with the 38Cs God gave ya', and keep the 38-caliber in your purse. Distracted men are easier to work."

Margaret's smile indicated she agreed.

"Dag's gonna love you," Geraldine said with a grin. "I'll tell him you resemble that chick who was on Rizzoli & Isles. Angie what's-her-name. Let's see what the shit head does with that."

Great! Pinned once again as an Angie Harmon look-alike. Only this time, she's a blonde. But, the more Margaret considered it, the prospect of interrogating Dagwood as a porn star wannabe intrigued her. Besides, why pass up an opportunity to blindside a lowlife degenerate?

CHAPTER TWENTY-TWO

Margaret eyed herself in the full length mirror inside Room 402 at the Days Inn in Philadelphia. An undercover Vice cop smiled back. She wondered how Driscoll would explain a Department expenditure for a Passion Red underwire push-up bra, a striking pair of fuck-me-now stilettos, and a plunging spandex bubble dress. She thought the platinum wig was more Anna Nicole Smith, than Marilyn Monroe, but figured both Playboy playmates would be smiling in their graves.

Resisting the temptation to call Driscoll and whisper breathlessly into his ear, she blew a kiss at her reflection and headed for the door. Next stop – Dagwood's den of iniquity.

The receptionist at Vixen Videos looked like a cross between the poster girl for Botox and a mime. And when she spoke her lips moved like those of the Tin Man's in The Wizard of OZ before Dorothy oiled them.

"Got a 2:30 with Dagwood," said Margaret, enduring the woman's visual frisk.

"And you're on time. Geraldine's friend, right?"

"Right."

"Dag's gonna love you."

"Why's that?"

"You're perfect. A blonde with big boobs."

"Turkish eye candy, huh?"

"Screw the Turks. You're a walkin' talkin' Barbie!"

Great. Now I'm a plastic doll. "Gee, thanks," she said.

Shooting Margaret a smile, the receptionist shimmied out from behind her desk, and disappeared through a door marked 'Private'. Tattooed on her right buttock, were Mick Jagger's trademark tongue and lips, unabashedly visible through a whisper of a skirt. When she reappeared, she led Margaret into Dagwood's office. It was oval, and shockingly red with ruby colored carpeting meeting walls of glistening claret. She expected an assortment of Skinema posters or photos of topless screen sirens, but the walls were bare. At the top of the oval, sat Dagwood behind an oddly shaped desk. Realization struck. *That's why all the red. What a douche! He's seated at what's meant to be a clitoris. And I'm standing inside a mock vulva!*

Leering, as though reading Margaret's thoughts, he stood and ambled toward her. 'Clench All You Want It's Still Going In', was emblazoned on his tee-shirt. Margaret, suppressing an urge to smack the bastard, smiled.

"Natural?" he asked, eyeing her breasts.

"All natural," she said, giving them a shake. "You like?"

"What's not to like?" He ran his index finger under each one. "Great tits like these are meant to be showcased. How is it you know Geraldine?"

"We danced tables together."

"Table tops?"

"Yeah, and sometimes below."

"Good. I like a girl who goes down." His focus was now on her lips. "Geraldine tells me you're new to adult video."

"A virgin."

"Is that so?"

"Virgin to the industry, that is."

He circled Margaret as though she were livestock. "Well, Miss Virgin To The Industry, I shoot hardcore. That gonna be a problem?"

"Nope." He had opened the door. Time to steer the conversation. "Deenie says you shoot more than porn."

"Deenie, is it? What else does Deenie say?"

"That she has nine lives."

A lecherous smile formed on Dagwood's face, now inches away from Margaret's. He closed his eyes and inhaled her.

"Scent. Quite the aphrodisiac, eh?" said Margaret.

"It lures the blind."

"Deenie tells me she and a chick named Sinthia are your specialty girls. Like me. Into all sorts of things." Margaret watched the man's eyes for a reaction. There was none. "Deenie, I know, but who Sinthia is I haven't a clue. I'm told I look like her."

"But can you move like her?"

"Honey, I move like a gummy bear in heat. Maybe you'd like to see me and Sinthia in action?"

"That'd be a little difficult."

"Why's that?"

Caution registered on the man's face. "You ask a lot of questions."

Margaret feigned embarrassment. "Just aiming to please."

"Where's a good exhaust fan when you need one?" Dagwood's face looked contorted.

"Exhaust fan?"

"I smell bullshit. I also smell cop. That door you came in? Use it."

"Now, listen pal, this cop will leave when she gets some answers." Margaret yanked off the blond wig.

"My lawyer talks to Vice."

"Good for him. I'm not Vice. In fact, I'm not from Philly so your hook into the Deputy Commissioner means squat. What do you know about the disappearance of Sinthia Loomis?"

"Fuck off."

Margaret grabbed hold of the man's testicles and squeezed. "Listen, dickhead, I'm not in a good mood. You'll talk to me or you and your lawyer will be sitting in a detention cell discussing your best defense against sexually assaulting a police officer. My breasts. Your fingers. Remember?"

"That's entrapment!" He winced as Margaret tightened her grip.

"Loomis. Sinthia. Talk," she said, applying pressure with each word.

Dagwood howled prompting Miss Botox to rush in. "I'm calling the cops!" she hollered.

"They're already here," he whimpered.

The receptionist threw her hands in the air, did an about face, and disappeared.

"OK, Dagwood, I'm gonna let go and you're gonna tell me what you know about Sinthia Loomis. Comprende?"

He nodded.

"Any funny stuff and six police officers will enter this room through that wall." As she let go the pimp cupped a hand around his aching scrotum. "Talk. Now." Margaret ordered.

"Wha'd'ya want me to say? Sinthia left. Vanished. I haven't a clue where she went." His breathing was labored. "You nearly killed me, lady."

"The price for groping me, asshole."

"Jesus! I may never walk again."

"Sinthia have a falling out with anyone before she disappeared?"

"No. She was the charm girl. Everybody liked her. If you're thinking I had anything to do with her leaving, think again. You know how much money I'm out since she split?"

Margaret knew that to be fact. "Wha'd'ya know about her life outside of this land of enchantment?"

"She didn't have one. She was a fixture here."

"Why leave?"

"Beats the hell out of me," he grimaced, trying to stand up straight.

"She ever mention plans about going anywhere?"

"If she had plans, she didn't share them with me. Wait! There was something. Maybe."

"Maybe?"

"A couple of weeks before she went missing, she told me she was thinking about getting a tattoo. I told her I didn't shoot trailer park video. My customers wanna see flesh. Not ink. She made a face and told me I wasn't the only game in town."

"She say anything more about the tattoo?"

"No, but she showed me what it would look like." Moving like a man who just had a gall stone removed, he hobbled to his desk and produced a sketch.

Truaillithe Fainne

"She tell you what it meant?"

"No."

Margaret eyed Dagwood. Was there something he was holding back? She didn't think so. And she didn't feel he was bright enough to murder the woman in the fashion she was killed. "Here's the deal," she said. "Deenie will be calling me weekly. If I get so much as a whisper that she's being mistreated, I'll track you down and run a box cutter through your balls."

He said nothing in reply, but as Margaret headed for the door, she was certain he'd gotten the message.

CHAPTER TWENTY-THREE

Truaillithe Fainne

Driscoll, seated behind his desk at One Police Plaza, studied the tattoo artist's sketch Margaret had brought back from Philadelphia.

"Truaillithe Fainne. Sounds French," Margaret said.

"A little, but I'm thinking Old Irish." Driscoll keyed the words into the department's Dell desktop seeking a translation. "Irish, it is," he said, pivoting the monitor for Margaret to see.

"Tainted halo? What the hell is that?"

"Beats me."

"Google it."

And so he did, producing the following:

- **Gaia Online :: *.Tainted.Halo.*'s profile**
ProgramFiles/Internetbrowser/Internetexplorer/
Loadfile:buttsecks.exe/systemfailure0Please-
Insert-Backup/Reboot/1347_Haxxorz/Buttsecks.
app *.Tainted.Halo.* ...
https://www.gaiaonline.com/
profiles/?u=619237907 – *16k* – Cached – Similar
pages -

- *Tainted Halo* <**EveryAngelHasAShadow**>

Tainted Halo's URL. http://www.bebo.com/ EveryAngelHasAShadow ..... Give *Tainted Halo* your luv for today. "Luv is the answer, but what's the question?" ...
www.bebo.com/Profile.jsp?- MemberId=8345628250 – Similar pages –

- ### *Tainted halo*
Tainted halo. Posted: Oct 04, 2004 at 0000 hrs IST. The Supreme Court's notice to Mr. and Mrs. Laloo Prasad Yadav is good news indeed, and bad. ...
www.indianexpress.com/oldstory. php?storyid=569703 – 30k – Cached – Similar pages –

- ### Kelly & *Tainted Halo* – Raven's Friends and Friendship Forums!
Feb 16, 2009 ... Kim & *Tainted Halo* Ravens Tagging Frenzy! ... Hi *Tainted Halo*! I'm excited to be paired with you this week. ...
ravensforums.com/forums/showthread. php?p=261708 – 139k – Cached – Similar pages –

- ### *Tainted Halo* – FanFiction.Net
Interact with writer, *Tainted Halo*, who has archived 11 stories for Yu Yu Hakusho, Final Fantasy VIII, Gundam Wing/AC, Megami Kouhosei, Fushigi Yuugi, ...
www.fanfiction.net/u/947509/Tainted Halo - Similar pages -

- ### myYearbook | **Tainted Halo*..LCDD
**Tainted Halo*..LCDD's Yearbook. Popularity: 21087 ... Name: **Tainted Halo*..LCDD. Gender: Female. This profile is set to Private ...

*www.myyearbook.com/?mysession=-
cmVnaXN0cmF0aW9uX3Byb2ZpbGNlcmlkPTEx
Nzk...* – Similar pages –

- ***Tainted halo, anyone? On Flickr – Photo
Sharing!***
Tainted halo, anyone? ... install the latest version
of the Macromedia Flash Player. *Tainted halo*,
anyone? By exiguousopificer. ...
*www.flickr.com/photos/84037577@
N00/3160463267/* - *53k* – Cached – Similar pages
–

- ***Tainted halo***
Tainted halo. Posted: Oct 04, 2004 at 0000 hrs
IST. The Supreme Court's notice to Mr. and Mrs.
Laloo Prasad Yadav is good news indeed, and bad.
...
*www.indianexpress.com/oldstory.
php?storyid=93003* – *30k* – Cached – Similar
pages –

Exploring each link was a tedious exercise in futility,
until Driscoll opened this one:

- **Tainted Halo ~ Every Angel Has A Naughty
Side** ☺

What blossomed onscreen were three sets of impossibly
perfect breasts jiggling in sync to a chorus of *O, Come All
Ye Faithful* with a message chugging along the bottom like
a TV network's news stream: Looking for a little swinger's
playtime in the city that never sleeps? Zooey, Priscilla, and
Sinthia invite you to call 869 LUVDOVES."

"I believe we've found our Sinthia," Driscoll said with
a smile. "Those cockeyed halos are a nice, touch. Don't ya'
think?"

"You don't wanna know what I think."

CHAPTER TWENTY-FOUR

Smoke encircled Loretta's face, drifting from a lipstick-stained cigarette she rolled between two fingers. She was on her break inside Arnie's Diner, a hellhole of a coffee shop, where her waitressing paid the bills. She knew the ban on smoking in a restaurant was strictly enforced in places like New York City and Albany. But that wasn't about to happen in Chesterville, New York, where many of its residents not only smoked tobacco, but chewed it as well.

Loretta's attention was drawn to the customer seated at the counter eating his breakfast. He'd only been in a few times, but was a hard guy to forget. Batty as hell. A recluse, she'd been told. Word was he belonged to some religious cult, but his plaid shirt and frayed jeans didn't point to any particular denomination. He seemed harmless enough, but had peculiarities. The fact that he waddled was one of them. She'd seen lots of struts in her day. But a waddle? The way he ordered his meal was another. The eatery's main draw was a bountiful breakfast at a reasonable price. To fill that bill, Arnie offered two eggs any style, two strips of bacon, a choice of freshly baked muffins, and coffee for $6.99. This guy would always order that; his eggs up with a blueberry muffin. But not before scrutinizing the other items on the menu like he was going to be tested on them. He never spoke. Pointing instead to what he wanted. She knew damn well he could talk, but for some cockamamie reason, chose not to. How did she know? Because his lips moved when he studied the menu. Like they were doing now, a newspaper six inches from his nose.

Oh, shit! He caught me staring! Loretta ruffled her apron in an effort to avoid his glare, but his unspoken threat was voluminous, as his intimidating eyes bore into her. After what felt like a full minute, he withdrew his stare, pushed his plate forward and placed a crumpled one dollar bill beside it. Getting off his stool, he leered at her, mouthed "Bye, bye now," and waddled out the door.

Through the diner's window, Loretta watched him climb behind the wheel of a vintage Cadillac. Its cab section was stunted making it look like it was designed to only accommodate two passengers. *Jesus! Is that an undertaker's flower car?* her inner voice asked. Under her steadfast gaze he veered the vehicle toward the parking lot's exit. The sight of him driving that type of vehicle was unusual enough but why was there a blue poly tarp covering its tail section? More importantly, what was under it? As if Loretta had willed it, the wind shifted, lifting the blue tarp; exposing the vehicle for what it was. A vintage flower car. More frightening though, was its cargo.

CHAPTER TWENTY-FIVE

"Kyle, put the sheriff on," was all Loretta managed to say before Arnie Krieger depressed the phone's switch hook. "Arnie! What the hell are you doing?"

"We don't need no trouble, Loretta. Calling the sheriff is the last thing you're gonna do."

"But I spotted a loon cartin' a friggen cross. You see the size of that thing? Had to be 25 feet! That nut's out to crucify someone."

"What I saw was a utility pole."

"Utility pole my ass! That was a friggen cross!"

"This is my shop, Loretta. And what I say goes."

Loretta glared at him.

"You forgettin' your last call, Loretta? When that towel-head muttered something into his cell phone and you told the sheriff he was detonating a bomb?"

Loretta had a few regrets. That one topped the list.

"You called the law on a goddamn State Assemblyman! New rule, Loretta. Unless someone's holding a gun to your head, no phone calls."

"Just admit it was a cross. You can give me that, can't ya'?"

Smiling, but saying nothing, Arnie did an about face and headed for his office. Once there, he un-pocketed the Post-it he'd used to record the vehicle's license plate number and deposited it inside his fire-resistant safe.

CHAPTER TWENTY-SIX

With his NYPD placard on the dashboard, Thomlinson could park anywhere. It was a privilege he cherished and one he had, on occasion, taken advantage of. He had scheduled a 4 p.m. acupuncture session with a healer, Doctor Heather Swensen. *That's a Danish name,* he reflected. *What do those who were once called Vikings in the 9th Century know about acupuncture? Does Doctor Swensen get off on pricking the skin of men? What kind of a vocation is that? Could she be a sadist? One who's found the perfect cover to inflict pain?* He couldn't quiet his mind. Thomlinson realized he was terrified. But how could a 225 pound hulk of a man dread an elongated Chinese needle in the hands of a Scandinavian chick? Why would he submit his body to such treatment, nay, mistreatment? *Would my testicles be safe from these rods?* He had read about the Chakras and their connection to energy channels, meridians that crisscrossed the human body. The question wouldn't be silent. Why sacrifice his skin to an alien technique that may or may not offer relief? But, he knew he was an addict and that addiction is never cured, only controlled. He couldn't risk the Department finding out he was slipping. It would only be a matter of time before he picked up again. His sudden "must have" attraction toward women was proof of that and he knew he needed help. If AA wasn't working, maybe acupuncture would.

He approached the high rise. Unnerved, he pressed the intercom button. After being buzzed in, he entered the lobby and walked toward a single elevator. "Out of Order...Take the Stairs" the sign read. *Damn it,* he thought. *Her studio's on the 6th floor!*

On the 4th floor an image came to mind that stopped him dead in his tracks. Visions of torture techniques devised by the Spanish Inquisition filled the panorama of his mind. In one, an executioner was hammering long nails into the body of a hapless victim believed to be a heretic. The temptation to turn and run pricked him. "For fuck's sake," he muttered, waiving his arm in the air to dismiss the apparition and continue his upward trek.

The aroma of incense teased Cedric's nostrils on the 6th floor landing. He approached the stylostixis practitioner's door. Finding no bell, he sheepishly knocked. There was a shuffle on what sounded like bare wood. As the door creaked open, Heather Swensen, clad in a Japanese kimono with dancing cranes, smiled. And when she did, her sparkling blue eyes dispelled all of Thomlinson's fears.

"Come in," she said, her voice just above a whisper. "Would you like some tea? It's perfumed with orange blossoms."

"That'd be nice. Have you got Splenda?"

"You drink your tea sweetened?"

"I do. But if you don't have Splenda, I'm good with Sweet'N Lo."

"I have no sweeteners," she said. "They can be very addictive."

"I suppose."

"And from what you told me on the phone, your addiction to alcohol is why you're here."

Thomlinson's response was a blank stare. His thought: *God, she has a charming voice.* He knew his fondness for the ladies, his new addiction, was why he was here. But, he wasn't about to divulge that. At least, not yet.

"When did you have your last drink?" she asked.

"It's been six years, three months, and thirteen days."

"You're the stuff heroes are made of."

"And you're the first damsel to call me a hero."

"No damsel in your life?"

"There used to be. There was this bar. Back in the day. Great place for picking up sirens."

"A siren is not a damsel."

"I've never been a one damsel man, Doctor Swensen."

"Maybe I can also help you with that. And, please, it's Heather."

"Only if you've got needles that turn guys into monogamists."

"I've been known to perform miracles."

"Alleluia, Heather! If that's the case, I'm all yours. Where do we go from here?"

"First, I'll explain how acupuncture works."

"I'm listening."

"In your case, I'll be focusing on what is likely an imbalance in your body that's causing your addiction. That particular concentration of care is what we call the NADA protocol. The name stems from the National Acupuncture Detoxification Association. I'll be inserting needles to target five points in your ear. In general, the nerves in our bodies form a gigantic network. Electricity flows through pathways we call meridians. When we're stressed, when we're traumatized, when we're depressed, the energy flow is interrupted and it coagulates. That's where the imbalance comes in. What the needles do is release the blockage. Does any of this make you anxious?"

"I gotta be honest, the thought of being a pincushion has me a little worried."

"Worried how?"

"Well, there's one fear in particular."

"And what's that?"

"I'm hoping none of those meridians lead to my ball sack. I'm very attached to my luggage."

"Your valise is safe with me."

"You promise?"

"I promise."

"That's comforting. May I ask you a question?"

"Of course?"

"You're an energy healer. That's what they call you, right?"

"That's right."

"I gotta say, you've got a pleasant aura about you."

"Thank you. That's very kind."

The doctor approached the samovar and poured tea into a porcelain cup. "Ok. What I'd like to do now is conduct a preliminary examination. I'll start by taking your pulse. Would that be alright?"

Thomlinson nodded and rolled up his sleeve, offering her his right arm. He watched her. Her touch was gentle.

"I'm checking your lungs, your stomach, and your adrenal glands," she said, moving her two fingers up the short expanse of his wrist. "How are you sleeping?"

"Good," Thomlinson said.

"Eight hours? Seven?"

"I'm a cop chasing down the City's crazies."

Heather Swensen smiled. "I'll jot down four. Sometimes, five. Allergic to anything?"

"Besides booze?"

"Aside from alcohol, yes."

"Nada."

"All good in the urination department?"

"Third floor, ladies and gentlemen. This is where this department store showcases winter coats, sweaters, and scarves. They're all on your left. A fine selection of urination can be found on the right," Thomlinson announced, parodying a department store elevator operator.

"Funny man, you are," Heather Swensen said.

"And, yes, all's peachy keen below the belt."

"Good to know."

After checking the pulse on his left wrist, she asked Thomlinson to stick out his tongue.

"That's a new one."

"The tongue reveals a lot."

"If you say so," he said, though it sounded like 'id ooo aye yo' with his tongue extended. He didn't want to know what she jotted down after her oddly erotic inspection.

"Alrighty, then. I believe we're ready to start. I'll step into my office for a minute, and while I do, I'd like you to undress. You can keep your underpants on."

Kicking off his shoes, Thomlinson stripped. Eyeing a stack of towels, he grabbed one and wrapped it around his waist. He hadn't noticed earlier, but there was soft rhythmic jazz streaming through an unseen speaker. *Was that Till Brönner's trumpet?*

The space was small but inviting. In the center of the room was the massage table shrouded in white linen. Its full size pillow was topped by the paper covering a patient often sees on an examination table in any doctor's office. As was the entire table top. An oriental screen depicting white clouds stood beside it. Clustered atop an oversized red lacquered Oriental style credenza, was an assortment of aromatic oils and several sleeves of needles, their tops accented in a variety of colors.

Heather Swensen reappeared and smiled. "OK. Please climb up and then lie face down on the table."

Thomlinson did as he was instructed, resting his face in a halo shaped cushion which forced him to stare at the bamboo flooring.

"I hope you're a fan of soft jazz," she said. "Many of my patients opt for a looping stream of Oriental Zen. I can switch to that if you'd like."

"Jazz is my kinda sound."

"Good. Jazz it'll be."

"That's Till Brönner's *Love Is Here To Stay*," Thomlinson said.

"Wow, I'm impressed." She inserted the first needle into the tragus of his right ear. The second into its antitragus. "You may feel a tingling sensation in the spongy formations that surround the ear's canal."

Sandalwood incense filled the small room. She must have just ignited the stick. There was enchantment in the perfumed air. And in the music. And in her voice, which was pleasantly haunting.

"I'm going to insert some needles in your back and down your legs as I detected wiry stress when I checked your pulse," she said.

She was right about the tingling. It felt as though a butterfly had landed in the middle of his back; then skittered down his right leg. As he stared at the bamboo flooring, her painted toes came into view. He watched those toes, her two bouquets of red carnations, float around him as another butterfly touched down on his shoulder, skipped down his arm, and came to rest on the side of his thumb.

Serenaded by the soft jazz, Thomlinson drifted into a beguiling trance.

"How are you feeling?" her voice chimed.

"Like I'm halfway to heaven," he said.

"You mean you're not there yet?"

"We're getting close."

"Maybe this'll help." She ran the palms of both hands up his spine.

"Ahhh, there's the stairway."

"The stairway?"

"To heaven."

Time flowed, unmarked and invisible. An altered state Thomlinson had never known. It felt amorphic and opaque, like some form of inebriation.

"OK, Cedric," the acupuncturist whispered. "I'm going to step into my office. When you're ready, get up slowly. You'll likely feel dizzy. Be very careful when you climb down from the table. When you're dressed step through this door and into my office. We can discuss a treatment plan."

Cedric felt as though he was coming out of anesthesia and wasn't quite ready to leave his blissful euphoria. It sure had been a nice trip. His ears detected a mellow sound. The jazz he'd listened to moments before had become softer. Someone was playing a flute. *"Was that Bobbi Humphrey?"* he wondered. After listening intently, he dismissed the notion. It sounded more Asian.

Gradually, he edged himself off the table. Once his feet sensed the floor, he straightened himself up. His body, it seemed, had lost its density. He no longer felt heavy. It was a peculiar sensation. Cedric laughed nervously at the notion he might be levitating. For God's sake, could he actually be floating above the planks of bamboo? Palming the wall to steady himself, he stepped into his pants. Levitating. Wow! Had he actually achieved the level of spiritual enlightenment reserved for the Buddhist Monks? Dismissing a inane urge to chant, he pushed open the door and approached Doctor Heather Swensen who was scribbling notes on a pad. "You're on to something, little lady. Five minutes ago I was floating."

"Of course you were."

"You mean that's supposed to happen?"

"If the session goes well, yes. You release the psychic weight you've collected. That stuff weighs ya' down."

"Heather, you take waste management to a whole 'nother level."

"I've never heard it described that way, but, yeah, I guess that's true. Thank you for the compliment."

"You're welcome. It's I who should be thanking you. How 'bout you be my guest at Scarborough's. It's a Trinidadian restaurant on Avenue U in Brooklyn. They make the best Pelau on the planet!"

"That's such a sweet gesture. But, I'm sorry, I don't socialize with my patients."

"Have you ever had Pelau?" he asked.

She said nothing but her eyes restated her 'no, thank you'.

"I understand," he said, immediately realizing his addiction was at play.

"And I'm staying clear of compulsions."

"Wha'd'ya mean?"

"Well, you know, Cedric, you have a compulsive personality. I'll speculate that it's part of the reason you're in AA. It's also why you're here."

"It is?"

"You shouldn't settle for a substitute."

"Wha'd'ya mean?"

"You're looking for a surrogate addiction."

"I am?"

"I'll speculate you're trying to go from booze to women."

Thomlinson was astonished by her intuitiveness. "What's wrong with women?" he asked, hoping to reroute the conversation.

"Nothing. A relationship with a woman is very healthy. But, based on what you've told me, and evidenced by your suggestion we have dinner after just meeting me, I'm of the opinion you may be looking to replace your addiction to alcohol with another."

Thomlinson was floored. Though he sported his best poker face, thoughts swirled inside his head. Had he told her he was chatting it up with women during his AA meetings? He didn't think he had. Did she know? If so, how?

"Cedric, I'm very flattered by your overture. I truly am. But if I were to become part of your thirteen stepping, I wouldn't be helping you."

"Wow, you're familiar with the term. Usually only someone in the program would know what thirteen stepping means. Are you a friend of Bill's?"

"I'm not. But you're not the first addict I've treated. Many of my patients have stepped beyond the scope of the program by putting down the drink only to pick up another poison. That behavior doesn't treat the addiction. It redirects it."

"Oh, God. Some luck I have. I pick a therapist who can see through me."

"That's what you need."

"You care that much, Heather?"

"I care about all my patients."

"Ok. All right. You win. I'm outed," Thomlinson said, glumly. "What the hell. Let's go for the cure."

"I have an opening next Thursday at 2.

"I'll be here."

Heather Swensen smiled. "Do you know the last words Buddha uttered on his death bed?"

Thomlinson shrugged.

"He was surrounded by his disciples. His favorite asked: "Lord Buddha, what is your final guidance before you leave us?" Buddha gestured for him to draw near. In his ear he whispered: "Work out your salvation with diligence.""

"Diligence. I have none. That's my problem," Thomlinson said.

"I know."

"You know?"

"Yes," she said with a smile. "And that's what we're going to be working on."

CHAPTER TWENTY-SEVEN

"Margaret, do you remember what this place used to be?" Driscoll asked, stepping inside the nineteenth century brownstone where the Tainted Halos had set up "house."

"I do. Where do you suppose they hid the holy water fonts?"

After walking down what once was the center aisle of St. Bonaventure's Church, Driscoll and Margaret came upon an anomaly that riled them. Gone was the raised marble table where Mass was celebrated with gold plated chalices, glistening patens, and sacrosanct ciboriums. In its place was a circular sofa that surrounded an oval bar where women, in plunging necklines and barely-there skirts, flittered about decadently dressed men who eyed them lustfully. Driscoll suspected the only incense would be found on the upper floors, in the aroma of amalgamated sweat and unbridled carnality.

Two blondes, in form-fitting religious habits featuring tunics and fishnet stockings, more suited for Catwoman than any nun Driscoll had ever encountered, were seated atop that bar singing an a cappella rendition of *Strangers in the Night*. In place of a coif, their Styrofoam halos suggested they were the pair the Lieutenant was here to see. When they finished singing, he approached. "I'm Lieutenant Driscoll," he said, producing his shield and Department ID card. "This is Sergeant Aligante."

"Hi! I'm Sister Priscilla," said the fairer of the pair.

"That's awful shiny," said the other, dabbing at her lipstick reflected in the shield's mirror-like finish. "I'm Sister Zooey."

"The name fits," Margaret said, drawing a look of disdain.

"We offer a discount for men in uniform," said Priscilla, scoping Driscoll from head to toe.

"I'll bet you do," Margaret said, sidling up to her boss.

"Ladies, too," Priscilla replied, her gaze still fixed on Driscoll. "Nice threads," she added, running a finger along the edge of the Lieutenant's Joseph Abboud jacket.

"Is this an official visit?" asked Zooey. "Or are you two looking for a little action?"

"Oh, brother," Margaret muttered, rolling her eyes. "Official," she said, producing a morgue photo of the Sinthia Loomis. "You know her?"

"Whoa! She looks dead!" Zooey shouted, silencing the bar and putting an end to her partner's flirting.

Priscilla grabbed the photo and produced a set of reading glasses from God knows where. "That's Sinthia," she stammered. "What the hell happened? Who did this to her?"

"We're hoping you could tell us. You knew her as Sinthia Loomis?" Driscoll asked.

Priscilla nodded.

"We're trying to determine who killed her," Margaret said, sympathetic to the anguish that marked the woman's face.

"Why would someone want to hurt Sinthia? She was a sweetheart."

"Is there someplace we can talk?" Driscoll asked, gesturing toward the crowd of gawking onlookers.

"Yeah. We can talk in there." Priscilla lead them inside what was once the church's sacristy.

Driscoll eyed the Aids-Awareness posters that lined the walls. *Looks a lot different than the vestries I remember as an altar boy,* he thought as the four took seats at a rectangular table in the center of the room. "We need to ask some probing questions about Miss Loomis. You up for that?" the Lieutenant asked.

Priscilla and Zooey nodded.

"How long have you known Sinthia?" Margaret asked Priscilla.

"Not long," the woman replied.

A cautious answer, Margaret surmised.

"She was one of us. A Tainted Halo," Zooey said. "Who'd wanna do this to an angel?"

"How long had she worked with you?" Driscoll asked

The two woman exchanged glances. The expression on their faces was a mixture of gloom and suspicion. Driscoll understood their hesitancy to readily open up to the police. He waited patiently for an answer.

"Two months," Priscilla finally said. "She'd answered our online ad seeking a female vocalist willing to sing in a swinger's club."

"She have a life outside of here?"

"Everybody's got a life outside of here," Zooey said, looking to Priscilla. Her eyes conveyed apprehension. Margaret was also well aware ladies in her their line of work weren't keen on being asked questions.

"What was hers like?" Margaret asked, sensing her uneasiness.

"Haven't a clue," said Priscilla.

"How 'bout you, Zooey? You and Sinthia ever get together outside of here?" Margaret asked.

When Zooey's lips tightened, Margaret recognized her unspoken discomfort. She'd witnessed it many times working Vice. "I'm guessing you hung up your halos at the door," she joked, hoping to dispel her trepidation.

"Huh?" Zooey asked, visibly perplexed.

"You said she was one of you. A Tainted Halo. I take it this was your only venue?"

"Our only what?" asked Zooey, looking more confounded.

"Yes, our only venue," said Priscilla.

"Either of you know where she lived?" Driscoll asked.

"No," they answered in unison.

"She'd show up. We'd do the routine. Three nights a week. That's about it," Priscilla explained.

Zooey flinched and Driscoll caught it. "And you?" he asked, watching blush fill her cheeks.

Zooey's lips tightened again.

"If you've got something to add, now would be the time," the Lieutenant urged.

"Sinthia thought she had a secret admirer," the woman whispered.

"What the hell are you talking about?" Priscilla asked, staring at Zooey.

"Someone who visited the club?" Margaret asked.

Another look between the two. Margaret read it as their feeling uncomfortable again. Talking about themselves was a lot easier than talking about where and who they worked for.

"Any information you can provide about this man will help us determine if he's responsible for your friend's death," Driscoll offered.

"He'd come in every now and then," Zooey said. "He'd also pop up on the street. Sometimes inside a store where Sinthia was shopping."

"Sinthia had a stalker? When were you gonna tell me this?" Priscilla asked.

"It didn't creep her out. That's why I didn't mention it. Sinthia felt the guy was harmless. Said he looked like a priest and was probably attracted to her costume."

"Costume? You girls parade around half naked on the street?" Margaret looked astonished.

"No silly, we wear the black and white get-up when we report to work."

"You mean the religious habit?"

"The what?" Zooey asked, sporting that confused look, again.

"She's talking about the get-up," Priscilla told her.

"Then why didn't she say so?" Zooey pouted, drawing an unseen eye roll from Margaret.

"The boss has us show up dressed like real nuns and just before we start singing we're supposed to strip down," Priscilla explained.

"You said she thought he looked like a priest," Driscoll reiterated. "And that she saw him on the street too. Or at a store. Can you be more specific?"

"Not really."

"She say what he looked like?" Margaret asked.

"Yeah. Said he looked like whozeewhatsis. You know. That silly goof on TV. Wears a red bow tie and a gray suit. Damn! What's his name?" Zooey looked to the ceiling as if seeking divine intervention. "Pee-wee Herman!" she hollered. "That's right! Sinthia said he looked like Pee-wee Herman."

CHAPTER TWENTY-EIGHT

Tilden stepped out of the Cadillac and saw that the tarp had shifted, exposing the cross. He wondered how long it'd been exposed and if anyone had seen it.

Dismissing the thought, he tugged on the cross until it cleared the tailgate and fell, hitting the asphalt with a thud. It wasn't likely anyone would notice it was missing. The grounds surrounding the abandoned church where he'd procured it were thick with brier. He was probably the only person to visit the site in months, maybe years. Besides, no one takes note of a flower car at a church. No matter how unique.

He was pleased he'd selected for his kill a working girl that resembled that bitch, Valerie, who'd reamed his ass, but was concerned the authorities had retrieved her corpse. Though there was no way in hell they'd trace her embalmed cadaver to him, he thought it best to obliterate his victims from here on out. This was not the time to take chances. Besides, he was looking forward to what he was planning as he'd never breathed in the aroma of burnt flesh. The anticipation gave him a rush.

CHAPTER TWENTY-NINE

Charcoal sketches of shadowy figures with ravenous eyes litter the walls of Room 312 at Mercer General Hospital in Trenton, New Jersey. The room was both home and studio to thirty-six-year-old Adrian Strayer, a ward of the city. Tall and lean, this Michelangelo with the mentality of a third grader sat crouched in a corner flailing his arms at his latest visitor, an apparition seen only by him. This was no isolated instance. Similar demons would visit Adrian throughout the day, posing a challenge to art therapist, Doctor Melanie Anderson, who'd been working with this haunted soul for the last six months.

"Adrian? Doctor Anderson called out as she entered the room with a box of pastels.

Distracted from his delusion, he squared himself and spoke: "I'm Adrian. Are you looking for me?"

On her last visit, he had answered to Patrick. Seamus, before that. Typical behavior for someone with a dissociative identity disorder.

"Yes, Adrian. It's Melanie. You remember me. Don't you?"

The man's lips quivered. "I think so."

"Who shall we draw?" she asked, watching him examine the artist's newsprint she'd spread before him. "Who will it be? Matthew? Philip? Would you like to draw Mark, again?"

"Mark's not my friend."

"I thought he was your best friend."

"He stopped talking to me."

For several months Adrian had portrayed the gallery of personalities that crowded his mind. Most often, Mark.

"You don't want to draw Mark anymore?"

"Mark's gone," Adrian said.

"Who, then? Matthew?"

"No."

"Why not?"

"He's gone too." Adrian shrugged. "Time to draw."

"All right. Who shall it be?"

"Ella"

The therapist was astonished. His artwork had always been influenced by the personalities inside his head. And they'd all been male. "OK. What color would you like to start with?"

"Black."

"All right," she said, bolstered by the belief that Adrian had peeled back a layer of unconsciousness where another entity existed. A female entity.

Eager to see where this would lead, she watched intently as Adrian began to draw. First an oval. Then a nose. Two symmetrically placed ears. And a mouth. She'd anticipated his usual distorted, expressionistic portrait, but this was simple and recognizable, although the eyes he'd drawn were closed. A body followed, as a female torso was connected to the face. When legs and arms were added, the figure appeared to be asleep.

Doctor Anderson, astonished by the realism, felt proud to be the muse behind his work. What he did next clearly indicated a breakthrough. But it also concerned her. With a piece of red chalk, he drew what looked like a rivulet of blood oozing from the subject's neck. Then added a bucket to catch its flow.

CHAPTER THIRTY

On the nineteenth floor of 115 Cadman Plaza, Fire Marshall Tony Ricci was pouring over his notes regarding a three-alarm blaze at Saint Therese's Roman Catholic Church where arson was suspected. When Engine Company 305 and Ladder Company 126 arrived on the scene, the church's north wall was being supported by a flame-ravaged portion of the eastern exterior. A common sight for New York City firefighters. What was not common was the charred remains impaled on a cross leaning against the church's door.

Since the unidentified victim was not the likely arsonist, Driscoll and his team had been called in to investigate the crucifixion. A crucifixion which, according to the medical examiner, may have been the handiwork of their embalmer as the remnants of a second locket was found under what once was the decedent's tongue. It, too, featured Saint Vitalis of Gaza, the patron saint of prostitutes.

The wrought iron nails which pierced the victim's wrists and tore through the metatarsal bones of the feet were unremarkable. They could've been purchased in any hardware store. The intensity and temperature of the flames left little physical evidence to assist with an ID. The body had been reduced to bone. Brittle bone. The condition of the few teeth that were present suggested the decedent may have never seen a dentist. The pelvic inlet was large, as was the sub pubic angle, which indicated the descendant was a female.

"The blaze broke out at 11:20 p.m.," Fire Marshall Ricci explained as Driscoll, Aligante, and Thomlinson listened. "That's two hours and forty minutes after closing in a tranquil neighborhood of one and two-family homes."

"Who called it in?" Margaret asked.

"The church's sexton. He was asleep in an adjacent building until a blast of intense heat woke him. The guy suffered third degree burns attempting to put out the flames. Claims he didn't hear or see anything out of the ordinary before the fire broke out. Nor did any of the area residents."

"Our guy stages a crucifixion. Sets the place on fire. And nobody sees a thing? I'd say we're after a ninja," Thomlinson remarked.

"A ninja who's changed his M.O.," Margaret griped.

"What's protocol on this?" Driscoll asked Ricci, not familiar with the reporting requirements of an arson investigator.

"Instances like these get reported to the National Church Arson Task Force. The Justice Department is also kept in the loop. Maybe this isn't the first time your guy's played with matches?" the fire marshal asked.

"Anything's possible. How'd the fire start?"

"He tossed a Molotov cocktail through a stained glass window. But we're not talking benzene. This guy loaded a glass canister with red phosphorous."

"Whoa! That's the same incendiary used in Vietnam. Our embalmer could be a veteran," Thomlinson suggested.

"Somebody clue me in. What's red phosphorous?" Margaret asked.

"It's a chemical blowtorch that American pilots used it to blanket enemy buildings," Driscoll explained.

"I thought they used napalm for that."

"Napalm was dropped on enemy personnel."

"And I thought **we** were the good guys," said Margaret, her face incensed.

"During the Vietnam War, Special Forces would drop a pellet of red phosphorous on the chest of bound prisoners then threaten to light it," Thomlinson added.

"What? The Articles of the Geneva Convention didn't apply to them?" Margaret looked appalled.

"The stuff burns at close to 3000 degrees," Ricci added. "Once ignited, it'll burn through steel."

"Where would someone get hold of red phosphorous?" Margaret asked.

"Good question," said Driscoll. "Cedric, you may be on to something. Could our guy be a disgruntled Vietnam vet?"

All eyes were now on the detective.

"I got a buddy, Wilfred. He's a Major at Fort Dix. Career man. Did a double in Da Nang. His wife makes a mean Catfish Creole. I'll give him a holler and put my feelers out while mooching a meal."

"Why a church?" asked Ricci.

"Maybe our guy's a defrocked military chaplain?" Thomlinson reasoned

"Could be," Driscoll said. "But whatever his background, he's not your garden variety arsonist. This son of a bitch is also one hell of an embalmer."

CHAPTER THIRTY-ONE

Before returning to the office, Driscoll parked the Chevy on Montague Street, where Margaret hopped out and ducked inside Avgerinos Restaurant to purchase lunch.

"Nothing says New York alfresco like a Chicken Souvlaki and a Coke," Margaret said returning to the passenger seat where she peeled back the waxed paper from her savory sandwich and handed half to Driscoll.

"You know, Margaret, I can't shake the feeling we're overlooking something," the Lieutenant said before biting into the Greek delicacy.

"OK. Let's break down his lunacy. He's arterially embalming his victims then sews a locket featuring the patron saint of prostitutes under the tongue. It suggests he's not a fan of the working girl, but why burn down a church?"

"Beats the hell out o' me."

"And why that church?"

"Maybe he's got a gripe with Sally Fields."

Driscoll looked at her wondering where she was going with an odd comment like that.

"What's Sally Field's got to do with it?" he asked.

"The actress. Sally Fields. She played the flying nun on TV. The church he torched was Saint Teresa of Avila. The original flying nun."

Driscoll's eyes widened, the expression on his face was one of utter bafflement. "That's Coke you're drinking, right?"

"Jesus! That's it!" she shouted looking like she'd just discovered the cure for cancer.

"It's all about Saint Teresa! She was no run-of-the-mill nun. She was a scholar known for her mystical literature. I'll bet there's a connection."

Though Driscoll was skeptical, he was curious. "How so?" he asked.

"She preached that the soul ascended into heaven in stages. I can't remember how many or what all the stages were, but the last one she called The Devotion of Rapture. It's when the soul separates from the body in a fiery glow and ascends into heaven. It's a stretch, but it could explain the fire."

"That would suggest the killer's more concerned with his victim's soul than her body."

"Maybe he's a priest?"

Driscoll looked up to the unseen heavens. "Please, God, say it isn't so."

"Does God answer you?"

"Sometimes. How is it you're so well versed in this Saint Therese and her Devotion of Rapture?"

"Therese is my Confirmation name. I remember how thrilled my sixth grade teacher was when I chose it." Margaret's face suddenly turned from exuberation to gloom. She looked as though she was about to cry.

"What is it, Margaret?" Driscoll asked, a sympathetic look on his face.

"Sister Mary Therese. That was her name. My teacher. My sixth grade teacher." Tears streamed Margaret's face. "She was there for me when I lost it one afternoon in church. The night before, my father . . . When my father tried . . ." Her chin hit her chest and her voice trailed off.

Driscoll knew she was re-living one of the many sexual assaults she endured as a child. "You're ok, Margaret. You're no longer a defenseless little girl. Your father's dead. He can't hurt you anymore."

The Lieutenant stopped talking and patiently waited for Margaret to regain composure.

"Some tough cop I am," she said, forcing a smile.

"That you are, Margaret. You're a helluva tough cop. And a very courageous woman." Driscoll took hold of her hand.

Silence settled between the pair.

But only for a minute.

"I need you to hold me, John," she whispered. "And I need you to hold me now."

Driscoll acquiesced.

CHAPTER THIRTY-TWO

Thomlinson, looking like a man on a mission, hurried into Driscoll's office. A roguish smugness filled his face.

"I've seen that look before. Whad'ya dig up at Fort Dix?"

A folder marked 'Military Dossier' hit Driscoll's desk. "That, Lieutenant, tells the story of one Albert Rafferty, PFC." Thomlinson grinned as Driscoll thumbed through the ten page report. "It seems Private Rafferty was a demolitions expert with a particular penchant for phosphorous."

"He use it to burn down any churches?"

"That's why the Major remembered him," Thomlinson said with a grin as he flicked his lighter to fire the end of a Macanudo.

Driscoll put down the report. He knew there was nothing in it that Thomlinson would've overlooked and preferred listening to the detective who was eager to share his findings.

"Rafferty was a loner," said Thomlinson, exhaling a cloud of cigar smoke as he straddled a chair. "His job involved torching enemy barracks, storage facilities and supply depots. He was good at it. Then one day, trouble found him."

"What kind of trouble?"

"A Buddhist temple was set ablaze outside of Luang Prabang in '68. Rafferty being the suspected torchman. Problem was, it wasn't the enemy's." The detective cocked his head and eyed the tip of his cigar. "General Lu Chow Lubang, head of Laos's anti-Communist forces, was a bit ticked off. A court martial followed and, although it was never proven that Rafferty was the arsonist, he was summarily discharged to appease the General."

"How old was he when he got the boot?"

"Twenty."

"That'd make him close to seventy now." Driscoll looked disappointed. "Hell, anything's possible. What'd he do in civilian life?"

"He was a janitor."

"A janitor? That doesn't fit the bill."

"He was a conscientious worker. Twenty-two years with the same employer. Never once called in sick."

"Who'd he work for?'

"Academia."

"Why do I sense you're holding something back?"

"Because, Lieutenant, you have the instincts of a seasoned cop. And, you can read me like a book." Thomlinson smiled. "My investigation yielded no record of Rafferty, anywhere, for the past fifteen years. I figured the guy was dead, homeless, or had mastered the art of disappearing. And then . . ."

"You hit pay dirt."

"That I did. Rafferty's last paycheck for janitorial services, dated September 3, 2013 had an employer's name on it. Care to guess what field?"

"I'll let you tell me."

"Pomona Institute of Funeral Services."

Driscoll grinned. "Be the perfect place to audit a class in Embalming 101. Wha'd'ya have on the institute?"

"Not much. Last graduating class was 2014. Closed down after that. But, certainly worth a follow-up. Oh, and on the subject of following ups, you'd asked me to look into a question someone had posted on that website you came across, *Embalming101.com.*"

"Right, the one involving two lovers getting in on in 1958 when the female suffers a heart attack. The guy wanted to know if he should sprinkle the body with myrrh, aloe and cassia and dig a grave," Driscoll said.

"Computer Crimes detectives tracked down the commenter through his IP address. He was a fifteen-year-old in Eldora, Iowa writing a term paper on the risks of heightened sexuality for first timers."

"Heightened sexuality? What would that have to do with the anointing oils?"

"I had the same question. Anyway, the kid nearly shit his pants when two uniforms knocked on his door," Thomlinson said with a grin.

"Kids, these days."

"You got that right."

The door opened and Margaret strutted into Driscoll's office, her face immediately soured by the acrid smoke. "The smoking of those things inside a building should be outlawed!"she declared, marching toward the window and opening it.

Thomlinson used the base of an artificial plant to snuff out the cigar, mouthed an apology to Margaret then leaned back in his chair, sensing she had something to say.

"Margaret, would you like to tell him? Or shall I?" Driscoll asked.

"I got it," she replied, then brought Thomlinson up to speed about her theory involving the soul separating from the body in a fiery glow before ascending into heaven and how it might explain why the embalmer crucified and torched his last victim at St. Therese's Church.

Impressed, Cedric considered rewarding Margaret with a cigar, but feeling the draft from the open window, decided against it.

"Any ID on the crucified victim?" Margaret asked.

"None. Considering what the fire did to the body, Pearsol thinks she'll remain a Jane Doe. But, if he's done it before, VICAP might be of help." Driscoll powered on the Department's Dell desktop. VICAP, an acronym for the FBI's **Violent Criminal Apprehension Program,** was a nationwide data center designed to collect, collate, and analyze similarities in crimes of violence, specifically murder. "I'll start by going back twenty years," the Lieutenant said, inputting **January 1, 1999** as his opening field, then added **Rafferty, Red Phosphorous, Crucifixion, Religious Buildings**, and **Female Victims.**

In a matter of seconds, the three officers were staring at a lengthy list of crimes. Raised a Catholic, Driscoll was particularly outraged by the barbarous and sacrilegious acts perpetrated against the religious that his search had uncovered.

02/06/1999 – Sister of Charity Novice Kidnapped

10/17/1999 – Boston Mother Superior Raped
Inside Convent

12/24/2000 – Carmelite Nun Sexually Assaulted

06/12/2001 – Indiana Priest Abducted, Tortured
And Left For Dead

That was just the beginning. Several pages followed. As silence filled the room, they scanned the list of atrocities.

"There's a special place in hell for these lowlifes," Margaret muttered.

"Amen to that," said Thomlinson. "I don't see a specific connection to a church, do either of you?"

"It's never that easy," Driscoll griped. "We'll need to delve into each one."

"That'll take a while," Thomlinson remarked, glancing at his watch.

"Something more pressing on your agenda, Cedric?" Driscoll asked.

"Not really. Determining the ID of this victim takes priority. Just need a minute to call and reschedule my appointment with my therapist."

"You're in therapy?" Margaret asked, her eyes wide.

"I'm seeing an acupuncturist. "

"Right, right. You'd mentioned that," Margaret said. "How's that going?"

"I've only had three appointments but it seems to be helping," Thomlinson replied, not going into detail.

"Good. I'm a firm believer in alternative medicine to treat muscular pain."

Having no intention of correcting Margaret's assumption, he smiled. "Just need a minute to call and reschedule," he said stepping out of the Lieutenant's office.

After hours of probing, the team discovered that most of the crimes originated inside convents. But, not all. In Selma, Alabama, a Franciscan Brother was shot and killed while protesting the mutilation of a black high school student by white supremacists. In Mississippi a crime did involve a church where on a sweltering afternoon in August 2001, a gunman interrupted Novena services, only to stave off police negotiators while holding hostage scores of terrified school children, four attending nuns, and a fear-riddled priest. When he aimed his Remington semiautomatic at a quivering nine-year-old, a SWAT team sharpshooter brought him down. The siege had ended, and no one ever discovered what motivated the gunman.

Although Rafferty's name produced no hits, what caught Driscoll's eye was an incident that occurred in the fall of 2004, in Callicoon, New York, a small town in Sullivan County.

The entry read:

10/19/2004 – Arsonist torches church. Penitent nun perishes in the blaze.

"That's fifteen years ago," said Thomlinson. "Right around the time Rafferty began flying under the radar."

According to the report, a fire had broken out at 3:00 AM, claiming the life of a Josephite nun, Sister Patrice Flood, age 44. Red phosphorous had been used as an accelerant.

"We've got a church, red phosphorous, and a nun. Coincidence?" Driscoll asked.

"Add Rafferty's disappearance and we're looking at four points of similarity. That doesn't suggest coincidence," said Margaret.

"Let's not overlook the fact that Rafferty worked at a funeral institute," Thomlinson added.

Driscoll wasn't about to argue, but what he found curious in the VICAP report was that the decedent had been found in her pajamas. What would a nun be doing in church in the middle of the night wearing pajamas? The report went on to say that her body was discovered curled in a fetal position inside one of the church's two confessionals. Smoke inhalation was blamed for her death. Officer Peter Winnicott of the Sullivan County Police Department was listed as first on the scene.

Something didn't feel right to the Lieutenant. The report wasn't formatted in the standard VICAP sequence. It read more like a newspaper clipping. Since there were no autopsy results, nor any subsequent investigation, Driscoll felt a conversation with Officer Winnicott was in order. Picking up the phone, he asked Communications to connect him with Sullivan County PD where he learned that Winnicott had transferred to the Monticello Police Department in 2005. He placed a call there and, as luck would have it, Winnicott, now a sergeant, answered.

"Monticello PD, Desk Sergeant Winnicott speaking."

"Sergeant Winnicott, this is Lieutenant John Driscoll of the NYPD. I'm investigating a case of arson in New York City involving a fire at a Catholic church."

"How can I help the Big Apple, Lieutenant?"

"According to VICAP you handled a church fire fifteen years ago in Sullivan County."

"I see you've done your homework."

"I understand a nun died in that blaze."

Winnicott didn't immediately respond. Driscoll heard what sounded like a cigarette lighter being engaged and then he heard Winnicott exhale hard, presumably after taking a long drag on a freshly lit cigarette. "A nun died in that fire, Lieutenant."

An odd response. His tone had changed, as well.

"The VICAP report looked a little sketchy."

"A nun died in that fire, Lieutenant, and no one gave a damn."

Driscoll, who wasn't sure why he'd elicited such a strong reaction, remained silent.

"You're right about VICAP being sketchy, Lieutenant. The sad part is you won't find any written report of what really happened," Winnicott added.

"Why's that?"

Silence lingered across the telephone line for an excessively long time as Driscoll waited for the officer to respond.

"Ya' know, Lieutenant? It's been fifteen years since they buried that poor nun and you're the first person to ask me about her death."

"The report says she died of smoke inhalation," Driscoll said, sensing there was more to the story.

"Lieutenant, may I call you, John?"

"Please do."

"Well, John, here's what happened that night. Make of it what you will. The call came in close to 3:00 AM. I had an hour left on an 8 to 4. By the time I got there, the fire was out. They found her inside the church, curled up in one of the confessionals. The blaze had consumed most of the church and although a good portion of the confessional was charred, the nun's body hadn't burned. I figured she'd climbed inside to avoid the flames. She was wearing blue pajamas. No shoes. I gotta tell ya', it's a strange feeling seeing a nun in pajamas. Anyway, I looked for the shoes. Couldn't find 'em. That raised a question. The church was surrounded by a gravel path, maybe ten feet wide. It encircled the entire church. Didn't make sense for her to go in there barefoot. I took out my pad and started making notes. That's when a priest, a Father Clement, called me aside and asked me to stop writing. Said he'd be removing her body and that the Church would be handling matters from here on out. I called it in and was ordered to back off, so I did. Looking inside the confessional, I could only see the back of the nun's body. It wasn't until they lifted her out that I got a good look at her face. She'd been beaten. Her right eye was swollen and so was her lower lip. They ruled the cause of death to be smoke inhalation. But it wasn't smoke that did that to her features."

"You think someone else was in that church."

"I do. And whoever it was, rearranged her face."

CHAPTER THIRTY-THREE

Sergeant Winnicott had asked the Lieutenant for the Department's fax number, saying he'd forward him further details about what he believed to be the nun's murder. The man was true to his word: a uniformed officer had just entered Driscoll's office with a fax.

Driscoll scanned the single sheet of paper. It was the autopsy protocol of one Margaret Flood, also known as Sister Mary Patrice, Order of Josephite Nuns.

Item H1196T27. Arrival Date: October 19, 2004. Margaret Flood. . . body is that of a well-nourished, well-developed, Caucasian female. Height: 161.6 centimeters, weight: 55.7 kilos. Initial examination shows marked discoloration surrounding the right orbital, measuring six and one-half centimeters in circumference. . . . swelling has formed around a laceration to the lower lip. . . . injuries to the face were sustained prior to death. No distinguishable marks or scarring to the extremities. . . examination of abdomen reveals well healed surgical scarring, eight and one-half linear centimeters . . . in line with the pubes . . . .

The coroner had listed smoke inhalation as her cause of death. For her manner of death, he had indicated 'undetermined'.

Driscoll picked up the phone and punched in a number.

"Medical Examiner's office. Pearsol, here."

"Larry, I'm going over an autopsy report on a Sullivan County woman who died of smoke inhalation. The coroner refers to a well healed surgical scar, measuring eight and one-half centimeters, in line with the pubes. What's could that be?"

"How old was the woman?"

"Forty-four."

"The location of the scaring suggests that someone operated on her uterus. Likely to be one of two possibilities. Hysterectomy or a C-section."

Driscoll's next call was to the Pinewood Novitiate, in Callicoon, New York, the site of the church fire. He spoke to Sister Beatrice Aloysius, the convent's Mother Superior. Having been newly appointed, she knew little about the incident.

"Sister, would you know the whereabouts of a Father Clement?" Driscoll asked, inquiring about the priest who had steered Winnicott away from his investigation.

"Yes, I would. He was the novitiate's Father Confessor for close to twenty years. That is until he suffered a stroke, the dear man. He still resides with us."

"Sorry to hear he suffered a stroke."

"It didn't affect his engaging personality, though. He makes you feel valued."

"God was kind."

"He sure was. I'd call him to the phone but the stroke took away his ability to speak."

CHAPTER THIRTY-FOUR

Driscoll was eager to meet with Father Clement. Letting Thomlinson and Margaret know where he'd be, he left the building, climbed behind the wheel of his Chevy and settled in for the three hour drive to Callicoon.

Though traffic crawled across the George Washington Bridge, the road opened up on the Palisades Interstate Parkway. Making his way along the meandering thoroughfare, he was lulled by the muffled sound of the car's engine and the steady hum of rapidly rotating tires. Just past the exit for Bear Mountain, he eyed a row of sycamores lining a winding path. It was while strolling a similar trail, that Colette had told him he was to become a father. A crooked smile formed at the recollection. But as the serene setting faded in his rear view mirror, his smile retreated as well. Rummaging through the cruiser's glove compartment, he retrieved a pack of Lucky Strikes, lit one, took a long drag and prayed the billowing smoke would obscure the uninvited epiphany.

Three hours and twenty minutes after setting out, the Lieutenant arrived in Callicoon. Making a sharp left off of Cider House Lane, he sighted the towering cluster of willows marking the entrance to the Pinewood Novitiate. Turning right, he entered the grounds and climbed a dirt road which meandered through a thickly wooded hollow of diminutive evergreens dwarfed by lofty oaks. The realization that evil had once disturbed this peaceful setting troubled Driscoll.

At the end of the cluster of trees lay a clearing, a small niche blanketed by a patch of blue sky. In its center, stood the small church, still encircled by gravel. Bright sunlight highlighted repairs made to the structure that'd once been engulfed in flames. To the right of the church were two buildings. The smaller one, he figured was the novitiate's dormitory. In front of the other, likely an administration duplex, he spotted a young woman in a gardening apron watering a row of impatiens. Parking the Chevy next to a rusting pickup, Driscoll headed toward her.

"May I help you?" she asked, sporting a vivacious smile that made the Lieutenant think of Meg Ryan.

"My name is John Driscoll," he replied, feeling it unnecessary to reveal a police presence. "I'm looking for Sister Aloysius. She's expecting me."

"Oh, Mother Superior. OK. I'll let her know you're here to see her. I'm Sister Catherine. Would you like to come inside?"

"I'd just as soon wait out here. It's a lovely setting."

"Yes, it is," she said with a smile before ducking inside the two-story sandstone.

High above the tranquil novitiate, Driscoll spotted a falcon circling. There was immense beauty in the sighting; the bird hovering effortlessly in ever widening orbits reminding Driscoll of a poem he'd studied in college, "The Windhover" by Gerard Manley Hopkins. His poetic reminiscence was interrupted though, when Sister Aloysius' voice sounded in his ear. "I see you had no trouble finding our little hamlet." She was a robust woman with gentle eyes submerged in a portly face that crinkled when she spoke.

"No trouble at all, Sister. Your directions were perfect."

"Come. Father Clement is anxious to see you. The poor soul. He gets few visitors. When he heard a high ranking police officer from New York was coming all this way to speak with him, he had Sister Ruth press his shirt and asked

Sister Angelica to purchase a stylish cardigan just for the occasion."

Driscoll smiled.

The nun led him to a trellis-enclosed portico in the rear of the Administration Building. There, in the center of the veranda, sat the priest, gently rocking in a rattan chair, staring aimlessly at the swirls of cherry scented smoke drifting from his pipe.

"Father, your visitor has arrived," Sister Aloysius singsonged as she and the Lieutenant made their approach.

Father Clement sported a boyish face, lined now with wrinkles. His placid, grey eyes were accented by luminous white brows. Smiling at Driscoll, he motioned for him to take a seat. Picking up a ballpoint pen, he reached for the writing pad he kept fastened to his chair by string. On it, he wrote: **I hope the incense from my pipe doesn't bother you. The Lord looks favorably on sweet smelling sacrifices.**

"I'll leave you in good company, Lieutenant," Sister Aloysius whispered. "I'll be back shortly with refreshments."

Whad'ya think of my new threads? The cleric penned. **Chic, no?**

"You're the cat's meow," Driscoll said, gesturing a thumbs-up.

The priest smiled. **What brings you all this way?** he wrote.

"Father, I'm here to ask you some questions about Sister Patrice and the fire that took her life."

Father Clement's focus remained steady, his eyes giving no indication he recognized the name.

"Do you remember her?" Driscoll asked.

Before the priest could respond, Sister Aloysius returned with refreshments.

"Father prefers tea in the afternoon. If you'd like something else. Coffee, perhaps? Or a Coke?"

"Tea is fine," Driscoll replied, watching the nun pour the steaming brew into two cups. Handing one cup to the

Lieutenant, she placed two spoonfuls of sugar and a touch of cream in the other. Shooting the Lieutenant a smile, she excused herself and left the porch.

Sister Patrice could have passed for Jane Wyman, the priest wrote.

Driscoll was relieved he remembered the slain nun. "What can you tell me about her, Father? And the night she died?"

It wasn't her fault.

"What wasn't her fault?"

The whole damn thing, he scribbled.

He appeared agitated. *What was that about,* Driscoll wondered.

You're a detective, yes? Why are you here, now? The fire was fifteen years ago.

"Loose ends."

A church was torched in New York City. I caught it on the news. You're thinking there's a connection. But after fifteen years?

"Loose ends," Driscoll repeated. "Something doesn't fit."

How can I help?

"Where were you when the fire broke out?"

Asleep. Inside my room in the rear of the administration building.

"Had the Novitiate received any threats before the fire? Any unexpected visitors? Anyone on the grounds who didn't belong?"

The priest shook his head.

"Sister Patrice. You said it wasn't her fault. What wasn't her fault?"

The cleric grew pensive, rolling his pen between two fingers, then tapping it on his pad several times before writing. **Kyle Rivers, our handyman, was a recovering alcoholic. One night he fell off the wagon and raped the poor girl.**

"Sister Patrice?"

The priest nodded. Sadness marked his face.

"What became of Rivers?"

Rotting in jail, he scrawled. **A good riddance!** he added, eyeing Driscoll. Tap. Tap. Tap, with the pen. **He impregnated her! We kept that out of the report. The Bishop felt the newspapers would make a mockery of the Church housing a pregnant nun. She eventually gave birth to a son.**

Driscoll now knew why the Church stepped in and halted Officer Winnicott's investigation. But, had they impeded the investigation of her murder?

"And the son, Father? What became of him?"

Put up for adoption. For some reason, that didn't happen. So he was raised by another Josephite at the Foundling. Harold MacKillop is his name."

"MacKillop?"

"The boy was named to honor Saint Mary MacKillop. She and Father Julian Tenison-Woods founded the Josephites in 1866."

Born to a nun. Raised by a nun. Was there any significance in that? Driscoll wondered. "Father, were you aware of anyone who may have wanted to harm Sister Patrice?"

The bruises on her face. You're wondering about those.

"Yes, Father. Her autopsy revealed she'd been beaten prior to her death, and was likely unconscious when she was placed inside the confessional. Can you think of anyone who could have done that?"

The cleric shook his head, but the look on his face betrayed him. Driscoll, a devout Catholic, was not about to challenge a priest. He knew the truth would eventually come out.

"According to the Fire Marshall, there were no other acts of arson in your area during the weeks that preceded or followed the fire. Lots of other churches but yours was the only one targeted," Driscoll pointed out.

You're thinking it may have had more to do with Sister Patrice than a random act of arson.

"Yes, Father, I do."

The priest, his eyes down, looked to be debating whether he wished to continue the conversation. As he tapped his pen repeatedly on his pad a look of contentment formed on his face.

On the day of my ordination I took a vow of obedience, Lieutenant. Fifteen years ago, that vow was put to the test when the Bishop insisted I never breathe a word about that nun's circumstance or untimely demise.

"Seems to me, you've revealed quite a bit in the last 30 minutes. You have a change of heart, Father?"

Call it what you will, Lieutenant. But, not to worry. A power greater than the Bishop will help me reconcile my conscience. In the meantime, if you're seeking justice for that poor nun, you'll want to speak to her son.

CHAPTER THIRTY-FIVE

Father Clement had directed Driscoll to 371 Baltic Street, a six-story limestone in downtown Brooklyn that served as home to the Order of Josephite Foundling. Sitting behind the wheel of his rain swept cruiser, eyes fixed on the graffiti-scarred orphanage, Driscoll was transported back in time where disconcerting memories of his own abandonment swirled inside his head. His father, a highly decorated police officer, was killed in the line of duty three months before Driscoll was born. But it was his mother's frightening departure that left him an orphan. Recollection of that dreadful morning in early August 1969 crowded his thoughts. Six days before his ninth birthday, Driscoll's mother threw herself into the path of an oncoming train, saddling him with feelings of anger, rejection and despair. It wasn't until he'd gained a better understanding of bereavement at the loss of his wife, that he entertained the possibility his mother's decision may have been triggered by a broken heart.

Intent on leaving his past behind him, he stepped out of the Chevy, raised the collar of his Burberry against the downpour, and headed for the orphanage. After ringing the bell embedded in the frame of a weather-scarred door, a soft-spoken woman, clad in a simple gray dress, welcomed him inside.

"I'm here to see Sister Clara," Driscoll announced.

"I'm afraid Sister Clara is in vespers. She won't be seeing anyone until this afternoon."

"She's expecting me." Driscoll produced his shield.

"Oh, I see. Well, if you'll have a seat in the reception area, I'll see what I can do."

The woman led the Lieutenant past a sterile refectory to a dimly lit room, its far wall lined with books. After switching on the light, she selected a leather-bound edition of The New Testament and handed it to Driscoll.

"I recommend Saint Paul's letters to the Corinthians," she said. "They can be very helpful to those who wait."

"And for those who don't?"

"Everyone waits," she said with a smile before disappearing from sight.

Driscoll placed the book on the chair beside him and meandered about the room. A cork bulletin board caught his eye. Fastened to it, were brochures offering a variety of social services to the unwed mother. All were laden with dust. On the opposing wall were several photographs depicting couples holding babies. The photos, presumably of adoptive parents, were faded.

Disheartened, Driscoll took his seat and paged through the text he'd been given. Interrupted by the sound of footfalls, he looked up to find a nun entering the room.

"I'm Sister Clara. You must be Lieutenant Driscoll," she said, extending her hand.

"I am," Driscoll answered.

"Let's go inside, shall we?" Sister Clara opened a door into a corridor of offices. Entering the third one on the right, she seated herself behind a cluttered desk.

The Lieutenant studied the depository of mismatched features that was the nun's face. Thin lips underscored a bulbous nose. Dense brows loomed above miniature eyes.

"I understand you and Father Clement discussed one of our charges. How is the reverend?"

"Affable," said Driscoll.

"If you speak with him again, let him know the sisters here are praying for him. Old age is often the playground for Satan."

"I'll be sure to tell him."

"So, Lieutenant, what is it you want to know about Harold? Has he gotten himself into trouble?"

"Just a routine investigation, Sister. How long was he under your care?"

"From birth through age eighteen."

"That's a long time. No adoption?"

Sister Clara studied Driscoll's face. "I was told Father Clement was up front with you about how Harold came into this world."

"He was, Sister."

"Good. Carrying a secret like that bores a hole in the soul. I'm glad he found the courage to disclose it."

"So, am I."

"Well, Lieutenant, in answer to your question, no, there was never an adoption process for the boy. You have to understand that when a couple is looking to adopt they're always curious about the child's parents. Rightfully so. But the Bishop had made it clear we were never to divulge the circumstances surrounding Harold's conception. What were we to do? We certainly couldn't make something up." A smile filled her face. "As time went on, Harold became very attached to me. I considered him a gift from God."

"Good to hear," Driscoll said, sensing there was more to the story.

"Do you have children, Lieutenant?"

"I did," said Driscoll.

"I'm sorry," said the nun, reading the sadness in the Lieutenant's eyes. "I'll bet you were a wonderful father. Harold could have benefited from a caring dad like you. Especially when he came into his teens."

"Problems?"

"He was getting into trouble on the street. The police would often escort him home. Nothing serious, mind you. A troubled teen is what they called him."

"And?" Driscoll spurred, suspecting there was more she wanted to disclose. He watched as Sister Clara's eyes narrowed. *Had she, too, been keeping a secret?*

"Of course we have no proof, but it certainly wasn't a ghost that desecrated the photos of our sisters," she said.

"Desecrated?"

"Several photographs of past and present sisters were displayed on the walls of our assembly hall. One night, someone removed several of them from their frames. A hole was burned into the chest of one of the featured nuns. Likely with a cigarette."

"Sister Patrice's, right?"

"Yes."

"Do you still have the photo, Sister? I'd like to examine it."

"I wish you could, but we destroyed it that day."

"Did you call the police?"

"We did. Their investigation didn't point a finger at anyone."

"What made you think Harold was the culprit?"

"I'm sure it was him. Earlier in the day I had told Harold about Sister Patrice. The boy was eighteen. I felt it was time he knew who his mother was and about all that had happened to her."

"How'd he take the news?"

"Not good. At first, he clenched his teeth and said nothing. After a minute or two, he took my hands, placed them on his cheeks and whispered, 'thank you for not abandoning me, like she did, the wretched whore'. After that, he left."

"He left the orphanage?"

"Yes, and I haven't seen him since."

CHAPTER THIRTY-SIX

Driscoll left the foundling home and slipped in behind the wheel of his cruiser. Unpocketing his cellular, he called Thomlinson. "Cedric, run an inquiry on a Harold MacKillop. He once lived at the Josephite Foundling in Brooklyn. Get me his last known address."

"Will do," said Thomlinson. "Oh, and Lieutenant, it's a dead end on our Viet-Nam vet, Albert Rafferty. He died in a boating accident in 2010."

"Good follow-up, Cedric. Maybe we'll have better luck on MacKillop."

Driscoll was on Atlantic Avenue, nearing Carroll Gardens, when Thomlinson called back.

"MacKillop has a short list of priors, Lieutenant. Mostly misdemeanors. But, get this. He disappeared from his last known job at M & R Demolitions a month ago and when he did so did a shit load explosives."

"Tell me it was phosphorous."

"It was."

"You got his current address?"

"248 Sterling Place. In Brooklyn."

"Good. You and Margaret get over to Judge Henley's chambers. I'll want a search warrant issued for that location. Sterling Place is in the 78. Reach out to their desk sergeant and tell him what we've got. He's to arrange back up, only. Make that clear. Back up, only. Once you've secured the warrant, you and Margaret are to meet me there."

"Car keys in hand, Lieutenant. I'll radio the Precinct. Barring no problems with the judge, my ETA is twenty-five minutes."

Driscoll made a wide left off of Atlantic Avenue and sped south on Court Street. By the time he reached Sterling Place, uniforms had cordoned off both ends of the street. Pulling alongside one of the precinct's patrol cars, a uniformed officer informed him that '248' was in the middle of the block. He placed another call to Thomlinson.

"Three minutes out, Lieutenant. Margaret is riding shotgun with the search warrant in hand."

"Good. I'm on the east side of Sterling where it meets Sixth Avenue. We'll go in from here."

"Roger that."

'248' was a four-story brownstone. Thomlinson raced up the steps. There were names listed below two of the three exterior bells. Neither was 'MacKillop'. He rang the nameless bell while Driscoll, with Margaret at his side, depressed the bell to a gated entrance on the ground floor.

No one answered the bell thatThomlinson had pressed. But the bell that the Lieutenant rang produced the sound of a barking dog. And, judging from its ferocity, Driscoll figured the dog to be big and unfriendly. His suspicions were quickly confirmed when the Rottweiler pounced, its jaws snapping viciously through a small opening in the steel separating them.

"Jangles, hush up," a woman's voice sounded. "Hush up, ya' hear?"

The dog whimpered and backed away.

"That's a good boy," the woman cooed, sidling up to the dog behind the entrance gate.

"I hope he stays that way," Margaret said.

"Not to worry, Ma'am. Jangles ain't never bit no one." Just shy of 3 feet tall, the petite dog owner held a milk crate in her left hand. Margaret figured she needed it to stand on whenever she opened the gate as its latch was well above her head. "I hope Jangles, here, didn't scare ya' none too much. He thinks he's a macho macho man, doncha boy?" she said, leaning over to pet the wriggling dog. The pooch mewled under her touch.

When Thomlinson, who'd waited out the dog's ferocious welcome, joined Driscoll, he and the tiny woman exchanged smiles.

"It's awful late. Whatcha' sellin'?" the homeowner asked.

"Ma'am, I'm Lieutenant Driscoll of the New York City Police Department," he said, producing his shield and Department ID card. "My two associates, are also with the Police."

"Wow! Mod Squad!" the woman shouted.

Despite the seriousness of their visit, Driscoll and Thomlinson grinned. Margaret, unfamiliar with the '60s prime time favorite, looked confused.

"We're here to see Harold MacKillop. He live here?" the Lieutenant asked.

"I knew it! I just knew it!" the woman said, shaking her head. "I warned him," she added, climbing atop the milk crate to open the gate.

"Warned him? About what?" Margaret asked, eyeing the dog who was laying quietly, his focus on a spider's web that had formed.

"You're here about his parking tickets, aren't ya'? That boy pays no attention to those signs."

"That's right, Ma'am. We'd like to speak with him. Do you know if he's in?"

"Ya' just missed him."

"Know where he went?"

"Beats me. But, I'm guessing he's out for the night. His van's gone."

"We'd like to see his apartment. Would that be ok with you?" asked Driscoll.

"Jeepers! I know the Mayor is tough on crime, but if this don't beat all. Sending you guys out at night over parking tickets. Boy, oh boy! Ain't that somethin'!"

"So, it's alright that we check out his place," Margaret said, ready with the search warrant if necessary.

"I guess it'll be OK. Heck, you're the law, right?"

"Right."

"You can come through here and up two flights. His door's at the top of the stairs. Lemme' getcha the key." The woman disappeared inside the house leaving them alone with the Rottweiler. "Don't mind Jangles," she hollered. "He won't be a bother as long as I'm around."

"I certainly hope you're right," Margaret muttered, eyes fixed on the pooch.

The woman reappeared with the key and handed it to Driscoll. "You guys will be three of only a few visitors to get inside his pad. He's not exactly a socialite," she called out as the three lawmen headed upstairs.

Thomlinson knocked on MacKillop's door loud enough to wake the dead. All indicators said he wasn't home, but no one was in the mood for surprises. After pounding on the door a third time, Driscoll used the key.

It was small apartment consisting of a bedroom, living room, kitchenette, and bath. Nothing about the place suggested he was their serial embalmer, but then John Wayne Gacy's home seemed pleasant enough until investigators looked under the floorboards and found the remains of his twenty-seven slaughtered victims.

"What do you suppose that's for?" asked Thomlinson, motioning to an assembly of wooden steps leaning against a paneled wall.

"Looks like a staircase to nowhere," Margaret said.

"Yeah, but we're not in the Fontainebleau. It's gotta lead somewhere," said Driscoll.

"I'd say MacKillop is a movie buff." Thomlinson grinned and pointed to a poster of Raquel Welch affixed to the opposing wall. "Remember what was hidden behind Miss Welch's likeness in The Shawshank Redemption?"

"The way out," Driscoll said, removing the poster from the wall exposing a sliding door. Positioning the steps under the door, the Lieutenant opened it, revealing a small room. Reaching inside, he palmed the wall, found a light switch, and flicked it on producing a dim blue radiance. "It's a photographer's dark room," he said, stepping into the cramped space where a cork board hanging above a stainless steel sink featured several 8 X 10 glossies of three local churches. Lying beside the sink was an assortment of photography equipment and an unprocessed roll of film. "Either of you know how to develop photos?" he hollered.

"I do," said Margaret. "I worked at a photo shop when I was in college."

"That's good enough for me. Get in here!"

Moments later, standing hip to holster alongside Driscoll, Margaret reached for the developing canister and a film-changing bag. Both hands inside the bag, she used a pen knife to open the roll of film and loaded it onto a plastic reel, which she slid into the developing canister. Removing the canister from the bag, she had Driscoll hold it while she filled it with developer. After tapping the canister against the side of the sink to remove the air bubbles, she reached for the timer and set it for seven minutes.

Time passed without either of them saying a word until Driscoll broke the silence. "This brings me back to my teen years," he said.

"Any particular memory come to mind?" Margaret asked, amused by his remark.

"There was this game we played," he replied, then quickly regretted bringing it up.

"This game have a name?"

"Let's forget I mentioned it."

"Fine with me."

Silence returned, accompanied now by awkwardness.

"It was called Seven Minutes in Heaven," Driscoll said.

"Huh?"

"The game. It was called Seven Minutes in Heaven."

As though on cue, the timer sounded.

"Looks like our seven minutes are up," said Margaret, stifling a laugh.

"What's so funny?"

"I can't help but wonder what might've happened had I set the timer for eight. But, I guess with Cedric in the next room we'll never know."

"Never say never, Margaret."

"If you say so," she said with a smile, as she proceeded to hang the film.

With their eyes riveted on the celluloid strip, a series of thumbnail images began to take shape.

"I wish they were larger," Driscoll said.

"I aim to please." Margaret placed the strip of film on a slide and inserted into the full size developer.

"I'm impressed."

"I'm glad. Ready?"

"Ready for what?"

"Lights out." Pulling on a string that hung from the center of the ceiling, she bathed the room in red. Turning on the developer, she adjusted the lens to achieve perfect focus, then turned it off. After placing a sheet of photographic paper across the lens, she turned it back on, counted to five and turned it off. Freeing the sheet of photographic paper from the developer's frame, she soaked it in a tray filled with solution. As she and Driscoll looked on, the silhouette of a building began to take shape.

"I know that church. It's St. Agnes in Brooklyn," the lieutenant said, alarm marking his face.

"And from the looks of things, his next target." Margaret pointed to an Official SkallyWagz Wall Calendar where someone had penciled in 'Burn, Bitches, Burn' at 9 PM that evening.

"Not if I have anything to do about it," Driscoll said, his eyes riveted to the madman's scribble.

CHAPTER THIRTY-SEVEN

"My parents got married at Saint Agnes, for Christ's sake! And if that calendar is correct, he's headed there now." Driscoll jammed the key into the Chevy's ignition, as Margaret and Thomlinson climbed in.

"What's his beef with Saint Agnes?" Margaret asked.

"It houses the retirement residence for the Order of Josephite nuns. Remember, his mother was a Josephite," said Driscoll.

"The guy's a bad dude, Lieutenant, I'll give you that. But he doesn't sound like our embalmer," Thomlinson reasoned.

"Why's that?"

"Would nuns need help getting into heaven?"

"In his mind they would." Driscoll floored the gas pedal, and activated the emergency lights. "Margaret, alert Dispatch. I want a team of plain clothes surrounding the church and convent. Arrange for fire trucks to be standing by. Both structures are to be evacuated."

"Done!"

It was 8:50 when Driscoll pulled the Chevy to the curb in front of St. Agnes's. Eyeing the team of plainclothes officers, he was glad to see Margaret's last command had been followed. Ordering Margaret and Thomlinson to join them, he hurried up the steps of the small church and ducked inside where the smell of burnt candles and furniture wax stirred childhood memories that were long forgotten, but embedded in his soul. *My house of spirits*, he mused walking down the center aisle and taking a seat. It was three minutes to nine. After absently paging through a missalette, he scanned the seemingly empty church, his eyes narrowing when he spotted a man step out from behind the altar. A frayed sweater and well-worn jeans clung to his lean physique. With unkempt hair hiding much of his face, the man approached the tiered assembly of votive candles, lifting an unlit one from its receptacle. Retrieving a small object from his pocket, he placed it in the empty base, then returned the one-inch candle and lit it.

That's how he does it. Driscoll surmised. *He tucks a wad of red phosphorus under a candle and the son of a bitch is long gone by the time it burns down and ignites the accelerant.*

"Police! Don't move! There's no way out, MacKillop!" Driscoll shouted, his 9-mm Glock 26 in hand. "If you're carrying a weapon, toss it across the floor. Do it now! Then kneel down and clasp your hands behind your head."

The man didn't budge, his eyes locked on Driscoll's.

"It's over, MacKillop. The church is surrounded. There're cops at every exit. On your knees. Do it!"

He was standing close enough to the candles to worry Driscoll. If he tipped them, they'd both be toast. "Step away from the candles, MacKillop, and drop to your knees. Hands behind your head. Do it now!"

"How the hell did you find me?" he asked, casting an odd smile.

"Step away from the candles. I don't want to have to shoot you."

"You'd be doing me a favor, Cop Man. I'm the bastard son of a fornicating nun. Mama spat me out and abandoned me like I was a foul smelling malignancy. You're looking at the twenty-first-century Jean-Baptiste Grenouille."

Driscoll caught the reference to the serial killer in PERFUME, Patrick Suskind's work of fiction, where, with a crude swipe of his umbilical cord, Jean-Baptiste tumbled into the offal below a fish stall's cutting block in eighteenth-century Paris. "The way I understand it, you were raised in the foundling. You weren't abandoned."

"To Mama, I **was** Jean-Baptiste. My father a drunk. My mother a whore."

"She'd been raped, MacKillop. How can you call her a whore?"

"Because I do!" he screamed.

"And killing innocent nuns will cleanse your stench?"

"I forced her into that confessional, you know. To repent for her transgression. But she refused."

"So you killed her?" Driscoll took a step closer.

"I redeemed her."

Now he's sounding like our embalmer, thought Driscoll. "And the nuns that live here in retirement? What sin have they committed?"

"The sin of being a Josephite. An order that should've punished her. Not conceal her wickedness."

"The sisters at the foundling. Are they accomplices too?" Driscoll drew closer.

"They get a bye because they took me in."

Driscoll lunged forward, grabbing MacKillop around the chest. A tussle ensued. Forceful blows were exchanged. Driscoll tackled him again, forcing him to the floor, hard, the back of own head crashing against inlaid marble. With his arms bound in the Lieutenant's grip, MacKillop used his leg to bring down the assembly of candles. A flash of fire erupted. The Lieutenant rolled away from the flames. MacKillop into them, crushing the few intact receptacles, igniting the phosphorus. As Driscoll looked on, the angry man's body was turned to ash by a rapid acceleration of flames.

CHAPTER THIRTY-EIGHT

Tilden, seated in front of his TV, was watching Judge Sanders deliver one of his
sensational sentences. Defendant du jour, Bob Matthews, had just been ordered to don a plywood sandwich board and march back and forth outside the entrance to the Pets R Us store inside the Nanuet Mall. Required to flash the nature of his crime, the board read: "I kidnapped ZooZoo, my mother-in-law's Pomeranian. May God have mercy on my soul." The judge's face suddenly disappeared from the TV screen, replaced by that of a shapely newscaster. Distracted by her low cut fuchsia blouse boasting ample cleavage, he missed her opening remarks. When the camera panned to the charred remains of a church, Tilden raised the volume.

"That's right, Phil," the buxom reporter said. "I'm back at the site of the three alarm blaze in Forest Hills, where it's believed an arsonist torched Saint Therese's Roman Catholic Church several weeks ago."

Tilden grabbed his remote and hit the rewind button, rolling back the live broadcast to where the news cameraman began filming the church. "Harold sure scorched that sucker," he muttered, a smile creasing his face.

As the newscast rolled on, Tilden's focus returned to the shapely reporter.

"When CBS2 NEWS first broke this story there was no indication of any loss of life," she said. "But sources now tell us there was a single fatality and that NYPD has reopened its investigation. However, One Police Plaza seems to be playing it close to the vest and are yet to respond to our inquiries as to the identity of the victim."

"And they never will," Tilden hollered. "After cleansing that prostitute's body of her sins, I crucified her as penance for the sins she'd committed before giving Harold the ok to illuminate the night's sky. They might have ID'd the harlot I'd tossed in the river, but they'll not find a shred of evidence on that one."

CHAPTER THIRTY-NINE

Angus pressed the gun against Mary's temple and grinned at Driscoll. "Where's your gallantry now, Mr. Cop Man?"

The Lieutenant said nothing, his eyes fixed on the brazen youth.

"These walls look a bit drab, no? I'm thinking a splash of your sister's blood would brighten 'em up," taunted the teen.

"You pull that trigger and I'll blow your head off," Driscoll said.

"I got more than one bullet in this gun, Lieutenant. The next one's got your name on it."

"Only vicious people kill the helpless, Angus. Vicious scum like you."

"Shut up," Angus said.

"Vicious scum. Who kill for selfish reasons."

"I thought I told you to shut up," Angus seethed through clenched teeth, eyes on Mary, the barrel of his pistol digging into her skull.

"Selfish. Vicious. Scum. That's all you are, Angus. Scum," Driscoll said slowly.

"I told you to shut the fuck up!" Angus screamed, turning his weapon on the Lieutenant.

The jarring dream rocketed the Lieutenant to wakefulness. For a few lingering seconds, though, he was still inside the shabby loft under the rusted span of the FDR Drive, which had become a safe house for two fugitive teenagers who'd terrorized his city years ago. The place where Angus, and his murderous twin, had abducted Driscoll's sister and demanded a safe passage to freedom in return for her life.

What the Lieutenant woke to was another nightmare of unimaginable magnitude. Yes, he had rescued Mary from the delirium of two psychotic killers, but he was no match for nature gone mad. A savage storm had rolled through the city overnight, knocking down power lines and uprooting trees. One of those downed lines had brought with it a transformer which burst into flames as it impacted his sister's house in Breezy Point, reducing it to fragments of charred wood and shattered glass. Its pine-paneled interior, along with all her furnishings were turned to ash in minutes.

To describe Mary as a complicated soul would be an understatement. The woman had been burdened with emotional baggage since childhood. Some creatively imagined. Some brutally real. Though she was under the benevolent supervision of a neuro-pharmacologist, Driscoll wasn't convinced she'd ever be healthy. He knew she picked up her medication and that she refilled it in a timely fashion because her pharmacist kept him in the loop. But, he had no way of knowing if she took the meds. He feared she may be stockpiling them. Or flushing them down the toilet like she'd done as a teen. Mary swore she had a handle on her demons and was doing fine living on her own in the small, but comfortable, converted bungalow in Breezy.

"What am I gonna do, John? Everything I owned was in that house," her voice echoed through the speaker of Driscoll's phone.

"It's only stuff, Mary. What's important is that you got out alive."

"Where will I live?" she whimpered.

"We'll get through this together, Mary. You'll live with me," he told her.

Driscoll knew her stay would be short-lived. His sister was plagued by the impulse to dissociate herself from everyone. The Lieutenant had also struggled with the chronic compulsion. Their insistence on distance stemmed from the tragedy he and his sister had endured as children. Driscoll was often visited by the haunting memory of that day, when, at the age of 8, after receiving a kiss from his mother, watched her climb the stairs to Jamaica's Long Island Railroad Station leaving him alone and confused on the street below. She'd told him she had to meet the 10:39 from Penn Station but hadn't explained why. Nor why he wasn't going up the steps with her. He heard the wheels of the approaching train screech and come to an abrupt halt. There was a scream, followed by rivulets of red liquid that cascaded down from the overhead tracks. Then another more piercing scream ripped through the stillness of the morning. John felt his body turn to stone. His young soul petrified in an incomprehensible moment that caused time to stand still as the summer sun froze in the lifeless sky. Two policemen, their walkie-talkies crackling, charged up the stairs. After what seemed like an eternity a woman descended the stairs in the company of one of the officers. They approached John with a question. "Aren't you the boy who was walking toward the station with the woman wearing a red scarf?"

"I am," he answered, knowing deep inside he'd never be kissed by his mother again.

CHAPTER FORTY

Driscoll was thankful Mary's mortgage company required proof that her homeowner's insurance was renewed each year. Despite being adequately covered, dealing with her insurance company's claims department would be an arduous undertaking for his sister. Both New York City's Department of Finance and of Buildings would have accurate details regarding the size and composition of the house, but how could she be expected to prepare a complete list of all her contents? Mary's dilemma notwithstanding, Driscoll had a maniacal killer on the loose so, in his stead, he hired a public adjuster to handle his sister's claim.

The Lieutenant was delighted to have Mary living with him, but he knew her compulsion toward detachment meant she'd be looking for another place to stay as soon as she hung her coat in Driscoll's closet. She loved her brother dearly and knew he'd never abandon her nor do anything to harm her. But, she had felt the same about her parents and look where that'd gotten her. A mom who chose suicide over life and a dad who'd been killed in the line of duty. Upon entering One Police Plaza, Driscoll headed for the Major Crimes Command Center on the fourteenth floor. Alone inside the elevator, he stared at his likeness in its partially mirrored wall. Weary eyes stared back.

When he entered his office, Margaret was there to greet him. Another woman in his life he was glad to see.

"How are things on the home front?" she asked.

"Mary's being Mary," he said, retrieving a travel size cylinder of Tylenol from his pocket. After popping two caplets in his mouth he washed them down with a swig of Poland Springs from a plastic bottle he kept stored in his desk.

"That water can't still be cold," Margaret remarked. "And you really should see a doctor about that headache. It's been a few days, no?"

"The Tylenol is helping. That being said, I'm good."

"Has your sister found a place to escape to yet?" There wasn't much about the Lieutenant's personal life that Margaret wasn't privy to. And to Driscoll, her life was an open book.

"She's waiting to hear back on a call she made to the Catholic Church's Diocesan Office where she volunteers. There's an apartment in Bayside where two Sisters of Mercy reside. They'll be away for a couple of months at their retreat house in Water Mill."

"Water Mill?"

"It's in the Hamptons."

"Nice. Maybe I shoulda' been a nun."

"It's not too late, Margaret."

"You think they'd welcome a Sister Mary Potty Mouth?"

"They'd warm up to you in time."

"You're damn right, they would."

Detective Thomlinson's face appeared in the doorway.

"You're just in time, Cedric. Margaret is considering entering the religious life," Driscoll said.

"As a bishop, no doubt," said Cedric.

"There's wisdom, right there, Lieutenant." Margaret grinned.

"How's your sister holding up?" Thomlinson asked Driscoll.

"One day at a time, Cedric. One day at a time."

"Works for me," he replied, having spent a good portion of his adult life in a twelve step program.

"OK. Let's get down to business. I found an interesting article in last month's edition of *Psychology Today*," Driscoll said.

"The poor man's therapist," Thomlinson remarked.

"Thankfully true, Cedric. And with the insurance industry raising deductibles and adding restrictions to this type of care I'm predicting the magazine will soon start publishing more than every other month."

"Amen," said Margaret.

Driscoll motioned for them to circle behind him, then pointed to an article he'd pulled up on his desktop computer: '*The Crowded Mind*' by Doctor Melanie Anderson. The title was featured under an artist's depiction of the human brain looking more like a jam-packed elevator than an anatomical organ. As Driscoll read from it what jumped out at his two investigators was Doctor Anderson's narrative concerning an incident involving her patient, Adrian Strayer, a thirty-six-year-old suffering from dissociative identity disorder. Strayer, who, according to Doctor Anderson, his art therapist, has the mentality of an eight-year-old, had used chalk to draw the figure of a woman who appeared to be dead. The therapist became curious when the patient added a red line which seemed to depict the blood that oozed from the woman's neck. Anderson's curiosity grew to concern when her patient added a bucket to catch its flow.

"The guy draws what looks like an embalming and her curiosity only grew to concern?" Margaret looked baffled.

"Concerned enough to call the police?" asked Thomlinson.

"No record of a call. Which is why I'm going to pay Doctor Melanie Anderson a visit," Driscoll said.

"Local?" Margaret asked.

"Trenton, New Jersey."

"Local enough."

"Lieutenant, it's got possibility written all over it. The only piece that doesn't fit is the guy having the mentality of an eight-year-old," Thomlinson mused.

"That may be so, Cedric, but he's got a multiple personality disorder. Perhaps one of those personalities is an adult," Driscoll said.

"Or he's faking it," said Margaret.

"And there's that," said Driscoll.

CHAPTER FORTY-ONE

Tilden wrestled with a sleep that eluded him. The vision of the prostitute he'd crucified at Saint Therese's Church continued to flash inside the recesses of his mind unleashing an uninvited memory.

Tilden took his customary place in line beside his trusted friend, Sean, outside Saint Barnabas Academy. The nine-year-old had a knot in his stomach. Although he had prepared his reading and knew it by heart, he was petrified. To keep from throwing up, he recited it again. "A reading from the Letter of Saint Paul to the Ephesians. 'Be ye therefore followers of God, as most dear children. And walk in love, as Christ also hath loved us...'"

"Tilden, shut it," Sean grunted without turning his head. "You know what'll happen if Scarface hears you."

"'... and hath delivered himself for us, an oblation and a sacrifice to God for an odor of sweetness...'" Tilden whispered. "'But fornication, and all uncleanness, or covetousness, let it not so much as be named among you, as becometh saints...' Oh, my God! I think I'm gonna throw up," Tilden sobbed.

"Keep it off my shoes and don't sweat the reading so much," Sean said.

"It's not gonna be good enough for Sister Agathon."

"Nothing's good enough for that battle axe."

"What's your Chapter, Sean?"

"Letter to the Ephesians, Chapter 2."

"Mine's Chapter 5. I know it by heart but it scares the hell of me that I've gotta recite it in front of her."

"Just don't look at the bitch."

"How am I supposed to do that?"

"I do it all the time. Just stare at the wart on her chin. That thing grows hair, ya know."

Tilden giggled, provoking an 'AHEM' from Sister Claude, who he hadn't seen approaching on the left. Mouth shut. Eyes fixed dead ahead, he waited for the nun to pass before resuming his conversation. "I got no sleep. I kept seeing Agathon with that freakin' glare of hers," he griped.

"You'll be ok, Tilden. You know what your problem is?"

"What?"

"You're a worry wart. Like the one on Agathon's chin. Three minutes up there and you're done," Sean said.

"Three minutes of hell. I threw up in bed this morning."

"I hope you got it all out 'cause if you throw up while you're up there, Ol' Aggie will make you lick it up."

"Zip it. Here comes the witch now."

Swinging her rosary like it was a police officer's billystick, she sidled up next to the two boys. Her face, jagged with acne scarring, was punctured by beady, mean eyes.,

"Master Tilden, embarrass me with your recitation and you're toast," she warned prompting what was left in Tilden's intestinal tract to liquefy.

The bell sounded, prompting the two rows of nine-year-old boys to proceed toward the school's entrance. Once inside the classroom, Tilden clenched his butt cheeks together and cut a deal with Saint Nicholas. He promised the patron saint of children he'd return to the store and pay for the three Milky Ways he'd stolen if the saint would keep him from crapping his pants. As if reading his mind, Sister Agathon dragged a piece of chalk across the blackboard. Tilden was certain he high pitch squeal was meant to drown out his plea to the heavens above. It also got everyone's attention. "Now children," ol' Aggie began, "you'll be privileged today to hear the very words St. Paul preached to the new Christians of Ephesus. Who can find Ephesus for us?" she asked, pointing to wall where the map of the Roman Empire had been pinned.

Silence filled the classroom as the students stared down at their desks.

"Sean, find it for me," she ordered.

As all color drained from the Sean Haggerty's face, he stood and ambled toward the map like a prisoner approaching the gallows. Since the legend at the top read 'Holy Roman Empire', he reasoned the City of Ephesus would be near Rome. Using an unsteady finger, he made an ever-widening circle in the center of the map, hoping Ephesus, itself, would somehow attach itself to his touch. When it didn't, he turned to face his classmates hoping for assistance. All he saw were blank stares. With his heart pounding, he closed his eyes and pressed his finger in what he prayed would be a miraculous direct hit.

"Sean, you heathen! Of all my students I was certain you'd know where it was. You're nothing but a disappointment. You should be ashamed of yourself!" She charged at the boy, and dragged his finger across the Ionian Sea, through Athens and Corinth, across the Aegean Sea, and slammed it into Ephesus. "Now, sit down!" she yelled. "Tilden. Chapter Five. Now!"

"I ca... ca... ca... ca... can't, Sister."

"You what?"

"Sister, I..."

"Now!" she bellowed.

Tilden slid out of his seat as his tears began to flow.

"Be quick about, Master Tilden! We don't have all day!"

He shuffled forward, butt cheeks clenched.

"Get a move on!"

By the time Tilden got to the front of the class a stream of diarrhea was trickling down his right thigh. When he turned around his face was beet-red and swimming in tears.

No One Will Hear Your Screams | 147

"You're not a mute, Tilden. Let's hear it!" Sister ordered.

"A reading from the Letter of Saint Paul to the Ephesians. 'Be ye therefore followers of God, as most dear children...'" Tilden whimpered, as his liquid excrement began pooling on the floor. The laughter that erupted, abruptly ceased when Sister Agathon raced around her desk and barreled toward the boy.

"Tilden, My God! Look what you've done! You've defiled St. Paul! Have you no shame? You must be possessed! There can be no other explanation!"

Tilden tried to speak but all that came out was a desperate rattle.

"Out with you, Satan! Be gone! Be gone, I command! Get out of my classroom!" she ordered then faced the class. "Children, turn away. Don't let the eyes of Satan's disciple fall upon you."

Tilden fled to the boy's lavatory and locked himself inside a stall. Falling to his knees, he struck two fingers down his throat, figuring if he vomited it'd stop his diarrhea. The bile he spit out seemed to form a face. Floating on the toilet's water, it stared up him. Could it be? Had he expelled Satan? Had he been possessed? Was Sister Agathon right?

"Help me, God. Please, help me," he pleaded as tears salted his lips.

As if in answer to his plea, Tilden heard the 10:45 bell.

"First Friday's Mass is at 11 and I'm serving! Thank you, God!" he shouted, grateful for the reprieve from Sister Agathon's classroom, albeit for just an hour.

Having only fifteen minutes, he cleaned up as best he could and raced to the sanctuary where he donned a while surplice and black cassock over his soiled clothes. Kneeling on the hard cold marble of the altar, he closed his eyes and offered his confession to Almighty God in sync with Father O'Leary. "I confess to almighty God and to you, my brothers and sisters, that I have greatly sinned, in my thoughts and in my words, in what I have done and in what I have failed to do, through my fault, through my fault, through my most grievous fault; therefore I ask blessed Mary ever-Virgin, all the Angels and Saints, and you, my brothers and sisters, to pray for me to the Lord our God."

When Tilden opened his eyes he discovered that Father O'Leary had left the altar. That'd never happened before. *Did Father get sick and rush to the bathroom?* He glanced at the few daily Mass attendees seated in the first row. They looked puzzled. When the sacristy door creaked, Tilden felt relieved. But, instead of Father O'Leary returning to the altar, Sister Agathon's face appeared in the doorway. With the curling motion of her finger, she summoned Tilden, who ambled toward her.

"My God, Tilden, have you lost your mind as well as your soul?" she grumbled, her face an inch away from his.

When Father O'Leary returned to the altar, Sister Agathon slapped Tilden repeatedly. *Crack! Crack! Crack!* The sounds echoed in the nave. The blows knocked the boy off his feet.

"How dare you duck my class and show up in Church possessed by wickedness?" she seethed. Grabbing hold of Tilden's earlobe, she dragged his convulsing body toward the sacristy's rear exit, like a lamb to the slaughter. "Blasphemy will not be tolerated in my class," she growled.

At the end of a frightful trek through a dark and descending corridor, Sister Agathon dangled a ring of keys in front of Tilden's face. Selecting one, she unlocked a rusted door that whined under rotting hinges. The nun then pushed Tilden into a room similar to the one he'd seen in a Dracula movie. Resembling the quarters where the vampire slept, it smelled like a crypt, giving off a stench of pulverized bone. An object, draped by a blanket, sat in the center of the room. *A chest of drawers, perhaps? A book case?* But, why was there a rope dangling above it? And to what was the rope fastened? The mystery was solved when Sister Agathon tore away the shroud and revealed a wooden cross. Lifting Tilden *over her head, she pressed him against the wooden beams. After cinching the rope around his wrists and ankles, she cranked a hoist, elevating the boy, the newly crucified boy, into the hollow below the arched roof.*

CHAPTER FORTY-TWO

Driscoll's headache persisted despite the Tylenol he'd taken an hour ago. Hoping the mundane act of driving would offer some relief, he climbed behind the wheel of the Chevy and set off for Mercer General Hospital in Trenton, New Jersey. Ignoring his GPS's directive, he chose West Street by way of Murray, instead of Canal, to get to the Holland Tunnel, thereby avoiding the throng of tourists and jay walkers shopping for electronic gadgetry along Bowery.

Bright sunshine greeted him as he exited the winding corridor into Jersey City. Entering the New Jersey Turnpike, he set his cruise control a notch above the 65 mph limit keeping an eye on a convoy of tractor trailers transporting the Meat District's hinds of beef to the outer burbs.

Doctor Melanie Anderson was checking her iPhone messages by the hospital's bank of elevators when Driscoll stepped off on the 3rd floor. "It's not every day, a country gal from Jersey gets a visit from New York's Finest," she said, sporting a Grace Kelly smile.

"Very nice to meet you, Doctor Anderson."

"Please, it's Melanie. And if you'll follow me, you'll understand why I met you at the elevator."

The therapist led the Lieutenant through an endless labyrinth of corridors. Driscoll wondered if they'd soon cross into Pennsylvania when she opened her office door and ushered him inside. Seating himself beside her cluttered desk, the Lieutenant eyed a kaleidoscope of drawings that had been Scotch taped to the walls.

"They all tell a story," Doctor Anderson said, taking note of the Lieutenant's focus. "My patients draw what they cannot tell me."

"That's a colorful array of voices. As I explained on the phone, I have some questions about your article and how it pertains to your patient, Adrian Strayer," said Driscoll.

"Fire away."

"Do you only treat patients who suffer from what you refer to as a dissociative identity disorder?"

"Thankfully, no. Multiple personalities target only a few of my patients. Good God, if they all suffered from it the volume in this room would be off the charts."

"Strayer, you've been treating him for a while."

"That's right. Adrian's been here for twenty-four years, but he's only recently begun to talk. He also has selective mutism," she said, pulling his binder from her desk drawer.

"I've never heard of that."

"It's an anxiety disorder. The individual is unable to speak, or so he believes. It starts in early childhood."

"That's interesting. What else can you tell me about Strayer?"

"They brought him here as a ward of the state when he was about 12. He'd been roaming the streets of Trenton for God knows how long where he begged for his meals. When he got caught stealing a couple of Hershey bars the shopkeeper called the police."

"How do you know his name?"

"We don't."

Driscoll studied her eyes.

"'Adrian' was scrawled in laundry ink on the waist band of his jeans when they brought him here."

"The jeans could have belonged to anyone. How do you know they were his?"

"Again, we don't."

"And Strayer? Where'd that come from?"

"According to his file, the admitting nurse, a Michael Larson, needed a last name. State Child Services had the boy listed as a 'John Doe'. Larson was a Civil War buff who regularly attended many reenactments as Medal of Honor recipient, Corporal Andrew Strayer. He penned it in as the boy's last name."

"According to your article, six months ago was when he started to talk. You'd indicated that a crowd occupied his mind. In whose voice did Adrian speak?"

"Peter's."

"Who's he?"

"He's an orphan."

"What'd he say?"

"He asked for a colored pencil and then drew this." The therapist handed Driscoll a sketch of a figure wearing a hood and what appeared to be a black robe. In the sketch, the figure had no face.

"Did Peter, through Adrian, say who he is?"

"You mean who she is. That's a religious habit he drew." The therapist handed the Lieutenant a second sketch. "This one has more detail," she said.

Driscoll studied the figure. It was definitely a nun.

"An orphan raised by nuns," Driscoll mused, out loud. "Did he draw any more?"

"That was it for Peter. After that, he became catatonic and withdrew inside Adrian's mind and never returned."

"Would Peter be a person in Adrian's past?"

"Perhaps. More likely a version of someone."

"What do you make of these?" Driscoll asked, studying the two sketches he'd been handed.

"I'm not sure what to make of them. In both the female figure appears to be dead. It could be an expression of hostility or simply something he witnessed or dreamed up in his head. I have no clue what the bucket of blood signifies.

The cross he drew on her chest would likely indicate the deceased was a nun."

"He drew a cross on her chest?"

"Yes. I'd realized after the article was published that they'd omitted that. Copy editor's choice, I guess."

"That's quite an omission. Had he ever done or said anything that suggested he'd been raised Catholic?"

"There's nothing in his file that indicates that. Nor has it ever come up in session. He came to us off the streets of Trenton. Lots of churches and parochial schools there. A good number of rectories and convents, too, I suppose. But, we have no way of knowing if he actually lived there. Aside from his presence on the streets."

"I see."

"Lieutenant, when you called my curiosity got the better of me. I must confess. I Googled you."

Driscoll smiled. "What'd you find?"

"It indicated your police unit is pursuing a serial killer. Is there something about Adrian's drawing that ties it to your investigation?"

"I'm not sure. But, I can't rule it out. Does Adrian have names for the personalities in his head?" the Lieutenant asked.

"Right now there's Mark, Matthew, and Patrick. And as I said earlier, Peter. But he disappeared. The female in his drawing he referred to as 'Ella'."

"Ella?"

"Does that name have significance?" the therapist asked.

"Not at the moment. I understand Adrian has the mentality of an eight-year-old. How's that determined?"

"Through a battery of tests and by clinical observation."

"Could he be faking it?"

"Possibly, if he were recently admitted. But, he's been here for decades. There's no way he could pull that off."

"These personalities. Could one of them be older?"

"Each one is unique but they all think and speak like an eight-year-old."

"What's security like for Adrian?"

"Trust me, Lieutenant, Adrian hasn't left this building since being admitted. In his mind I'm sure he's travelled around the globe, but he's been here all the while."

"You said Adrian hasn't drawn any other females. Only Ella. Is that right?"

"That's right."

"His artwork. Is that his only form of communication?"

"The art is an ice breaker which allows him to express his feelings. He and I then talk about those feelings. In depth."

"What did he say about Ella?"

"He chose not to talk about her. Which may indicate his memory is distant or she stirs feelings he's not ready to discuss. Time will tell which it is. I'm betting on the latter."

"Why's that?"

"When he finished the drawing, he threw his chalk against the wall and pressed his chin into his chest."

"Whad'ya make of that?"

"That's a display of anger. Intense anger."

CHAPTER FORTY-THREE

Driscoll sat behind the wheel of the Chevy collecting his thoughts. He had more questions than answers. Contrary to what he'd been told, had Adrian managed to get out of the hospital undetected to perpetrate the heinous murders? What's the significance of his sketch, where a woman wearing a cross is being bled? From the neck, no less. Hadn't Harold's arson been fueled by his perceived abandonment by his mother, a vestal bride of Christ? Did Sinthia's abduction and killing have something to do with her wearing a religious habit to the swinger's club? My God, had someone declared war on nuns?

After popping three Tylenol tablets in his mouth, he washed them down with a sip of 7 Up from the bottle he'd purchased at the hospital's gift shop. Grabbing his cellular, he called Margaret.

"Hey, John! How'd it go at the hospital," she asked.

"The therapist was helpful. She agreed to keep us in the loop if and when this Strayer character gets another visit from Ella, the subject of his artwork. Who, by the way, was depicted wearing a cross."

"That's new."

"I'd like you to go downstairs to the property clerk and retrieve everything we collected at Harold MacKillop's apartment. We may have missed something."

"You thinking he may be our embalmer as well as an arsonist?"

"Not sure. But this lead at the hospital now suggests an assault on a nun, albeit on paper."

"Could it simply be coincidence?"

"You know how I feel about those."

"I do."

"Instinct tells me Strayer's artwork is a piece to a puzzle."

"And MacKillop's belongings may hold another?"

"Correct."

"I'll get on it right away."

"Bring Cedric up to speed."

"Will do."

CHAPTER FORTY-FOUR

Seated across the scarred oak table inside the precinct's Property Room, Aligante and Thomlinson sorted through the contents of the box of personal effects that had been collected at Harold MacKillop's apartment.

"You know there are two things I've been dying to ask you," Margaret said, her elbows on the table, her eyes on Thomlinson.

"Fire away," the detective responded, looking puzzled.

"Do the needles hurt when the acupuncturist sticks you?"

The question unsettled Thomlinson. The last thing he wanted to do was deceive his long time friend. Sure, Margaret knew he'd been battling alcoholism for years. Hell, everyone in the department was aware of his fight with the sleeping tiger. But, the last time he'd brought up acupuncture in her company she went on to say something about alternative medicine being a viable option to treat muscular pain Would a simple "no" put an end to the questioning? he wondered. Knowing Margaret, he doubted it.

"The thought of being a pincushion had me a little worried at first," Thomlinson conceded. "But, in truth, I hardly felt anything when Dr Swensen inserted them."

"Good to know."

"What's your second question?" Thomlinson asked, his eyes narrowing.

"Have the treatments helped you resist the temptation to pick up a drink?"

The look on the detective's face was one of astonishment.

"I thought you thought…."

"I know," Margaret said, cutting Thomlinson off mid sentence. "It's not easy to open up about the demons that wreck havoc in our lives. I had mentioned muscular pain because I detected a guarded look in your eyes when I broached the subject of your treatment."

"I could lean over and kiss you right now, Margaret."

"But you won't. Just know you're not alone, ok?"

"OK"

"Back to the case, Cedric?"

"You mean back to being us?"

"Yep."

"You got it." The pair turned their attention once again to Harold MacKillop's personal effects.

"He won't be needing these," Margaret said, holding up an unopened pack of latex condoms.

"He may have been radicalized. Could be partying right now in that strip joint in the sky with 72 virgins. Those rubbers would have come in handy. Ahh, heaven!" the detective beamed.

"The guy torched a church, Cedric. He's not in heaven."

"Where is he, then?"

"Hades."

"Whad'ya suppose he used these for?" Thomlinson asked, examining two child-sized masks, one of Casper the Ghost, the other, Howdy Doody.

"He coulda' been a pedophile."

Margaret was grossed out whenever she had to paw through a dead man's clothing, particularly when he favored Speedos over Hanes tighty whities. Revulsion filling her face, she grabbed the carton containing his underwear.

"You better hope they bagged the hamper separately," Thomlinson said with grin.

"Zip it."

Gingerly picking up a yellowed and frayed Fruit of the Loom pair of boxers, she grimaced. The cotton underwear had seen better days. "Hold still Margaret, that'd make a great post on Facebook," Thomlinson said, aiming his iPhone. "I'll hashtag it #NYPDSargeantOnAPantyRaid!"

"You snap that picture you'll be eating these," she growled, rolling the underwear into a ball.

"Looks like our boy had an appointment every Wednesday at 7 p.m.," Thomlinson said, holding up MacKillop's SkallyWagz Wall Calendar.

Margaret sidled up next to the detective as he ticked off the weeks back to January. "Yep, every Wednesday," he said.

"Wha'd'ya suppose the 'G' is for?" Margaret asked, staring at the notation: '**7 pm – G**' that'd been circled in red.

"G. His main squeeze?" Thomlinson pondered aloud.

"Thousands of girl's names begin with G," Margaret griped.

"Two thousand if he swung from both sides of the plate. I say we pay another visit to Jangles Hideaway."

"Jangles?" asked Margaret, looking puzzled.

"The mean Rottweiler with the tiny woman on the other end of his leash."

"Right. MacKillop's landlord. Let's go."

Ten minutes later they were met by the growl of the beast.

"He's assessing his prey, Margaret. Which one of us will he have for dinner?"

"Don't fuck with me, you vociferous brute. I aced my last qualification at the firing range." Margaret stared down the dog.

Jangles whined before retreating.

"Well, look at that. Beauty cured the beast. I think he's got the hots for you, Margaret," said Thomlinson.

"I'm not into dogs."

The landlord poked her face into the cubby hole under the brownstone's stoop and smiled.

"I see you remember us," said Margaret.

"Where's the dapper gent who was with you last time?"

"Back at the office, ma'am. May we come in?"

"Sure. What brings ya'back?"

"We have some follow-up questions about your former tenant," Margaret explained.

The little woman stepped onto the milk crate, unlocked the gate, and ushered the pair into a living room where all the furniture was covered with sheets.

"I keep the good stuff covered unless I'm expecting company," she said, pulling a sheet off an outdated and frayed couch. When the dust settled, Margaret and Thomlinson sat.

"We believe Mr. MacKillop went someplace specific every Wednesday night at 7. Any idea where he might have gone?" Thomlinson asked.

The woman shrugged.

"Did he go out often?" Margaret asked.

"Nah, one or two nights a week, maybe. If that. And he rarely had any visitors. Not exactly a social chum, if ya' catch my drift."

"Any lady friends?"

"Ain't never seen him with one. Wait a minute. Did you say Wednesday night?"

"Yes," said Thomlinson.

"Thanksgiving's always on a Thursday, right?"

"It is."

"Well, like I said, it was next to never he had anyone visit. But last Thanksgiving was my turn to have the neighbors over. The night before. A Wednesday. I was stuffin' the bird when I heard Harold ushering a crowd of people up to his flat. That never happened. I stuck my head out into the hall and asked him what was up. He said his therapist was on vacation and he was hosting weekly group, whatever that meant."

CHAPTER FORTY-FIVE

Margaret and Thomlinson hurried into Driscoll's office to report what they had discovered only to find the Lieutenant looking forlorn.

The smart looking blue suit Thomlinson was wearing along with the navy blue dress Margaret had on looked like they'd been cut from the same fabric.

"You ok, John," Margaret asked.

"I will be. I just returned from my sister's apartment in Bayside."

"So the Catholic Church came through for her," Thomlinson said.

"They did. They also stocked the fridge and gave her cash to shop for new clothes. I have a feeling I won't see much of Mary from here on out."

"That's the apartment she'll be staying in for only a couple of months, right? Until the nuns return from their retreat house, no?" Margaret asked.

As Driscoll eyed his two similarly clad investigators, a smile creased his face.

"Mary's stay of only a couple of months has been extended, Margaret. She's done so much volunteer work for the Church's Diocesan Office in Brooklyn, they're going to accommodate her permanently."

"Bayside's only a forty-five minutes drive," Thomlinson said, consolingly.

The Lieutenant's smile faded.

"Yeah, but Mary will be Mary," Driscoll said, glumly. "Whad'ya come up with on our dead arsonist?"

"MacKillop had scheduled a group therapy session every Wednesday. Where and with whom, we don't yet know," Thomlinson said.

"A lot of good it did him. He still had a penchant for torching churches," Margaret groaned. "His landlord, who asked for you, by the way, told us he had a crowd over one night for Group Therapy."

Driscoll's eyes narrowed as he began to contemplate the significance of that detail.

"A Group Therapy session inside his apartment? There had to have been contact between the patients for that to happen. With no house phone or computer in his apartment, MacKillop likely used a cell phone, no?" Driscoll asked.

"Absolutely. And bank statements we found inside his dark room show he was paying Verizon Wireless monthly," said Margaret.

"Good luck getting any help from them. Especially if MacKillop was using an iPhone. Remember, Verizon sided with Apple when the FBI demanded they create a 'back door program' that would allow them access to the locked iPhone used by the San Bernardino terrorists," Thomlinson said.

Driscoll turned his attention to his computer screen where the arsonist's file was open and did an electronic search. He found was no mention of a cell phone in any of the investigative reports. "The guy gets torched in a spontaneous blaze fueled by a heavy-duty accelerant where CSU is able to identify remnants from a leather wallet, some credit cards, and a plastic ball point pen, but no phone?"

"They were all over his van. If he'd left it there, they'd have found it," Thomlinson reasoned.

Margaret nodded in agreement.

"Phones are like appendages these days. If it's not in your pocket, it's in your hand," said Thomlinson.

Driscoll thought back to his last encounter with the arsonist inside St. Agnes' Church. He had tackled him, forcing him to the floor. Could the phone have been knocked out of his pocket on impact? He picked up the desk phone and called the church.

CHAPTER FORTY-SIX

Driscoll killed the engine of his Impala after pulling to the curb across from the small church. Inside the cruiser, his thoughts drifted to better times when his parents were young and devoted. When family was everything. Gazing at the 19th century brownstone, he became a young boy again, a freshly laundered surplice folded reverently over his arm as he hurried up the church steps, eager to serve as an altar boy at St. Agnes' 10:15 Mass. All churches in the Diocese had switched to English as the official language for the Celebration of The Eucharist, but Father Windsor, a venerable antiquarian, hosted a monthly Mass in Latin and young John had once been awarded the honor to serve in that ancient ritual. Thrilled by his election, he gladly skipped little league try-outs and a couple of after school stickball games so he could memorize the entire Mass in the ecclesiastical language of the early Church.

Stepping out of the cruiser, darkness settled, rocketing him to the grim present and the realization that an abomination had recently taken place only yards away. The Lieutenant shielded his hands inside the large pockets of his Burberry, as if the gesture would guarantee his safety, and approached the church. The team of plain clothes officers, the bomb squad, the K9s, the patrol cars and the fire trucks, had all retreated, restoring silence to the crime scene. A bed of St. Petersburg irises in bloom caught Driscoll's eye. *Life prevails,* he thought. But, pushing against the massive oak door, the lingering smell of the long extinguished fire rattled him.

"It's good to see you again, John," Monsignor Sean Hennessey's voice echoed in the nave of the church.

The priest was a bulk of a man with the swagger of John Wayne and the good looks of a present day Tyrone Power.

"Likewise, Sean," Driscoll said, taking hold of the cleric's outstretched hand. "How was your getaway to the tropics?"

"Well, I guess you could call Florida the tropics. Nothing like an expensive single malt at the Tequesta Country Club to make me forget the fire. Did you know single malt is the Scots version of holy water?"

"In fact, I did," Driscoll said with a grin. "After we wrap this up, you and I should pay a visit to Glasgow"

That prompted a smile on the Monsignor's face.

"It only takes me twenty minutes to pack. We priests travel light," he joked. "But seriously, John, I owe you a great deal of thanks. Had it not been for your brave effort this place would now be a pile of ash."

Driscoll smiled.

"The firefighters deserve most of the credit," he said.

"But it was you who had them standing by."

"Thank you and you're welcome." Driscoll unpocketed the plastic tube of Tylenol. "Can I trouble you for some water," he asked.

"Sure." Hennessey headed for the sacristy. Upon his return he handed Driscoll a Dixie cup.

"Thanks, Sean." Driscoll downed another dose of pain killer.

"After your call, I checked the drawer in the sacristy where lost items are placed. Plenty of sunglasses. A couple of rosaries. But, no phone. It could've been overlooked. Our sacristans are high school kids. Volunteers who give us 50% of their time. The other half is spent texting or snackchatting, whatever that is."

"It's snapchatting," said Driscoll, stifling a grin.

"Whatever."

"I'm thinking the phone may have fallen from MacKillop's pocket during our scuffle. And our mêlée was right about there," Driscoll said, moving toward the area where the votive candles had been knocked over.

The floor was marble, giving way to hardwood slabs that ran under the wooden pews to his right. A plaster wall to his left supported a confessional booth.

After checking below and around six rows of pews and finding nothing but two nickels and a torn movie theater ticket, the Lieutenant returned to where he'd first stood. Looking at the confessional, it appeared flush with the floor. But, as he approached, he saw that the base met the floor only at its corners. Its center was notched across the bottom, leaving an open expanse measuring a quarter-inch or so in height.

Activating his iPhone's flashlight, Driscoll knelt and directed the beam under the confessional.

"I'll need a hand moving this, Sean."

"Dear Lord, it's under there?"

"We'll know in a minute."

The two Irishmen tilted the confessional. There, lying on the unwaxed strip of marble, was an iPhone.

"Shut the front door," exclaimed the cleric.

CHAPTER FORTY-SEVEN

Tilden heard the faint, but unmistakable, AT&T jingle emanating from his iPhone. Most of the time it sat on the table by the front door. He rarely used it. He could count on one hand the number of outgoing calls he'd made. His last incoming call was weeks ago when Louise let him know she'd miss Group Therapy because of a migraine. The phone's chirp meant he had a voice mail.

Curiosity piqued, Tilden retrieved it. Only the caller's number appeared on the Voicemail screen. Hitting 'PLAY', he brought the phone to his ear. He didn't recognize the caller's voice. It sounded as though he was crying. Convinced some sad sack had dialed a wrong number, he pulled the phone away from his ear and eyed the 'DELETE' tab. As he was about to erase the voicemail, the caller's voice grew louder. Clearer. Recognizable. It was John from Group. And as Tilden listened intently, the voice hollered: "That fucking cop killed Harold. Harold! Your best friend, Tilden! He's dead! Harold's dead!"

Tilden stopped breathing. In less than a minute, his brain shut down. Like a marionette without a puppet master, he collapsed to the floor.

CHAPTER FORTY-EIGHT

Driscoll was pleased MacKillop's iPhone, though locked, was an older model, and hoped its age would make it easier for his in-house technicians in Computer Crimes to retrieve its password. The last thing he wanted was to alert the higher ups. NYPD Brass were adamant against calling attention to an investigation involving accessing data from a private phone. It was well known that the FBI had hired hackers to retrieve information from an iPhone used by Rizwan Farook, one of the shooters in the San Bernardino terrorist attack. Although their action was in the interest of national security, they still drew criticism and Driscoll knew his arsonist posed no such risk. At least, he hoped he didn't.

His techs had the device for five days. He'd give them two more. If they were still unable to get into the phone, he wasn't sure what he'd do. Surely, he couldn't seek the help of Moira Tiernan, a tech savvy whiz kid, who'd once assisted him in tracking down a serial killer, a bone thief who lured his female prey over the internet. The feisty teen would find her way in before the Lieutenant could blink. Moira was a rebel at heart. It wasn't enough for her to simply unmask the madman years ago. No, she had to take it to the extreme and, without telling a soul, electronically set herself as bait. The result? The murderous psychopath shattered every bone in her body. Driscoll recalled all too vividly his race to the hospital where Moira lay encased from head to toe in a plaster sarcophagus. "Kids these days," he muttered.

His desk phone rang and what the caller had to say wasn't encouraging.

"So, if your next attempt at configuring a password fails, the phone stays locked forever?" asked Driscoll.

"I'm afraid so, Lieutenant."

"Alright, thank your team for their efforts and have someone return the phone to me."

The news set his conscience in a whirl. Should he involve Moira in his new investigation? There may be useful data on the arsonist's phone and that electronics wizard would gain access in minutes. After she located the data that'd be the end of her involvement. Would he be putting her at risk? After all, her last involvement almost got her killed when a crazed murderer abducted her. But, what if there was information on the phone making it clear why these women were being targeted and by whom? Shouldn't he utilize every available means to find that out? By not doing so, wasn't he putting some unknown victim at risk of possibly being targeted by this murderous fiend? Such a quandary. Since NYPD would never authorize dollars paid to a hacker he had no choice but to find one himself. And no one was better than Moira. For the sake of stopping this madman's reign of terror he'd contact Moira to simply discuss the possibility of a minimal and supervised assist. A very supervised assist. Under no circumstances would she come in contact with this madman.

Parking the Chevy outside Moira's basement apartment in Astoria, Driscoll felt like an intruder. Shouldn't he have called first? Why break all the laws of courtesy? Will she be home? And if so, will she open the door for him. She might dial 911 and report him as a prowler. After descending the steps, a whiff of cannabis teased his nostrils. Was it an analgesic to help with her pain? Maybe. But could it also mollify her resistance? He heard the melodic sound of a Japanese flute through the door, which ceased the moment he knocked. There was a shuffle of feet followed by the clanking sound of a deadbolt lock being opened. In the crack of the door, a security chain dangled while arctic blue eyes stared at him.

"How are you, Moira?" he said, paternally.

Her eyes narrowed. She closed the door, only to release the chain and open it again. Without responding to his question, she motioned for him to come in.

Driscoll squeezed past her and entered the cramped room where a Persian cat, enthroned on a cushion, stared at him. He looked for a place to put the two cups of organic coffee and the two chocolate croissants he'd picked up at Le Pain Quotidien. Clearing a pile of vinyl LPs from a small bamboo table, he placed them down and took a seat at one of two chairs.

"You're still a fan of chocolate, I hope."

"I am," she said, taking the seat across from the Lieutenant. Biting into the crusty dough, she fixed curious eyes on Driscoll.

"The physical therapist still helpful, Moira?" He was relieved she was at least responsive.

"She is. I won't be up and dabbing anytime soon, but I'm walking without a cane."

"No cane That's good. What's dabbing?"

Moira held back a grin. A somewhat devilish grin. She reveled in dropping words that members of the older generation would be clueless as to their meaning.

"Dabbing's the latest dance craze."

"Dabbing. That's cute. What else keeps you busy?"

"Mother's opened a yoga studio where she teaches yoga to pregnant women. I help with the books and by drumming up clients. Why are you here?" she asked, taking a sip of coffee, her eyes still studying him.

"I was in the neighborhood," he answered, knowing she saw through his lie.

"You should join us at yoga."

"I'm not pregnant."

"It works wonders on overstressed and overworked policemen who've hit a wall in their investigation."

"Touché," said Driscoll,

Moira smiled.

"In fact you could invite my mom to your precinct a couple of times a week. She'd boost morale and get the crew to stop smoking and drinking. How's Cedric, by the way?"

Ah, she remembered Cedric's battle with the bottle, he mused, impressed by her subtle craftiness. His rambunctious fourteen-year-old assistant had grown into a spirited and astute young adult.

"Not a bad idea," he said. "And Cedric is doing well. In fact, he sends his regards."

"I see. And did Margaret also know you were going to be 'in the neighborhood'?"

"I keep my team well informed."

A hint of a smile told the Lieutenant she, too, was enjoying their lighthearted duel. "Just imagine, Lieutenant, you're on the threshold of being the top cop who brought 21st century relaxation technique to New York's Finest."

"That would take a little doing. But there is a huge storage room that's hardly used. I'll see what I can arrange."

"Good! This coffee is delicious, by the way."

She'd become more relaxed. She appeared to be less on the defensive.

"Indonesian beans from Sumatra," Driscoll said.

Moira stared at the Lieutenant, her eyes level with the steaming brew.

"I'm sure this visit is not to promote coffee. How 'bout you tell me why you're really here."

"I need your help."

"I've heard that before." She put down the coffee and bolted upright. "Excuse me, time to feed the cat. He's OCD and if I'm off by 5 minutes he turns into a Bengal tiger with a thing against males."

"You know why I'm here, Moira. I'm after another very bad dude."

"You're always after a very bad dude."

She disappeared through a door which Driscoll presumed led to a kitchen.

"This one's a demon," he hollered.

"Aren't they all?" she yelled back.

"I suppose so," Driscoll muttered to himself.

When Moira reappeared, she was wearing a red silk scarf around her neck.

"I'd love to talk more about your problem, Lieutenant, but I'm late for my weekly appointment with my therapist," she said.

"Your physical therapist?"

"No. My shrink."

She's seeing a psychotherapist and I pick today of all days to drop by. She'll do nothing but rant about me. Any chance of her helping me is gone! Damn it, why didn't I call first!

"How you getting there?" he asked.

"Access-A-Ride."

Driscoll's guilt took another hit. Thanks to him, she was at the mercy of the City's poorly managed transit system for the disabled. "How 'bout I drive you?"

"How would I get back?'

"I'll wait for you," he said, praying her session would cover something other than his visit.

"You're moonlighting for UBER now?"

"C'mon. Let's go."

"Well, you've upped your game with the high end croissants. I'll give you that. You got a Beemer outside?"

"No, but the Chevy's linked to Pandora and I'm sure we can stream in some of that Japanese flute you were listening to."

"Give me a minute to roll a joint."

"Cute, Moira. Real cute," he said, grabbing his keys.

CHAPTER FORTY-NINE

"Why the fuck would you think I'd be interested in helping you track down this demon you're chasing?" Moira asked, as soon as she slid inside Driscoll's cruiser.

There's no doubt she and her therapist will discuss me," Driscoll thought as he pulled away from the curb. "Why do I think you'd be interested? To tell you truth, I'm not sure. But, I'm hoping you will. Remember, without your help the first demon may still be on the loose."

"Who's to say he isn't? His body was never recovered," she said, a chill coming over her.

"Trust me, he isn't coming back."

"Michael Myers came back. Again and again and again."

"You're confusing the movie world with real life, Moira. The Long Island Sound doesn't give up its dead. After I shot him, the water claimed him. And that's where he'll stay."

"He visits me every fucking night, Lieutenant. That's alive enough for me," she muttered, tears beginning to flow.

A sad silence settled between them as Driscoll pulled into a parking space outside the therapist's building. He understood the oppressive dread that had taken hold of Moira. She was still broken. Her bones may have healed but her spirit was fractured with an uncertain prognosis. Driscoll felt paternal, and wanted to salvage innocence from her world of carnage. Had he not felt the same way about his daughter, Nicole, who, at fourteen, had lost her life because of the recklessness of a drunk driver?

Fighting back the urge to embrace her, Driscoll got out of the cruiser, walked around to the passenger side and helped her out of the car.

"Are you really going to wait for me?" she asked.

"I said I would."

"There's a Starbuck's a couple of blocks over."

"Not to worry, I'll be alright."

He watched Moira limp toward the building's entrance. His heart faltered as she negotiated her way through the revolving door. Climbing back in behind the wheel, he turned off the ignition, adjusted the Chevy's seat to a comfortable position, and took in his surroundings. Her therapist's office was in Long Island City, where buildings were shedding their industrial concrete skin in a frenzied re-gentrification. Bodegas that had once sold a cup of coffee for a dollar were being replaced by nouveau chic storefronts offering a cup of organic Joe for five bucks. Though some residents who'd managed to hold on to their rent stabilized apartments have argued that the coffee at the bodega was better, the convenience store owners never had a dozen customers lined up for a cup of Henri and Brian's Organic Aloha Blend.

The thought of coffee made him mindful of Moira's suggestion. Figuring Starbucks would be a good distraction, he got out of the car. After walking the two blocks, he ordered a double espresso, hoping the caffeine might help diminish his headache which was no longer softened by the acetaminophen. Sitting on a veranda overlooking a vast lawn, he watched a group of children flying kites. The afternoon was mild and welcoming. The children's laughter suggested hope was alive but he knew beyond the scenery of a leisurely afternoon, horror in human form stalked the five boroughs. He, the watcher, saw what most didn't see and employed every strategy to ensure they never did.

CHAPTER FIFTY

"I had a visitor today," Moira began.

Doctor Hannah Adelman knew something was up as Moira had abandoned the arm chair for the therapeutic sofa. "Why shouldn't you? You're popular."

"From a cop."

"Will you be dating him?"

"Not this one."

"Why not?"

"It'd be like dating Dad."

"What's wrong with that?"

"It was Lieutenant John Driscoll."

"Oh, him," the therapist said, a look of curiosity marking her face.

"He wants my help. Again!"

"What kind of help?"

"To catch another killer."

Doctor Adelman had known all too well the nightmare her patient had lived through. She was maternally protective of her brutalized prey. "It must be a major homicide, no? Could this be the crucifixion case that everyone's talking about?"

"I don't know."

An unsettling quiet overtook them. It was obvious to Doctor Adelman that Moira's mood had turned inward. "Well, are you gonna give him a hand?" she asked, intentionally provoking her patient.

"Don't you remember what happened last time?" Moira grumbled.

"I do."

"Then why ask if I'm gonna help him?"

"C'mon, Moira, you know you get a charge out of traipsing on the edge," Adelman prodded, knowing she had stirred a cauldron of raw feelings.

"Who's side are you on?" Moira griped, inflamed by the characterization.

"You're the one who tracked down his last boogeyman."

"I don't like where you're going with this."

"Would you rather we discuss the weather?"

"You know, Hannah, you're beginning to piss me off."

A few miles north of the city dark clouds were gathering for a summer monsoon. A booming drum roll of thunder shattered their precarious silence.

"Maybe we should talk about the weather," Moira said.

"I could use an espresso." Adelman walked toward her De'Longhi double serve machine. "Would you like one? It's organic."

"Sure. Why not?" Moira said, looking distraught.

While the therapist fiddled with the coffeemaker's plastic knobs, Moira bit down on her lower lip and closed her eyes. "I fucked up. Big time! There's more to the story than what I had told you."

Psychotherapists, in general, knew patients sometimes lied during their sessions and also kept secrets. Throughout Moira's treatment, which started right after her ferocious attack at the hands of a serial killer, Adelman had sensed her patient had provided her with a homogenized version of the incident. Was she tactically concealing an ugly motive? Perhaps Driscoll's barging into her precarious, but settled, life had stirred her psychological 'sand', the fractured morsels of trauma she'd unconsciously buried deep inside her mind. If so, she was grateful for Driscoll, her agent provocateur, because of him, and the turbulence he had created in her patient's inner world, Moira's therapy could advance; targeting areas in her psyche, hitherto untouched.

"I didn't just sit behind a laptop tracking down his boogeyman," Moira confessed. "I set a trap for the killer, using myself as bait. I paid no attention to every command Lieutenant Driscoll made. His orders meant nothing to me. He warned me to stay clear of the actual pursuit. Did I listen? Hell no! Screw his warning. I dove right in. Invincible Moira on a mission. Moronic Moira is more like it. I made myself fucking bait! Can you believe it? Bait! All because I wanted to get closer to the killer."

"Why?" Adelman asked, knowing her patient was on the brink of revealing a deep hidden secret.

Moira let her head fall between her legs and fell silent for a full two minutes. When she sat upright, her face was flushed and her lips were clenched together. "That boogeyman…"

"Go on Moira. How did that boogeyman make you feel?"

"That boogeyman turned me on," she whispered, her eyes trancelike.

"His killing got your juices flowing," Adelman pushed.

"They did. I wanted to fuck him. Still do," Moira said, looking pointedly at the therapist. "Happy now?"

"Yes. I am."

"All this longing to be fucked by a madman. Means I'm fucked in the head, right?'

"Aphrodite wasn't."

"Aphrodite?" Moira asked, incredulously.

"Every Greek god would have given up eternal life just to nail her. Do you know who Aphrodite chose?"

"Apollo, the hottie."

"She chose Ares, the God of War. The ultimate serial killer."

Moira looked baffled

"You don't see the connection?"

"I'm not sure what I see."

Adelman banged her coffee cup on the table. "Some women lust after killers. They turn them on."

"Oh, my God," Moira said, her eyes like saucers.

CHAPTER FIFTY-ONE

Checking his watch, Driscoll returned to the counter at Starbucks, ordered two coffees to go along with an apple turnover. After a minute's wait beside his Impala, the revolving door delivered a smiling Moira.

"My therapist was happy with my progress. Whatcha got in the bag," she asked, sliding into the passenger seat.

"An apple turnover and a couple of house blends."

As Moira bit into the fruit stuffed pastry she became a little girl in Driscoll's eyes. Her tears had dried and her nubile smile had returned.

"It's not gonna work, you know?" she said, dispelling his dreaminess.

"What's not going to work?"

"Sweetening me up with goodies so I'll help you."

"No, Moira. I gave it a lot of thought while I was at Starbucks. I have no right to ask you to put yourself in harm's way. I'm very sorry I did."

"No reason to be sorry, Lieutenant." Tears welled in her eyes. "It's me who owes you an apology. I should have listened to you. And I didn't. You're not to blame for my injuries. I am. I'm the one who fucked up. I was delinquent and defiant. But, most of all, I was a know-it-all fourteen-year-old out to prove to the world how smart I thought I was."

Driscoll was blown away. *Where the hell did that come from?*

"You've carried too much guilt for too long," she continued. "I'm sorry I gave you such a hard time today. Seeing you brought it all back to me and it will take time to sort things out in my head." Were those tears she now saw in Driscoll's eyes she wondered before collapsing into his open embrace.

CHAPTER FIFTY-TWO

Driscoll had no desire to join Moira's flying circus. But how could he turn down Doctor Adelman's request that he attend Moira's next scheduled appointment, especially since she'd reached out to him the day after he'd driven her to her last appointment? But why had she extended the invitation without explanation other than to say it was critical? Not that he had anything against the mental health field, after all he had benefited greatly under the care of a compassionate counselor in the aftermath of the loss of his daughter and his wife's vanishing into an eternal coma. Since Adelman was adamant that he attend and his investigation would likely remain at a standstill until he gained access to MacKillop's phone he accepted.

"Is it really essential that I be here?" Driscoll asked the therapist as soon as he stepped inside her office.

"It's very nice to meet you, Lieutenant. Moira has told me so much about you," Doctor Adelman said, sidestepping his question.

Driscoll wasn't sure how to respond. He looked to Moira, who smiled, then back to the therapist. "Has she now?" he said, sporting a curious grin as he took a seat.

"Moira thinks of you as a father figure."

"Oh, really?"

"Absolutely. And as such, it's important you know that Moira has confided in me more than she has with anyone else. She's chosen me as her advocate to secure for her the serenity she deserves."

"In this calamitous world serenity has gone the way of the rotary phone."

"I'm sure that feeling stems from the horror you see every day in your line of work. But one's journey should never be abandoned."

"I was into him, that bone collector," Moira muttered, almost inaudibly.

"Don't go there, Moira," Adelman cautioned, visibly alarmed.

The Lieutenant again looked to Moira, then back to the therapist, who shook her head and raised an eyebrow. Driscoll fiddled with his tie, unsure of what to do or say. After what seemed like an eternity of silence he felt compelled to speak.

"You were into Godsend, Moira? The killer who stole his victim's bones and nearly killed you?" he asked as the look of astonishment filled his face.

She gave no reply

He eyed Moira, but she avoided his stare. Turning back to the therapist, Driscoll asked: "What the hell is she talking about?"

Adelman clenched her lips giving him the impression it wasn't her turn to speak.

"He flayed them and gouged out their ribs. It turned me on," Moira murmured, looking as though she were in a trance.

"Jesus Christ, Doctor! How long have you known about this?" The Lieutenant's face had reddened. His eyes darted back and forth.

"She only confided it to me in her last session."

"She's been sitting on this for ten years?"

"I'm afraid so. If it's any solace to you, her revelation followed your recent visit which means you've helped in her treatment."

Driscoll shook his head in disbelief before his face collapsed into his hands.

"Can she be cured?" he asked, his focus now on Moira, whose eyes were fixed on the wall.

"A fixation like this is incurable. The aim of my treatment is to help Moira manage it."

"She doesn't seem like she has," Driscoll said, looking to Moira who said nothing.

"I believe she will. Let's be thankful she's not corresponding with anyone on death row," Adelman said. "Many like her do."

Driscoll thought of Richard Ramirez, the so-called Night Stalker who, after being convicted of murdering thirteen people and sentenced to death, married his pen pal. "Does Moira have any incarcerated friends?" Driscoll asked.

"Hey! I'm sitting right here," Moira shouted. "You two have been talking about me like I'm not in the room. Well, I am in the room! And you, Lieutenant, are here because Hannah told me your presence would help. Trust me, I'm here to get to the ugliness. And if it means exposing it to you, so be it. I'm as wacky as it gets, Lieutenant. Who's got a cigarette?"

Driscoll reached in his jacket and produced a pack of Marlboros. Looking to Adelman, who nodded, he gave Moira a cigarette. After lighting it for her, he lit one for himself, leaned back in his chair and exhaled. "She was fourteen years old, Doctor. You're telling me your average young teen could get that worked up?'

"Must madness afflict only the age appropriate?" Adelman asked.

"I chase grownups, Doctor. Adolescents, even the anything-but-average ones, are out of my league," said Driscoll.

"I was never your average anything," Moira shouted, before exhaling a cloud of smoke.

"Evil is not age specific."

"I'll give you that," Driscoll said.

"OK. Now that everyone's on the same page. Moira, I must insist you stay clear of any and all of this policeman's investigations," Adelman said.

"Amen to that," said Driscoll. "Moira, there's no way you're going anywhere near this case."

"Too late for that," Moira said, poking her finger through a column of smoke rings. "I've already hacked what was on the guy's phone."

CHAPTER FIFTY-THREE

"Moira, you've got thirty seconds to tell me why I shouldn't lock you up inside the holding cell downstairs," Driscoll barked, his head pounding.

"Not sure I like how you spruced up the office, Lieutenant. I'm guessing you had help." Moira turned her eyes on Margaret. "Sergeant Aligante, is this your idea of feng shui?"

Margaret looked as though she were about to respond but held back.

As if sensing her hesitancy, Moira walked toward an art deco cabinet. Caressing its lacquered surface, she shot Margaret a thumbs down.

"Sorry you're not a fan of my taste in furniture," Aligante replied, disingenuously.

Moira pushed aside an artificial dieffenbachia and sat on Margaret's conception of elegance.

"Get your fat ass off my cabinet!" Margaret yelled.

Moira, grinned. Happy she'd provoked the sergeant, she slowly slid off, and returned to her seat across from the Lieutenant.

"Moira, your thirty seconds is now down to twenty," Driscoll said.

"A battleship gray file cabinet takes the art right out of Art Deco, Lieutenant. How 'bout I rustle up a Chinese wood screen with dancing cranes. Add a little color and panache," Moira suggested.

Margaret narrowed her eyes, inwardly seething.

"You're down to ten seconds," said Driscoll.

"Dancing cranes would clash with the Lieutenant's seaside artwork," Margaret said.

Moira eyed the framed silk print and gave Margaret another thumbs down. "Driftwood At Riis Park' is no Picasso. And lemme guess, the mechanical cockatiel that was perched in the corner when I was here years ago flew the coop when you splashed the walls with Dullard Blue. I'm betting you got a department discount at Home Depot when you peeled off twelve bucks for the paint, right? What, the City wouldn't shell out the big bucks for Behr so you went with Glidden? Hey, that rhymes with Tilden!"

"Who's Tilden?" Driscoll asked.

"You're looking for the arsonist's sidekick, no? A sawbuck says Tilden's your man," Moira said.

"Moira, tell me you didn't hack into my files," the Lieutenant growled.

Moira pouted her lips.

"Oh, dear Lord," Margaret muttered.

"You two should be grateful I did hack the files. Why'd your techies waste so much time on the arsonist's phone."

"You conduct an unauthorized and illegal search of an ongoing NYPD investigation and we should be grateful? Do you realize the penalty for what you did?" Driscoll shouted.

"Hey! I'm not the bad guy, here. You're the one came knocking on my door. Had you not, I'd have no reason to access the files. Anyway, you now have what you need. I should get a 'thank you'," she said.

"Thank you?" Driscoll mocked.

"Don't forget, your suspect is the meanest dude of them all. And I'm helping you."

Driscoll pounded his fist on his desk, startling Moira. The Lieutenant then pointed a reprimanding finger at her. "First of all, young lady…"

"Are you for real? Now you're gonna 'young lady' me?" Moira fired backed, taunting the Lieutenant.

"Enough!" Driscoll hollered. "You can forget my visit, Moira. After hearing firsthand what you said in that session with your shrink, you're sidelined. You hear me?"

"Her shrink? You accompanied her to a session with her shrink?" Margaret looked.

"Whoa! Talk about confidentiality. Why don't you announce it over the intercom, Lieutenant? 'Ladies and gentleman, this is Lieutenant Driscoll speaking. I'd like you all to know that Moira's very private psychotherapy is going well and that you're all invited to her next session where more secrets will be revealed.'"

Margaret's eyes widened. She looked to the Lieutenant, "You went to see her shrink?"

Driscoll was livid. "I was invited to the session, for God's sake!"

"Doesn't he look cute when he gets upset?" Moira whispered to Margaret.

Driscoll's glare shut her down.

Margaret shook her head as Moira feigned misery.

"Alright, ladies, let's get back on point. Moira, after you hacked into my files, where'd you go from there?" the Lieutenant asked.

"I checked out your Computer Crime technician's attempts to get the password for the guy's phone."

"That's two departments hacked!" Driscoll griped. "When did this start?"

"When you drove me back from my therapist's session. That first day when you knocked on my door."

Driscoll shook his head in despair.

"You mentioned a Tilden? Who's Tilden?" asked Margaret.

"Beats the hell out of me. He's the only name listed on Harold MacKillop's phone's Reminders app."

"What's a Reminder's app?"

"It's an iPhone feature that lets someone set up electronic alerts when they want to be reminded to do something.

He had one set for September 17th to wish Tilden a happy birthday. There's a list of contacts but it won't do you any good," Moira added.

"Why's that?"

"They're all service listings.

"Wait a minute. How'd you get a list of contacts and access to this Reminder app? I never gave you his phone," Driscoll said.

"I didn't need it. In fact, neither did your technicians, but I'm sure your police higher-ups wouldn't approve of them doing what I did."

Driscoll's eyes narrowed.

"Here we go," Margaret groaned.

"Just what did you do?" Driscoll asked.

"I had your guy's phone number and that he was with Verizon. Every iPhone user backs up contacts. Unless you're an idiot."

"She's talking about us, you know," Margaret said to Driscoll before shooting Moira a glare.

"C'mon guys, the last thing anyone wants is re-creating a contact list for a lost phone," Moira said.

"And?"

"Like I said. I didn't need the guy's phone. I simply hacked into Verizon's Cloud."

"My files. The Department's files. And Verizon," Driscoll fumed. "You proud of your crime spree?"

"A trifecta!" she said, grinning.

"Wrong sport. And because none of the data you pilfered can be legally used in our investigation because of the exclusionary rule, you struck out."

CHAPTER FIFTY-FOUR

Dead eyes stared back at Tilden as he examined his face in the mirror. A patchwork of scaly skin and ruptured blood vessels framed his hellish reflection. *Jesus H. Christ! I look like shit.* "Two weeks of binge drinking over the loss of a friend will do that to a man's mug, I suppose. But it's time now to settle the score with Driscoll, your executioner, Harold. In grand fashion," he said, peeling back the tarp strewn across a stainless steel gurney.

"Welcome to hell, Aggie," he taunted, as the bound and sedated Sister Agathon stared up at her captor. "Or should I be calling you ex-con Aggie? Karma spares no one, ya' know. The Bishop must have been thrilled to strip you of your habit and excommunicate you twenty years ago. Imagine that? Sister Agathon tried and convicted of child abuse. Several counts! Oh, and a little thing called involuntary manslaughter. Shame on you Aggie."

A moan escaped the listless woman's lips.

"It took me awhile to track you down. But track you down, I did." Tilden disappeared to the corner of the room only to reappear dragging a large cross. It produced a loud 'thud' when he let it fall to the floor.

Another desperate moan from the inert captive. Louder this time.

Tilden grabbed hold of her legs and yanked her from the gurney. The woman's body crashed to the floor creating a dull thump accompanied by the crackling sound of bone being shattered. Agathon let loose a scream as the jagged edges of three ribs protruded through her chest.

"How 'bout I play your favorite tune?" Tilden asked. "You know, the one you had us listen to every day in class? It'll be a suitable farewell."

Agathon's eyes opened. As did her mouth from which erupted the desperate scream of captured prey.

Tilden wadded a corner of the tarp, stuffed it down her throat and focused on finding the musical selection on his phone. "Ahhh, here it is. Saint Matthew's Passion, by Bach." He hit 'PLAY'.

The solemn timbre of violins echoing through the cavernous cellar painted a look of dread on Agathon's ashen face. Her expression blossomed to horror when Tilden dragged her body onto the cross and reached for the iron hammer and the rusted railroad spikes he'd collected at the Amtrak crossing in town. "Sister, you're about go through what you put me through in the dungeon at Saint Barnabas. Welcome to déjà vu all over again. Only this time I'm wielding a mallet."

Using his right knee, he held her left arm firmly against the cross beam and hammered his first nail a half inch above Agathon's wrist, making certain it penetrated her forearm between the radius and ulna. Blind to the agonizing plea of her eyes; deaf to her muffled screams, he heard only the snug sound his nail made when it breached the wood. Pleased with his handiwork, he reached for her right arm. To his surprise, she resisted.

"Christ didn't resist. Nor shall you," he griped, pinning her bicep against the wood; pounding the second nail with fury. The force of her howl dislodged the wadded tarp from her mouth. Immune to her strident wailing, Tilden forced her ankles together, pressed them against the base of the cross and whacked away at the final nail, pulverizing the bones of both tibias.

Her body firmly fastened to the cross, he stripped her naked, then, in a moment of piety, dismissed the notion of defiling the catacomb between her legs.

Alone with his newly crucified captive, he silenced Bach's concerto on the iPhone, dropped to his knees, and brought his nose to within an inch of Agathon's. As her laborious exhalation fanned his face, he grinned.

CHAPTER FIFTY-FIVE

The "Bell Tower" alarm tone on Driscoll's iPhone woke him at 4:04 a.m. "What is it now?" he griped, rubbing his sleep crusted eyes.

At 4:45, hopeful his head, which continued to ache, wouldn't explode from the relentless whipping sound the NYPD's helicopter made as it cut through the night's sky, he stared down at the immense city below still shimmering with lights. "I'm too old for this," he groaned.

Thirty turbulent minutes later, the chopper banked right and descended toward its bumpy touch down on the Mohansic Golf Course in Yorktown Heights, 25 miles north of New York City, in Westchester County.

Lieutenant Christine Talmadge, the gum chewing head of the Detective Bureau at Yorktown PD, handed Driscoll a container of Starbuck's coffee as he stepped clear of the chopper. "I had them add a shot of espresso, Lieutenant, you're in for a long day," she said, motioning toward the idling patrol car that would transport the pair to the newly established crime scene three miles away.

Illuminated by high intensity police lights, the cross dangling from the Baptist Church Road Bridge made Driscoll feel he'd walked onto the set of one of Clive Barker's horror novels adapted for the screen.

"Why crucify a woman?" Lieutenant Talmadge asked, staring at the atrocity from the muddy shoreline of the reservoir, several yards from the bridge.

"I plan to find out," said Driscoll.

The sight of the impaled corpse above the reservoir with outstretched arms reminded Driscoll of the towering stone statue of Christ the Redeemer overlooking Rio de Janeiro from atop Mount Corcovado. It filled him with eeriness, an almost mystical emotion he hadn't experienced in a very long time. The altar boy inside him had been stirred. The crucifix had always had an impact on Driscoll's soul. It represented total commitment and unquestioned faith. How had this sacrilegious staging instantly set off torrents of spirituality inside him? It was as though the perpetrator was privy to all that Driscoll held sacred. Was the Lieutenant's soul his target? If so, he had hit his mark. Driscoll had never felt such a personal vulnerability while approaching a crime scene. Would the executioner know that? If so, he must have had a soul at one time. Such a glaring paradox as the author of this vile montage lacked both soul and conscience. His staging pointed to a religious mind at odds with itself. Why malign the holy crucifixion? On this cross was a woman's body. What did that signify? What heresy was being acted out by a brazen killer with a shocking flair for horror? What grandiosity blinded him? He had to have known this gory scene would be flashed across countless television screens. Streamed across every social media platform. Plastered on the front page of the New York Post, the Daily News, the New York Times, the Corriere della Sera in The Vatican and every other newspaper in Europe and beyond. And who was this brutalized woman horrifically on display? Was she a sacrificial lamb of some demonic cult festering in Westchester, the most affluent county in the country? According to Origen, the 3rd Century theologian, the devil is the consummate impersonator of Christ. Was Satan, himself, at play here?

"Are you ok, Lieutenant?" Christine Talmadge asked, noting Driscoll's trance-like intensity as he studied the crime scene from the reservoir's bank.

"He chooses a bridge so he can pull over and drop the cross in seconds," Driscoll replied, giving voice to his thoughts. "Any traffic cameras up there?"

"The proposal's been before the City Council for years. But since the bridge gets very little traffic during the day and next to none at night, it's never been approved."

"He had to have known there'd be no cameras."

"You figure a local?"

"Certainly familiar with the bridge," Driscoll said. "Alright, let's get a closer look at the body."

Talmadge gave a thumbs-up to four uniformed officers who unfastened the parapet hook from the bridge's guardrail and slowly pulled up the linked chain that had kept the crucified victim dangling above the water.

"Now you'll get to see what our crime scene detectives saw close up and understand why I called you," Talmadge said, slipping on a pair of latex gloves and handing a pair to Driscoll as they made their way to the bridge.

When the large wooden cross containing the crucified remains was lifted over the bridge's guardrail, the Lieutenant's eyes narrowed. Her executioner had fastened something to her. It was the front page of the New York Daily News which featured a photo of Driscoll. It had been nailed into the victim's chin, just below her gaping mouth. *Why place it there?* Driscoll wondered. *Had he intended to have it appear as though she was announcing the paper's headline?*

TOP COP SNUFFS OUT CHURCH ARSONIST

CHAPTER FIFTY-SIX

Chief Medical Examiner Larry Pearsol thought he'd seen it all. But, never, in his wildest imagination, had he ever thought he'd be performing an autopsy on the corpse of a crucified woman. And, like the impaled Christ emblazoned above the altar of Saint Malachy's on West 49th, this corpse was ashen.

"33AD," he muttered, eyes scoping the elderly victim.

"33AD?" Driscoll asked.

"Our savior's crucifixion. Your guy's fixed on it. He replicated the whole thing." Pearsol turned to face the Lieutenant. "I've got two years to go before retirement and you bring me this?"

"Look on the bright side, Larry. The case will make you Medical Examiner of the year."

"Like hell it will. I've had a quiet career of dedicated public service and I'm planning to exit without fanfare."

"Understood. What's the body tell us?"

"Plenty. Let me get the electronic protocol out of the way, first." Pearsol depressed the 'RECORD' button on the Department's Uher digital unit: "Item D297F26. Arrival Date September 18, 2017. Jane Doe. Remains consist of a fully developed female measuring 158.75 centimeters . . . all extremities are attached . . . initial examination reveals a five centimeter semi-translucent glaze of adhesive which covers the subject's rippled flesh between the carotid artery and the jugular vein . . . both forearms have been penetrated with what appears to be railroad spikes; as are both ankles at the joint . . . further micro analysis required . . . DNA and pathology examination to follow...."

Pearsol hit 'STOP', placed a gloved finger on the deceased's neck, and motioned for Driscoll to have a closer look.

"The latex sealant covering this stretch of skin is identical to the adhesive used by your embalmer, Lieutenant. I won't know until I open her up whether the crucifixion or the embalming killed her. On a positive note, this one wasn't turned to ash like the victim at Saint Therese's."

"If he'd torched her it would've interfered with his elaborate staged invitation. This killer is devolving, Larry. The trigger being my killing his accomplice. His vengeance, directed at me, has caused him to change whatever the hell his mission was."

"He's a dangerous guy, Lieutenant."

"He's also a bit of movie director. Designed the scene just for me. I'm betting he crucified her first, kept her breathing so she could relive what Christ went through. The witness and victim in one."

"Her skin says a lot. She's in her eighties. Jaundice. That happens when blood flow crawls. I see a spine curvature. Hanging on the cross didn't help. Those nails between the ulna and the radius hold her on as gravity pulls the body down. The lungs are then restricted. And look, this mother fucker pierced her side, just like what the centurion did to Christ. Whack City," said Pearsol. "Where are you on the ID?"

"Nothing yet. Margaret's checking Missing Persons. May take a while. The body tell us anything else? Other than that this psycho has reduced her to a skeleton encased in dead skin?"

"She's a ghost, alright. But no matter the age everyone's got a network of nerves that reveal a lot. Check these eyes," he said, rolling back the lids.

No One Will Hear Your Screams | 197

"Why so bloodshot?"

"That's from the pain she felt when he hammered in the spikes. You're guy did it like the Romans did. The nails were pounded between the radius and the ulna, smashing through bone, nerves, veins and arteries. When a trauma like that occurs, adrenalin floods the system, blood pressure rockets and small capillaries burst."

"The agony of Christ's cross played out in the 21st Century." Driscoll looked as though he wanted to spit.

"See that? That's an occipital contusion to the skull. I'd say she was bludgeoned with a blunt object, likely causing unconsciousness," Pearsol added.

"That'd be during her abduction, I'd say. She probably never saw him coming," Driscoll reasoned.

The M.E. sensed Driscoll's growing malaise. He knew the Lieutenant had seen many unclothed homicide victims over the course of his career, but there's a sacredness to old age and he knew Driscoll was affected by the nakedness of this elderly woman. Recognizing the impropriety and uneasiness that marked the Lieutenant's face, Pearsol covered the victim's breasts and abdominal area with a sheet. Driscoll, who had reverence for the human body, particularly that of a woman of advanced age, was thankful for the gesture, and expressed his gratitude with a nod. As a public servant, the Lieutenant was someone who viewed the human body as a living relic which deserved dignity. Hadn't God fashioned man in his likeness, as revealed in the first Book of Genesis? As a homicide commander, Driscoll's not in pursuit of the burglar, the forger, or the garden variety car thief. His life's mission has been the pursuit and apprehension of homicidal miscreants who've degraded and defiled the human body. This spiritual component inside Driscoll had been forged early in life through many years of Catholic indoctrination. Who better to have as a guardian than a tireless civil servant with spiritual leanings?

"The absence of callous on her hands indicates she wasn't a laborer," Pearsol continued. "Her fingernails are well maintained. There's no sign of dye in her hair. The cut is no-frills. Somewhat boyish. If Central Casting was looking for an octogenarian librarian, she'd fit the bill. No trace of stretch marks on the abdomen. I'd say she never gave birth."

"Any sign of sexual assault?"

"None."

"He sew another locket under the tongue?"

"No locket. But I did find this under the tongue." Pearsol produced a gleaming medallion secured inside a clear evidence bag and handed it to Driscoll.

"This medal features Saint Brigid," the Lieutenant said, eyeing the one inch oval.

"Last time it was a locket. Containing a photograph of a different saint, right?" the M.E. asked.

"Right. Saint Vitalis of Gaza, the patron saint of prostitutes."

"I'm no detective, but I doubt we're looking at a prostitute," Pearsol said, eyeing the corpse.

"I'm inclined to think you're right."

"I'll know more when I complete the autopsy but could we be looking at the work of a different killer? A copy cat, maybe?" Pearsol asked.

"Can't rule it out. But my instinct says 'no'.

"I'm sure, as psychotic as his actions are, he's got a reason for inserting religious ornamentation inside his victims."

"No doubt. But why a different saint this time?" Driscoll mused.

"Brigid. That's a saint I've never heard of."

"She was a bright-eyed Irish girl who many believed was the reincarnation of the Celtic goddess, Brigid. She was born in County Louth in the 5th Century. Not your average child growing up."

"Not sure anyone's average, these days," said Pearsol.

"You're right about that, my friend."

"And Brigid?"

"Her father, a pagan chieftain, woke one day to discover young Brigid had given away much of his wealth to the poor. Shortly after that, she was veiled."

"Veiled?"

"She entered the convent and became a nun."

"I'm sure her father was pleased she was out of the house."

"She's credited with the miracle of curing two girls of mutism. Because of that, the Church of Ireland hails her as the patron saint of children."

Driscoll immediately thought of Moira who had narrowly escaped death at the hands of a crazed bone stealing killer the Lieutenant eventually took down. *Where was Saint Brigid then?* he wondered. More importantly, where was he?

CHAPTER FIFTY-SEVEN

Inside the deserted park, the carousel shimmered in the morning light. Its horses frozen in mid gallop. Mute. Their hollow eyes keeping watch over the empty park. On a golden stallion sat Moira, an equestrian rider, waiting for him. The crushing sound of gravel under foot announced his arrival. Rushing toward her swing set, she hollered: "Gimme a push! I wanna touch the stars."

He tossed his coat on the grass. "Ready yourself for blastoff, little girl. Liftoff in 3 ... 2 ... 1!"

Her jubilant squeal echoed through the desolate park.

"Higher!" Moira screamed.

"Any higher you'll be in orbit."

As Moira sang the lyrics to David Bowie's Space Oddity, he joined in. "Earth to Major Moira. This is Houston. Time for re-entry."

"Not yet, Dad."

'Dad'. The word stopped his breathing. Not trusting his legs, he headed toward the bench and straddled it.

Moira leaped from the swing, rushed to his side, and wrapped her arms around him. Overwhelmed by her closeness, he studied her face. Warmed by what he recognized as genuine tenderness, he looked into her eyes, and smiled.

"I have something for you," he said, producing a small jewelry box.

"What is it?"

"Open it."

Moira's eyes widened at the sight of the small woven cross. "It's beautiful and so delicate. I love it."

"Do you know what it is?" he asked.

"No. Tell me."

"That's Brigid's cross. Saint Brigid is an Irish saint who watches over children."

Driscoll watched Moira's expression transform from blissful joy to intense anger. She let the cross fall to the ground and used the heel of her shoe to pulverize it.

"That was your job," she scoffed. "And you failed."

An ambulance's blaring siren cut through the stillness of Driscoll's bedroom, shattering his dream, releasing him from his nightmare.

CHAPTER FIFTY-EIGHT

After spending forty-five minutes in the waiting room of Madison Avenue Radiology & Associates for what turned out to be a fifteen minute CT scan of his head Driscoll was eager to get back to work. After easing the Chevy into a parking space outside of 520 1st Avenue, he cut the engine. As the hustle and bustle of New York City droned on around him, he closed his eyes and thought back to last night's dream. Its opening, before it had turned to nightmare. The playful exchange with Moira warmed him as much as it saddened him. He missed his daughter. He'd always catch a glimpse of Nicole's soft smile in the curve of Moira's lips. A trace of her childlike voice when Moira spoke. The hint of Nicole's marvel in Moira's eyes. All treasures. Gift wrapped, last night, albeit brief, in a nocturnal fantasy.

Wiping a tear from his eye, Driscoll stepped out of the car and ducked, once again, inside the multi-story building that housed the City Morgue. Heading toward the elevator, he bumped into Jasper Eliot, the Chief Medical Examiner's assistant. "How's your mom?" he asked him.

"We're meeting with her oncologist at Sloan Kettering in a little while. I'm on my way there now. I don't have a good feeling about it," Eliot added, his face etched with dread.

"I'll keep her in my prayers," Driscoll said.

"Thank you, Lieutenant. If you're here to see Larry, he's grabbing lunch at Benjamin's. It's a pub on East 22nd."

Shooting Driscoll a crooked smile, Jasper Eliot rushed out of the building.

Driscoll wondered why Pearsol would choose an eatery a mile and a half away. Figuring it likely meant good food, he stepped outside and into the stream of pedestrians rushing North on 1st Ave figuring a brisk walk would do him good.

Waiting for the walk sign to go from red to green on East 20th, Driscoll felt a rush of dizziness. Closing his eyes, the feeling disappeared. When he opened them, the vertigo was gone. Paying it no mind, he continued uptown.

The oversized American flag fastened to the restaurant's South wall, which was illuminated brightly by a Pre-American Revolutionary style lamp, made him feel he had stepped into a Colonial Era tavern. A Black Walnut bar, supported by expertly carved minutemen, added a museum quality to the room. The wait staff, dressed in period garb, hurried from table to table, delivering large pitchers of foaming ale to a three-piece suit clientele.

"What's good?" asked Driscoll, surprising the M.E. who was seated solo at a lace draped table near the rear of the eatery.

Larry Pearsol stood, smiled, and shook the Lieutenant's hand. The two men then sat.

"You'll wanna have the Alexander Hamilton brisket, John. Especially if you've scheduled a duel for later this evening. It's the perfect last meal. Go heavy on the horseradish. And if you have it with a Doctor Brown's cream soda, you'll think Katz closed their deli on East Houston to open a bar in the Flatiron District. How the hell did you find me?"

Before Driscoll had a chance to answer, a pony-tailed waiter appeared with a menu.

"I'll have what 'she's' having," Driscoll said, delivering the line as though he was Rob Reiner's mother on the set of *When Harry Met Sally*.

The reference to the hilarious scene inside Katz Deli wasn't wasted on the waiter, who, stifling a laugh, managed to deadpan: "You got it, Estelle."

"You're a funny man, Lieutenant. Orgasmic, in fact. How'd you find me?" Pearsol asked.

An uproar at the bar caused Driscoll and Pearsol to turn their heads. A round of high-fives by a dozen enthused patrons was all they saw.

"So, how'd you find me?" the M.E. asked again, a little louder this time as the din made by the happy bar patrons hadn't died down.

"Jasper Eliot told me you'd be here. He's off to Sloan Kettering with his mother to discuss the results of her recent medical tests."

Pearsol put his hands to together, a gesture Driscoll read as a silent prayer.

"Sometimes this death business we're in sucks, Lieutenant."

"Amen to that," said Driscoll.

"You went to my office looking for me. Your coming here means it's more than a craving for a bite to eat."

"It is. We've ID'd your Jane Doe. She was a nun."

Pearsol's eyes widened. "Whoa! He killed a nun?"

"A former nun. Sister Mary Agathon. Excommunicated for child abuse which led to manslaughter. As Henrietta Strauss, she served 18 years. Which is why we got a hit in VICAP."

"Ahh, FBI's data base of sin," Pearsol said, studying the Lieutenant. "You look a little glum, my friend. Everything ok in your world?"

"Just a little sleep deprived, Larry. I appreciate you asking."

The M.E. nodded.

"Do you remember Moira?" Driscoll asked, immediately wishing he hadn't.

"Who's Moira?"

"A young woman I know. I had a dream about her last night. An upsetting dream. She's in her twenties now. When I first met her, she was barely a teen. A whiz kid. You remember the killer who was stealing the bones of his victims?"

"We're going back. That case was ten years ago, no?

"About. Moira helped track him down."

"Yeah, yeah, yeah. I remember now. Didn't the killer abduct her? And break all her bones?"

Driscoll needed no reminding of that dreadful outcome. His focus turned to the happy

crowd ten feet away as if to dispel his regret. "The bastard did one helluva job on her."

"You took him out, right?'

"I did."

"Hope she's ok now?"

"We keep in touch. She healed well."

"If she's looking for work I could use an assistant who knows her way around a keyboard."

"She's got a job."

Pearsol studied the eyes of his long time friend.

"I hope it's doesn't involve helping you again."

Driscoll silently stared at Pearsol.

"Oh, boy. I know that look. She is, isn't she?"

"She was."

"Let me see if I've got this right. A teenager, who helped you track down a serial killer, became a victim of said serial killer."

Driscoll simply nodded

"And after having every bone in her body broken you had her up close and personal with another one?"

"It's complicated."

"Show me something that's not." Pearsol gestured for the waiter.

"Time for the check?" Driscoll asked.

"Hell no. You think the Alexander Hamilton was good, wait'll you taste their desserts."

When the waiter hastened over, Pearsol asked him, "Do you still serve those lemon zested blueberry tarts?"

"Made fresh today."

"Good! I'll have mine alamode. John, you'll wanna do the same."

Driscoll nodded.

"What was that German wine you served me the last time I had the tarts," Pearsol asked the waiter. "Kinda semi-sweet."

"You had the Liebfraumilch, Sir. This week we're featuring a Hans Schiller selection."

"Ahh, the perfect wine for the occasion," he replied, shooting Driscoll a wink. "Bring two glasses."

The waiter gave him a thumbs-up before heading off.

"Why is it the perfect wine for the occasion?" Driscoll asked.

"Liebfraumilch. German for 'beloved lady's milk'. It's impossible to find. This place held on to a few cases. The wine was originally produced in the vineyards of the Church of Our Lady in Worms. If our victim was a nun, who better to grace our table than the Virgin Mary?"

"You know you missed your calling, right?"

"And what would that be?"

"You belong in Hollywood directing religious themed movies. Just look at what you've orchestrated here," the Lieutenant said, as the waiter solemnly poured the wine.

"You can't fault a guy who spends his waking hours in the company of rotting corpses for sprinkling some laughter now and again."

The two men took a sip of the Liebfraumilch.

"Hey, you're right about the wine," Driscoll said. "It's… it's …."

"The word you're looking for is heavenly."

"More like seraphic," Driscoll said. "Sláinte," he added, raising his glass.

"Cheers," Pearsol replied.

They enjoyed another measured sip in silence.

"Larry, inviting the Virgin Mary to join us with such flair suggests you were a saintly student at parochial school."

"Parochial school, yes. Saintly? Not according to Sister Priscilla."

"C'mon! How could she not be a fan of young Lawrence of Astoria?"

"You've got me confused with Peter O'Toole in Lawrence of Arabia, who she also wouldn't like."

"Why not?"

"He was male."

The comment made the Lieutenant smile. He, too, had experienced growing up Catholic inside countless parochial school classrooms where the nuns made it evident they were not fans of men.

"Sister Priscilla sounds like a tough nun," Driscoll said.

"A brute. She reigned over the Fifth Grade like Gaius Caligula. She had it in for the boys. Especially me. She had this secret drawer in a rotting oak desk. Kept it locked and wore its key around her neck as a pendant. On occasion, she'd open the drawer and introduce me to her 'Board of Discipline'. Never did I see her use it on any of the girls. And trust me, they weren't saints. I once passed a caricature of Sister Priscilla to my heartthrob, Muriel, who was seated behind me. Muriel giggled, but Priscilla, who had the ears of a schnauzer, didn't. And that was the beginning of a long and painful relationship between my butt cheek and her hardwood paddle. My flesh was scorched and flayed. But that was just a preamble for what was to come. It was Christmas Eve. You know, when the magic is supposed to begin." Pearsol brashly downed what was left in his glass. "We boys wore uniforms back then, light blue shirt, tan belted khakis, and a dark blue tie. I'd never gotten the hang of tying a knot the right way. The tie always ended up too long, hanging several inches below my waist. I'd stuff the elongated tie in my pants. Only that day, I'd forgotten to stuff it. Sister Priscilla, seated at her desk in front of the class was reading aloud from her favorite novel, the Catechism. She was going on and on with the 'Thou shalt nots' when I noticed my tie was hanging past my crotch. I quickly tucked the damn thing into my pants. When I looked up, I realized I was in her crosshairs. 'Pearsol, thou shalt not nudge your disgraceful appendage in my Religion class,' she seethed. A peal of laughter erupted, but ceased when she stood and marched toward the classroom's 'Science Corner' where she opened the lid on one of the small cages, and extracted a mouse. A fat one. With it thrashing about below her two fingered grip, she stormed over. Yanked me out of my seat. Unbuckled my belt. Pulled open the waist band of my pants. And dropped the wriggling and clawing rodent into my briefs. That thing wanted out! And in its attempt to escape, it made mince meat out of my balls. I was ten fucking years old! This wasn't something I could discuss with my parents. They were pious and would've sided with the goddamn nun! I deserved justice so I set out to kill her. No fucking way would I return to that classroom, her chamber of horrors, with her in it. The nights that followed saw me laying awake plotting her execution. There were no goddamn jingle bells that Christmas. Being an altar boy had its perks. One of them was being familiar with the labyrinth of passageways behind the sacristy. I knew I could get into the convent through a sliding door in one of those passages. No one ever took note of an altar boy going in or out of the area. Especially a few minutes before early morning Mass. Five days after the sacred celebration of the birth of Christ, armed with a box of kitchen matches, I slid open the closed, but never locked door. I knew where her room was as I'd once been commandeered into helping her carry home school supplies. The hallway was carpeted so my footsteps were silent. The sound of snoring streaming through her door's keyhole brought a smile to my face. I struck a match. Slid it through the hole. And then another. And another. And another. And another. The unexpected blaring of a smoke detector scared the shit out of me. I bolted out of there with my heart pounding so hard I thought my chest would explode. Who'd have thought a 9-volt battery would wreck a perfectly executed plan. I'm not boring you, am I, Lieutenant?"

"Hell, no. That's quite an admission. What happened next?"

"I raced home. Barreling up Crescent Street, I spotted a police car in front of my house. I did an about face, and bolted for Astoria Park where I shimmied under the fence and into the enclosure where the Parks Department stored their trucks in winter. The area was gated so they always left them unlocked. After climbing inside the cabin of a Chevy Long Bed, I squeezed into the hollow behind the passenger seat and hid. For three days. Three days, Lieutenant! All the while praying my mother wouldn't find my diary."

"You kept a diary?"

"More like an account of what Sister Priscilla had done."

"So you wrote it all down."

"Damn right, I did. If I ended up dead I wanted the Daily News to let the world know what that bitch did to me."

Driscoll was impressed and his expression showed it.

"Pretty smart ten year old," he said.

"More like a lucky ten year old. Maybe one with a death wish. Nobody knew where I was."

"But you're here to tell the story. Death wish or not, something intervened."

"More like someone. I had finally fallen asleep after being awake for 72 hours. I thought I was dreaming when I heard voices calling out my name. When I opened my eyes two flashlight beams were crisscrossing the windshield. I nearly shit my pants when a voice hollered: 'Lawrence, if you're in there, come out now.' Scared out of my wits and on the brink of delirium, I unlatched the door. A policeman's gloved hand grabbed me by the shoulder and yanked me out. It took me a full minute to stop trembling and only then did I realize I was swaddled in my mother's arms. But I feared that was temporary and that my day of reckoning had come. I was about to pay for burning down the convent and killing all the nuns inside. I surrendered to my fate by passing out. But, when I woke up, I was not standing before a judge. I was not in a jail cell; nor strapped into the electric chair. I was at home, in my room, in my bed, with my mother sitting beside me, holding my hand. I could see she'd been crying. I could also see she'd found my diary,'cause there it was on the nightstand. I told her I was sorry. She said, 'for what? 'For the fire,' I said. 'What fire?' she asked. In that moment, I realized the convent didn't burn down. The nuns hadn't died. My vocation as an arsonist may have fallen short, but I quickly learned that Sister Priscilla was not only let go, but defrocked. My parents had pressed charges against her, the school, and the church. Are you ready for the best part, Lieutenant?"

"Hell, yeah!"

"The Daily News came to my house the next day and interviewed me. And because of the article they published about Sister Priscilla's brutality, the Diocese launched an investigation of the entire teaching staff in Brooklyn and Queens."

Driscoll felt a high five was in order. He looked to the spirited crowd at the bar. They're enthusiasm had ebbed.

"So you're a happy man," Driscoll said.

"I'm glad my frantic parents had reached out to my buddy, Mike, who gave up my likely hideaway, but I'm not happy about the scar that still marks my balls. You wanna see it?"

Driscoll's eyes widened as he shook his head.

"What kind of a crime investigator chooses not to examine the evidence?"

"A wise one. I'm guessing that's the last you saw of Sister Priscilla."

"I see that bitch every day."

"She's still haunting your dreams? That can't be good."

"It's better than good."

Driscoll looked puzzled.

"Every time I insert my scalpel into the flesh of a cadaver, I imagine it's the living and breathing Sister Priscilla. Every single time. It's not easy doing what I do, John. Most coroners call it quits after a few years. Not me. Because of that nun's cruelty, I wake each day eager to strip her of all dignity. Sink my blade into her flesh. Carve out her vital organs. Drain her of her blood. Over and over again."

CHAPTER FIFTY-NINE

"Good morning, John. How'd the brain selfies go with the x-ray guy?" Margaret asked, stepping inside Driscoll's office.

"Won't know for a few days."

"I've got a theory about your headaches. Wanna hear it? "

"Tell it to the x-ray guy."

"I think you're…"

"Oh, Jeez. I'm gonna hear it anyway."

"C'mon, you've had these headaches for five weeks. I've given what I have to say a lot of thought."

Driscoll closed the file he was reviewing and smiled at her. "OK. I'm listening," he said.

"All work and no play . . ."

The Lieutenant leaned back in his chair. "I know where this is going," he said, as a gentle smile formed.

"Face it, John. You're struggling with whether or not we should be an item."

"That's very enticing but what you're suggesting would have us playing hooky from a police investigation and let's face it, Margaret, were we to get romantically involved you'd need to transfer out of Homicide."

"I realize that," she said. "Besides, saying goodbye to your headaches our sharing some intimacy would put you in a better frame of mind when we're back on the case."

"Your Groupon at Motel Six about to expire?"

"They'll keep the light on for us."

"I'm sure they will. Find Thomlinson."

"Oh, that's kinky. But, I don't think my Groupon covers a ménage à trois."

"Cute. Find Thomlinson. We've a case to solve."

"Alright. Alright. But, all work and no play…"

Margaret left, leaving Driscoll to his thoughts. The anticipation of a romance was appealing. A splendid escape from the grind of the investigation. A chance to briefly hit 'pause' on the countless uncertainties, anomalies, and discrepancies in evidence collection. He could take Margaret in his arms, apply his lips on her alabaster skin, lose himself in the caramel of her eyes. So why was he opposed to the yearning? The visuals of such bliss were intoxicating. Were there traces of loyalty to his beloved Colette, who passed away years ago, but was omnipresent in his soul? Surely the sin of adultery couldn't apply to such a post mortem narrative. Or could it? Had his heart been buried with his spouse? A promise of perpetual faithfulness preserved in a life of celibacy? His rational self rebelled against such deep-rooted Catholic school indoctrination. Did Margaret sense his inner strife? Speaking of strife, was she truly ready to transfer to another department should they pull the trigger and get romantically involved? Could the persistent headache be the result of a clash of conscience with his romantic cravings and not the head injury he sustained while wrestling that crazed arsonist to the floor inside St. Therese's Church?

Driscoll put his thoughts on hold as Thomlinson and Margaret entered.

"Cedric Thomlinson at your service, sir," the Detective quipped, straddling a chair while Margaret, taking her seat beside him, nonchalantly opened another button on her blouse exposing a hint of black lace from her bra. Her wily invitation was not missed by the Lieutenant.

"Ok, it's time to get down to business," Driscoll said, shooting Margaret a look. "While screenwriter Sylvester

Stallone may be best known for his role in *Rocky*, a favorite screenwriter of mine also starred as the lead in his own movie. In *Dead Man's Shoes*, Paddy Considine plays a soldier, who, after returning home from war, discovers his brother had been abused by local drug dealers."

"And this is relevant, how?" Thomlinson asked.

"The study of Criminology suggests we analyze prior crimes, even fictional ones, to help us understand recent ones," Margaret said.

Thomlinson's eyes widened. A broad smile creased his face. "Looks like someone paid attention in Criminology 101," he said.

Margaret grinned.

"The relevance, Cedric, is in the motive. The ex-soldier confronts and kills his brother's tormentors. Remember, nothing fuels murderous tenacity like revenge," said Driscoll.

"That's quite a line, John. Maybe you should be a screenwriter," Margaret suggested.

She's certainly a charmer, thought Driscoll. "Nothing says revenge more than the latest developments in this case. We've got the brutal murder of an excommunicated nun who'd served time for child abuse and manslaughter by an executioner who's apparently angry with me for killing his probable accomplice, an arsonist."

"I see the significance," said Margaret.

The Lieutenant held back a grin. One that said he was impressed with Margaret's concentration on the case and her blatant attempt at brownie points.

"I'm glad you do, Margaret."

Her smile was her 'thank you'.

"After interviewing that art therapist in Trenton I'm pretty certain Adrian Strayer, who's art work depicted a nun being embalmed, never left the hospital," Driscoll continued. "But who's to say he didn't have a brother?"

Interrupted when his desk phone rang, Driscoll answered it.

The Lieutenant's face went through a transformation. It looked as though he was about to pass out.

"What is it, John?" Margaret asked, detecting his sudden paleness.

"That was my neurologist. They forwarded him the cat scan of my brain. I have a subdural hematoma. It's gotta be from when I hit my head while wrestling with MacKillop."

"Oh, my God!" Margaret, murmered, her heart racing.

"They're sending an ambulance to take me to Montefiore. They need to operate."

"When?"

"Now."

CHAPTER SIXTY

Driscoll didn't know where he was. He had awakened in a blanket of fog where everything was coated in gel. In the midst of the opaque whiteness, a silhouette was crystallizing. Its brown eyes were fixed on him. He couldn't identify the face. Voices echoed. A man's. Then a woman's. The man was dressed in white. His form stretched to the ceiling. What was he was muttering to the woman? He only caught traces of it. It's volume strong, before fading.

"Glad to see you made it, John," a woman's voice reverberated.

"I don't think he's out of it, yet," a man said. "We'd better let him sleep."

Driscoll watched the figures fade. Then disappear. Within seconds slumber had its hold on him. As did his dream.

"What are you reading? A newspaper?" Margaret said, placing the file on the Lieutenant's desk. *"No one reads them anymore. Everybody goes to Google News on their phones."*

"Wow! They reopened Kennedy's," Driscoll said, his head buried in the paper.

"That must be a bar. Manhattan?"

"No. It's my favorite restaurant. It's in Breezy Point. It'd been closed for several months for renovations."

"Jeez!"

"And now it's back!"

"I'm sure you had a lot of memories there. You lived in Breezy, right?"

"For twenty years. Margaret, grab your purse. We're going to dinner. At Kennedy's. Now."

"What? Really?"

"Why not?"

"For starters, they probably have a different chef. Who knows what the menu looks like."

"Trust me, it's even better. The article says Aiden's still there."

"Who's Aiden?"

"A gastronome. Their chef extraordinaire."

"What makes him an 'extraordinaire'?"

"Oh, Margaret, he's a maître saucier."

"A maitre what?"

"And I know just what to have him prepare for you. Imagine shrimp simmering in melted butter, wrapped in prosciutto from Parma, then doused with a béchamel sauce."

"Wow! That sounds better than sex."

"What? Now Aiden's my rival? Forget Kennedy's. I'm taking you to Wendy's."

"Like hell you are. Breezy Point here we come."

"I see why they call it Breezy Point," Margaret said, stepping out of Driscoll's cruiser, and feeling the briny breeze rifle through her hair.

"They've really done a great job renovating this place," Driscoll said as they approached the restaurant.

"Is that a widow's walk," Margaret asked, pointing to the stylish enclosure on the roof. "It'd be nice to climb up there."

"Why? You expecting Captain Ahab?"

"I'm perfectly fine on the arm of my Lieutenant," she said, snuggling into his embrace.

"Right answer, Margaret. For that you get the Crème Brûlée."

"You mean there'd have been no dessert if I'd gotten it wrong?"

"Dessert goes to the deserving."

"Gee, you really know how to charm a woman."

"Ain't it the truth," he said with a wink. "Margaret, it's time now to prepare your taste buds for a heavenly treat."

"Dee-lighted," she said, opening the door for him.

"Margaret, that's a first."

"What is?"

"You're the first woman to open the door for me."

"Could be I'm just hungry."

"OK, that's a bubble burst," Driscoll muttered, ushering her into the foyer.

"Good evening, folks. What time is your reservation?" a voice asked.

"I didn't make one," said Driscoll.

"I'm so, so, sorry, sir. But we're completely booked," the hostess said.

"You didn't make reservations?" Margaret looked astonished.

"Well, I was distracted... by you!"

"So now it's my fault?"

"Uhhh... yeah. It's your fault."

"Oh, for Chrissake. You'd planned on Wendy's all along." Driscoll grinned.

"Why are you smiling?"

"You know I always have a plan B."

"Yeah, Arby's."

"Margaret, you have no faith."

"Don't get me started."

Driscoll turned to the hostess. "Is Olivia on tonight?"

"Yes, she is?"

"Who's Olivia?" Margaret asked.

"Plan B," said Driscoll, then turned to the hostess: "Would you please call her."

"It's not gonna help you get a table. Olivia does the scheduling."

"Tell her there's a City health inspector here about a cicada infestation in the kitchen," said Driscoll.

"What the hell is a cicada?"

"She'll know."

"Are you out of your mind?" Margaret cried out as the hostess raced up the stairs.

"I told you this was gonna be a fun night," Driscoll said with a grin.

"A fun night? You call this a fun night? Where the hell are the shrimp? You promised me shrimp!"

Driscoll's face lit up as he spotted Olivia hurrying down the stairs. "There she is!"

"John? John Driscoll? Jesus, it's good to see you!" she shouted. "Wait! You're working for the health department now?"

"No. But she is," Driscoll said, motioning to Margaret.

"Ahhh, so, you're the brunt of his teasing, too." Olivia smiled and extended her hand.

"I suppose I am. My name's Margaret. It's nice to meet you."

"John, lemme guess. You need a table and you knew this rouse would get me downstairs, right?"

"That was his "Plan B," Margaret said.

"Honey, this man's got the whole alphabet up his sleeve."

"Time to get serious, Olivia. I have a very important question to ask," Driscoll said.

"Oh, my God. What now?" Margaret groaned.

"I understand Aiden's still working his magic in the kitchen. Is he on tonight?" the Lieutenant asked.

"He is, indeed."

"Good. Can you take our order?"

"We haven't sat down yet," Margaret griped.

"A minute ago you were complaining about no shrimp. And now it's about a table?"

Margaret shook her head in resignation.

"Does Aiden still make those delicious shrimp wrapped in prosciutto?" Driscoll asked.

"Ahh, Béchamel et Crevettes," Olivia said, perfecting a saucy French accent.

"That's the one."

"That dish earned him a culinary award, you know. Shall I place an order for two?"

"Please do. And we'd like a bottle of Vouvray."

"You got it. Oh, and he's prepared baked brie and medallions of pork tenderloin as appetizers. I'll bring you a small plate."

"Perfect."

"Good! Come with me. I'll seat you at Table 7. It's got the best view of the bay."

Olivia was right. The night's view of the New York skyline was spectacular.

"You know, Margaret, we got the VIP table without a reservation and I didn't have to go to Plan C," said Driscoll.

"You amaze me. You really do."

The restaurant was bustling. A sultry voiced soloist was doing a good job channeling Diana Krall's *The Look Of Love* as a jazz quartet added a fluid accompaniment.

"You see that red light just above what looks a little like a castle?" Driscoll asked as the pair stared at the illuminated NY skyline in the distance.

"I see it."

"That's the Empire State Building."

"You know, I've never been up there," said Margaret.

"Really?"

"Not once."

"We ought to do it."

"As long as we do it together."

"Of course together."

"Good. I wouldn't want to end up like Annette Bening."

"Annette Bening? What the hell are you talking about?"

"You've never seen the movie 'Love Affair'?"

"Annette Bening in Love Affair?"

"She plays this singer who meets a former football player. Though they're both in a relationship, they fall in love."

"Who plays the guy?"

"Warren Beatty."

"Aren't they married?"

"In real life, they are. Not so in the flick. Anyway, because of their circumstance they agree to put their feelings on hold for awhile and suggest..."

"They suggest if they're both available in six months they meet atop the Empire State Building," Driscoll said.

"It's three months. But, you said you didn't see the movie."

"I didn't."

"Then how did you know that?"

"Because Irene Dunn and Charles Boyer made the same pact."

"Wait. What?"

Driscoll smiled, reached across the table and took hold of Margaret's hand. "The movie you watched was a remake. The original starred Irene Dunn and Charles Boyer. And no, Margaret, an accident isn't going to strike you down and leave me standing atop the skyscraper wondering what became of you. We'll visit the tower together."

Margaret smiled, and shook her head lovingly, her eyes locked on his.

"Those eyes, Margaret. I melt when you gaze at me like that."

"I'm glad."

"Me, too."

CHAPTER SIXTY-ONE

After leaving Driscoll's room, Margaret headed for the bank of elevators. It was nearing 3 p.m. She'd head for the diner down the street. Having skipped breakfast and lunch, she was famished. Time to trade the antiseptic smells of the hospital for those of the diner's kitchen.

"Magazine?" The voice startled her.

Pivoting, she eyed the man. His face was heavily scarred, distorted. His pudgy hands held an assortment of reading material.

"I've got Better Homes and Gardens, USA Today, People, Glamour, Us Weekly. I also got some religious books, if salvation is your thing."

"I'll pass on salvation. You got a National Enquirer in there?"

"Ahh, you're into scandals. Are you a night crawler?"

"What's a night crawler?"

"Like in the movie."

"What movie?"

"*Nightcrawler*. It stars Jake Gyllenhaal packing a camcorder. He's got a police scanner in his car. So if there's an accident or a domestic disturbance he gets there before the police and films it. He then sells the live footage to a local news channel. It's like the stuff you see in the National Enquirer."

Margaret pressed the 'down' button, holding her thumb on the illuminated circle

"I'm not a fan of camcorders," she said.

The man smiled, displaying an oddly yellowed display of crooked teeth. "So you're just into scandals?" he asked.

"Sort of."

"Ahh, so it's up to me to guess your job, eh? I'll say you're a mortician."

Margaret's eyes widened.

"You're not Alexandra Mosca, are ya? You kinda look like her."

"Who's she?"

"A funeral director. High profile. One of the first women in the United States to achieve that title."

Running her hand down the sleeve of the navy blue Tahari cropped-Jacket dress suit, Margaret smiled. "First to achieve the title? That's impressive," she said.

"A few years back she posed for Playboy."

"Get out."

"No lie."

Margaret's smile broadened. "She posed for Playboy and you think I resemble her?"

"You do."

"Nice to hear. I'll take a copy of USA Today."

The man fanned through the assortment of magazines and found what Margaret had

asked for. "You can tell a lot about a person by their reading material," he said, flashing his oddly shaped teeth.

"Oh, really," Margaret said.

"Take you, for example. You prefer national news over Hollywood gossip."

Margaret scanned the small corridor of the hospital. "There better not be a hidden camera somewhere shooting the return of 'This Is Your Life'," Margaret warned, jokingly.

"And you're a fan of old TV Shows."

"You don't quit, do you?"

"I'm sorry. Have I crossed the line?"

"Not at all." Margaret shot him a smile, grabbed the magazine and ducked inside the elevator that had just arrived.

As soon as Margaret entered Pete's Diner the tempting aroma of home cooking brought a smile to her face. She chose a seat at an empty booth by a window overlooking the parking lot. A matronly waitress with Clairol blond hair appeared with a menu and a glass of iced water.

"Would you like to hear our specials?" she asked.

"Is the Reuben one of 'em?"

"Top o' the list."

"Good. Can I get the rye bread toasted?"

"You bet. You like your mustard domestic or hoity-toity?"

Margaret looked puzzled. *Is that a brand name?* she wondered "Hoity toity?"

"Dijon," the waitress said, feigning a French accent.

"Definitely domestic. And lots of it."

Using a pencil she retrieved from behind her ear, the waitress jotted down the order, verbalizing it as she did. "Reuben. Rye down. Plain mustard. Heavy."

"You'll want a cream soda with that. Doctor Brown's?" she asked

"None better."

"You got it."

The Reuben was a bust. The corned beef was dry, the sauerkraut, questionable and the mustard was bland. Thankfully, Doctor Brown came through. Leaving most of the sandwich on her plate, she added a bag of UTZ Salt'n Vinegar potato chips to her tab, left a decent tip, and exited the diner.

Hoping Driscoll would be awake, she hurried back to the hospital. On entering the Lieutenant's room she was surprised to find a visitor sitting beside his bed. "Moira? What are you doing here?"

Moira's face was pale. She sat quietly, wringing her hands. "I saw the bulletin on NY1. Is he going to be ok?"

"He'll be fine."

"I dropped everything and raced over here. I really should have stopped for flowers."

"He's allergic to pollen."

"*She's picked one helluva time to be a bitch,*" Moira muttered under her breath as her eyes zeroed in on Margaret. "Except yours, I suppose," she said, pointing to a vase of irises.

"There's no need for you to stay, Moira. I've got this covered."

"I'm not going anywhere."

"You have a job, don't you?"

"I wrapped up early."

"Your boss ok with that?"

"She's my mom. And, yeah, she's ok with that."

Silence settled between the two.

But not for long.

"I see you brought a book. Do you plan to read to him?" Margaret asked.

The sergeant's voice was less confrontational. Moira read it as a cease fire. "I think he'll get a kick out of it," she said.

"He's a finicky reader. What's the book about?"

Moira held up the paperback for Margaret to read the title.

"Saint Paul's Epistle to the Romans," Margaret recited. "Oh, brother."

"You got an issue with St, Paul? Or just me?"

"You never struck me as the religious type."

Though Margaret's tone was less threatening, Moira remained guarded. "There's a type?" she asked.

"Of course there is," Margaret said.

"Then I'm the type. When I graduated from The Academy of Mount Saint Ursula with honors, they asked me to give the valedictorian speech," Moira boasted.

"I had no clue."

"And you call yourself a detective?"

"I call myself 'Sergeant' and don't push your luck."

Moira rolled her eyes. "For what it's worth, this isn't my book. Some guy dropped it off."

"What guy?"

"Said he was a hospital volunteer."

"Did he have facial scars?"

"Yeah."

"A volunteer's badge?"

"I didn't see one."

"I didn't see one either," Margaret said. "Let me see that book."

Moira handed it to her. While doing so, a leaflet became dislodged and fell to the floor which Moira picked it up. "Wow! Saint Paul is quite the adman," she said.

"Adman? Wha'd'ya talking about?"

"This fell out." She handed the church bulletin to Margaret. "He's still seeking converts to Christianity. That bulletin's dated last week."

"So it is," Margaret said, her focus interrupted when Driscoll stirred.

"Hello, ladies, what'd I miss?" the Lieutenant slurred, confusion marking his face.

"Oh, John, you're back!" Margaret gushed.

"Back from where?" he asked taking in his surroundings. It took a moment for him to realize he was in a hospital bed but his voice was stronger.

"Hi there!" said Moira.

"I've been here all day. She just got here," said Margaret.

"I see nothing's changed between you two. How 'bout you both holster your sabers while one of you explains why I'm harnessed to an IV drip?"

"Sounds like a job for you, Sergeant. I'm heading down to the cafeteria for a cup o' joe. Lieutenant, I'll bring you back a cappuccino," Moira added nearing the hall.

"Don't let the door hit you in the ass on your way out," Margaret shouted.

"Margaret, where the hell am I?" Driscoll asked.

"You're in the hospital, John. In the Critical Care Unit."

Driscoll scanned the room. He blinked his eyes rapidly, hoping he was dreaming. When he realized he wasn't, he looked to Margaret. "Why am I in a hospital?"

"You had surgery."

"Surgery? Was I shot?"

"No, John. You had a blood clot removed from your brain. It's what was causing those headaches. You remember the headaches, right?"

"Vaguely. Have you really been here all day?"

"Yep. Since they rolled you into surgery early this morning."

"What time is it now?" he asked, his eyes darting around the room looking for a clock.

"Just after 4," Margaret said.

"I'm thirsty."

"There's a vending machine down the hall." Margaret stood, eager to help in any way. "What can I get you?" she asked.

"Tullamore Dew."

"You're in a hospital, John. The only alcohol they serve comes with a sponge."

"I'll have a Mission Orange."

"Mission Orange? I haven't seen that in years."

"Then I'll have a Tab."

"Oh, my God! You're stuck in the 60's! What did that surgeon do to you?" She lovingly brushed her hand across his forehead.

"Stuck? Whadya mean, Margaret?"

Concern filled Margaret's face. She sat back down. "What year is this? What's today's date? And who's the President?" she asked.

"It's December 7, 1941."

"John, Pearl Harbor was not attacked today. You sit tight. I'll be right back. I need to find that surgeon," she said, back on her feet again.

"Relax, Margaret. I'm only kidding. Get me a ginger ale."

Margaret glared at him.

"What?" he said.

"Dammit, John. You had me worried."

"Sorry, Babe. I'm still a little out of it."

"And only because of that I'm going to cut you some slack," she said, stifling a grin over him calling her Babe. *Still a little out of it, indeed.* "Alright. I'll be back in a minute with your soda. If that smartass returns, send her home."

Driscoll smiled at the thought of waking to find two women at his bedside. Both fawning. Alone now, he took in his surroundings. He figured the bouquet of irises on the windowsill were from Margaret. Moira being more the balloon type, though there was no balloon. Next to the window sat a table stacked with magazines. Beside it, a leather chair. He heard footsteps. They were Margaret's. She handed him an opened can of ginger ale which contained a straw. Driscoll took a long swig. "You have no idea how good this tastes," he said.

"That's good to hear. Your headache gone?"

"I'm a little sore. Not quite a headache. More like a sting. Right here." He placed a finger on the top of his head. "Jesus, Margaret! Where's my hair? And what the hell are these metal things?"

"They had to shave your head before the surgery. And what you're feeling are staples. Ten of 'em. They hold that maddening brain of yours inside your noggin."

"Wha'd'ya mean maddening?" he griped, running his finger along the row of metal stitches.

"Would you prefer 'challenging', 'inciting', 'provoking'?"

"OK, Margaret, I get it. But as soon as I'm out o' here, I'm going shopping for a hat."

"Why? You don't like the Kojak look? I think it adds charm."

"I'm not charming enough?"

"Who could be more charming than you?"

"Apparently, Telly Savalas. How long you figure I'll have these staples?" Driscoll moved his finger from one staple to the next. *Margaret was right. There are ten!*

"What's the rush to remove them?" Margaret asked. "Think of the benefits."

"Benefits?"

"You're sure to pick up Showtime and HBO. No charge. And maybe some other intergalactic signals. I'm told ET is also very charming."

Driscoll looked at her and shook his head. "You're on a roll, Margaret."

"All kidding aside, I'm sure they'll let you know before you're discharged when they'll take the staples out. In the meantime, stay clear of magnets."

"Ya done?"

"I think so."

"Brain surgery, eh? You think it made me more intelligent?" Driscoll asked.

"Do you feel more intelligent?"

"I think I do," the Lieutenant said, taking another swig of ginger ale.

"Smarter than the scarecrow from the Wizard of OZ after he got his 'brain'?" Margaret asked, teasingly.

"I thought you were done."

"And….. Done!"

"It's good that we're sharing a laugh. Long day for you. Emotional, I'm sure," Driscoll said, taking note of the moisture collecting in the corners of Margaret's eyes as she stared at him.

"Yes. 'Emotional' would describe my day, John."

"It means the world to me that you're here. More so, that you've been here all day," the Lieutenant said, smiling softly.

Margaret returned the smile. "I was surprised to see Moira. But more surprised that your sister wasn't here. Did you let her know you were in the hospital?"

"I didn't. But I did list her as the person to contact had there been any complications. She's not stable. She's . . ."

"Sssshh. No need to explain. I know her circumstance. You did the right thing. You always do."

"That's sweet of you to say."

"Sooooo… You had brain surgery. Did you see God?" Margaret asked, her hands casually folded in her lap

"Was I supposed to?"

"Some patients who've had cranial surgery claim they saw a light that spoke to them. There's a lot written about it."

"I can't say I saw a light. There was a lot of mist."

"Like that twilight zone- type place psychics talk about?"

"I had neurosurgery, Margaret. I wasn't at a séance."

"Well, there are some similarities. I've been to a séance."

"Why'd you go to a séance?"

"I tried to reach my dad."

"What? Why in God's name, would you do that?"

"I wanted to give him a chance to make amends. To free his soul from eternal damnation. And he did."

Driscoll smiled, realizing the experience had given Margaret some relief. "Impressive. Maybe I should meet with your psychic."

"Why?"

Driscoll's eyes closed. Tears formed. Margaret realized she'd stirred a memory she wished she hadn't. Before she could change the course of the conversation, the Lieutenant responded.

"I'd like to see my daughter. We never had a chance to say goodbye."

Margaret took hold of his hand and squeezed it.

"Ahem," Moira said as though clearing her throat as she entered the room. "Wow. You're looking better, Lieutenant!"

"Thank you. How's the coffee in the cafeteria?"

"It's no Au Bon Pain and they don't make cappuccino," she muttered taking a seat.

"I'll let them know they need to up their game during my exit interview," Driscoll said, sporting a grin.

"Sergeant, did you read to our recovering patient?" Moira asked, pointedly.

"Read to me? Margaret, what's she talking about?" Driscoll asked.

"A hospital volunteer dropped off a book for you," Moira explained.

Margaret handed Driscoll the copy of Saint Paul's Epistle to the Romans.

"I'm just out of surgery and you hand me St. Paul?"

"I'm guessing he was out of Fifty Shades of Grey."

"Funny gal you are, Margaret. What's this?" he asked, pulling out the bulletin from between two pages.

Margaret watched a pallor spread across the Lieutenant's face. "What is it, John?"

"This bulletin's from St. Agnes's. It's a recent one."

"And?"

"That's the church where I took down the arsonist. Our killer. He's been here."

CHAPTER SIXTY-TWO

The rusted mirror framed by the bamboo medicine chest was cracked, splitting Tilden's face in two, offering a glimpse into his severed soul. He was having difficulty removing the latex that clung to his nose, cheeks and forehead. Had he left it on too long? He hadn't anticipated finding a second woman seated beside Driscoll's bed after having toyed with the dark-haired woman at the elevator. Soaking the cotton pad with a stronger astringent, he applied more pressure and watched his nose pierce through the disguise. Choosing a burn victim as his cover while he killed the Lieutenant was not only a stroke of genius but a masterful and lurid tribute to his friend and accomplice, Harold, whose untimely demise demanded his death be avenged.

"But it wasn't avenged," his inner voice reminded him. *"That cop's still alive because you were stymied by that girl."*

Tilden closed his eyes, willing that reality away. When he opened them, an empty silence settled inside the hollow of his head, while, in the mirror, a face stared at him. It was that of Valerie's.

Narrowing his incandescent eyes, he stared at the uninvited specter with her dull brown irises and Maybelline painted face. "Women, who needs them," he muttered. "Hear this, bitch. After I settle the score with that bastard with a badge, I'll resume my annihilation of the likes of you."

CHAPTER SIXTY-THREE

"Some bachelor pad," said Moira collapsing into Driscoll's modular sofa. "Ahh, Roche Bobois," she cooed, running her hand against the soft leather.

The Nota Bene corner ensemble, boasting pigmented corrected cowhide, sat below a framework of windows, offering a breathtaking view of New York's lower harbor.

"Roche who?" Margaret asked.

Moira stared at Margaret and said nothing which infuriated Margaret. "I asked you a question, Missy," Margaret snarled.

"He's an aficionado extraordinaire when it comes to living room furniture," Moira replied, turning her nose up. "Our Lieutenant has excellent taste," she added, smiling at Driscoll.

"John, she's buttering you up. She must want something," Margaret warned.

"Roche Bobois. Go ahead, Margaret, let's hear you pronounce it," Moira said, mockingly.

"Moira, I don't know why you're here." Margaret stared at her know-it-all nemesis.

"Obviously, because of my feng shui."

"OK, ladies. It's time to put away your daggers. And that's an order." Driscoll barked.

Their silence said they understood. Not happily. But, that they understood.

"Let's get down to business. Because of my surgery, the Department took me off the case for a month. They said it would stress me out. So, we're meeting here. The fact that we're meeting at all stays between us. Moira's joining us simply because of her encounter with our suspect. Understood, Moira?"

Her nod suggested she did.

"Cedric, how 'bout you bring us up to speed on the investigation?" the Lieutenant asked.

"We figure the suspect heard about your rush to the hospital on NY1," Thomlinson began. "He sure has it in for you."

"Sure, I killed his buddy."

"And his accomplice," said Thomlinson.

"Not anymore," said Driscoll.

"It's the last time NY1 will feature a bulletin like that. They told their entire audience where you were recuperating after surgery for Chrissake," Margaret grumbled. "After my visit to Spectrum News on 9th Avenue, their *Crime* editor, was re-assigned to *Real Estate*. And the hospital has established new protocol regarding visitation."

"Forensics is analyzing the prints found on the book and the church bulletin," Thomlinson continued.

Moira looked confused. Rather than interrupt with a question she raised her hand.

"Yes, Moira," Driscoll asked.

"Fingerprints are detectable on paper?" she asked.

"Not to the naked eye. Two chemicals, ninhydrin and diazafluoren, are used to produce prints from skin oils left behind," Driscoll explained.

"Cool!" said Moira.

"The hospital's security cameras caught the suspect entering the Rosenthal Building carrying a brown shopping bag," Thomlinson said. "Here, have a look," he added, producing his Galaxy S9 and playing the clip he'd made while viewing the hospital's feed.

The video revealed Security checking the shopping bag.

"That bag likely contained the magazines and the book," Margaret said.

As the video continued, a security guard is seen giving the man a Visitor's Pass. The man then walks toward a bay of elevators. In the next segment he's upstairs talking with Margaret. After Margaret is seen getting on the elevator, the camera shows him heading to the Lieutenant's room. He's then seen entering it.

"The guy waddles like a duck," Moira noted, retrieving her iPhone to investigate the anomaly. "Could be Emery-Dreifuss syndrome. Metaphyseal chondrodysplasia. Spondylolisthesis. Hypophosphatemic rickets. Koller syndrome. There's more."

"You're an interior decorator and a diagnostic expert?" Margaret asked.

"Apparently she is," Thomlinson said, earning Margaret's glare.

"Bookmark that search," Driscoll instructed.

"Done," said Moira giving the Lieutenant a thumbs up.

"Moira, what'd the guy look like?" Driscoll asked.

"His face was scarred," Margaret said.

"He asked me. Not you."

"But, I've been trained to observe."

"Was that before or after you left him and got on the elevator?"

"I thought I told you two to knock it off," Driscoll barked.

"He had a pale face," Moira said. "Like chalk. Looked like a ghost. Yes, he was scarred. Looked like a burn victim. Brown hair. Dull. Unwashed. His eyes. Like bugs."

"Wha'd'ya mean, like bugs?" Thomlinson asked.

"He had roach eyes."

"So. They were brown," said Margaret.

"No. Black. All pupil. No color."

"Did he have antennas, too?"

"The word you're looking for is 'antennae', Margie."

"For the last time: zip it," Driscoll said through clenched teeth.

"Sorry," Moira said.

"Won't happen again," said Margaret.

"How old was the guy, Moira?"

"Forties, maybe? Fifty, max."

"Aside from the scarring, did he remind you of anyone?"

" Wha'd'ya mean?"

"I know where you're going with that question," Margaret said. "He didn't look anything like Pee-wee Herman."

"She's right," Moira said. "But, what's a likeness to Paul Reubens have to do with anything?"

"A witness reported he looked like him."

"He didn't," Moira and Margaret said in unison.

"No way he'd show his actual face inside a facility with cameras. Especially if he's up to no good. He had to have been wearing a disguise," Thomlinson reasoned.

"If that was a mask. It was a damn good one," Margaret said.

"Agreed," said Moira.

"Someone talented enough to stage a crucifixion rivaling any of Clive Barker's *Hellraiser* flicks, would know how to perfectly transform his face for the camera," the Lieutenant reasoned. "Especially, inside a hospital he'd chosen as his new killing field."

"With you as his prey," said Margaret.

CHAPTER SIXTY-FOUR

"You never saw him?"

"Nope," Moira said as she sat squirming on her therapist's couch.

"You told the Lieutenant and his team that you did. Why is that, Moira?" Doctor Hannah Adelman asked, her legs crossed, her eyes focused on her patient.

"You know why."

"That I know why is not important. It's only essential that you know why."

Moira closed her eyes, leaned back on the sofa, and pulled her knees into her chest.

"Silence isn't always golden, Moira," Adelman said as she walked toward her De'Longhi double serve espresso machine.

"Here we go again," Moira groaned.

"Where is it we're going?" she asked, her back to her patient, a technique she used to unconsciously instill trust.

"Jesus Christ! Driscoll once had a bird that spouted one liners just like you're doing. I feel like I'm in the room with a parrot instead of a mental health professional."

"And now we're talking about birds," the therapist said, using the swivel jet feature of the coffee machine to froth her low fat milk. "You'd say anything to delay your cure, wouldn't you?" she added.

"There's no cure for the likes of me."

"So, why are you here?" Adelman asked, returning to her seat, demitasse in hand.

"I have no fucking clue. You're the doctor. I'm hoping you'll pull a rabbit out of your hat."

"Oh. So, I'm no longer a parrot. I'm once again a mental health provider. But you'd rather I be a magician?"

"That's right. It's gonna take a pretty big wand to cure me of my addiction. Which, by the way, I've grown fond of."

The therapist took a sip of her coffee and stared at her patient. "It's obvious you lied to the police about seeing the serial killer because you had an ulterior motive."

"And we're off to races, again. I feel like I'm at the Spanish Inquisition?"

"Your addiction is at work here, Moira. It's in overdrive. You can see that, can't you?"

"Yes. Yes. Yes. I'm an addict. I've admitted it. Again and again and again. What more can I say?"

"I'm sorry," the therapist murmured.

"You're sorry? For what?"

"For acting like a desperate mother instead of a seasoned psychotherapist. And for breaking all the rules of my vocation. You deserve a more professional counselor."

"Broken rules? What rules?"

"I'm guilty of dispassionate concern. I'm getting too involved."

"What the hell are you talking about?" The look on Moira's face was one of astonishment.

"You deserve a more professional counselor," Adelman said.

Panic seized Moira. "Wait. You're cutting me off?"

"There are better shrinks out there, Moira. I'm sorry I failed you."

"Oh. So, I'm too much of a sick puppy and you're giving up on me?" Moira waited for an answer. There was none. All she saw was Adelman silently sipping her espresso and staring at her. "Well, fuck that. And fuck you." Moira stood, grabbed her bag and headed for door.

"There are better psychologists out there, Moira," the therapist said.

Moira, her fingers inches away from the doorknob, turned on her heels. Her face was awash with tears. "I don't want to work with anyone else," she whimpered.

"I'm sorry I failed you."

"Don't say that. It's only since I admitted my lust for killers that I'm having a hard time accepting your care. It's you who deserves better."

"Together, we can work it out. But we can't if you leave."

Moira returned to the sofa and collapsed on it. "Please teach me, Hannah, how to put it all in your hands."

Adelman stood, and took a seat beside her patient.

Moira trembled. Throwing herself into the arms of her therapist, she wept.

When her patient stopped crying, Hannah Adelman asked if it would be alright to pick up where they'd left off.

"Yes," Moira said.

"Tell me again what you told the police about the man."

"I said he looked like a ghost. You know. Pale face. Transparent like. And that he waddled when he walked. Like a goose."

"So you did see him."

"No. Not really. What I saw was him on the hospital's security camera which Detective Thomlinson had downloaded to his phone. I also told them that he had bug eyes."

"Did he?"

"I have no clue."

"Why tell them he did?"

"To bust Margaret's chops."

Adelman said nothing, but her look conveyed disapproval.

"It's a minor detail. It's not like it's going to lead to a conviction."

"I suppose so, but it's still a lie."

Moira stole a glance at the wall clock. She disliked being called a liar, even though she opened with a lie, then distorted the truth throughout the session. But, there was no way she'd let anyone, even her shrink, know she'd spent time conversing with the man while she sat beside Driscoll's hospital bed. Though he was a non-entity at the time, he now stirs a longing she hopes to satisfy. For Moira, it was beyond sexual. What turned her on was the predatory proclivity of the men Lieutenant Driscoll pursued. The mere thought of the hunter stalking and capturing his prey got her off.

CHAPTER SIXTY-FIVE

Moira defined 'addiction' as the abuse of drugs or alcohol. She'd been taking Vicodin for ten years and not once had she taken more than the prescribed dose. And so, she felt she was no addict. The fact she was turned on by 'the bad boy' was simply a preference. Besides, Driscoll's police files revealed their suspect had targeted a porn star and an ex-con. He had a type. Why shouldn't she?

She opened her laptop and scoured through her 'acquired' NYPD files again. Had she overlooked a detail that might identify this crazed embalmer? Had the Lieutenant? There was a complete dossier on Harold but very little on his accomplice. Only Driscoll's assertion that the two had been collaborating. If they were, how did they communicate? "Accomplice" wasn't listed in Harold's iPhone. Or was it? She studied the list of names in the arsonist's iCloud file where he'd backed up his contacts. *Abbott's Plumbing and Heating. Carey's Car Service. Frank's Electrical. Jonathan's Roofing. Michelson's Drain Service. Oscar's Firewood. Thaddeus & Company, Moving and Storage. Zeus's Pizza.* Though all appeared to be business contacts, none of the phone numbers ended in 00. *That's odd*, she thought.

She took another look at Harold's file. "He rented an apartment," she said aloud. "What renter needs a roofer?"

Convinced she was looking at a coded address book, she grabbed her phone and called each number.

Though the first and second number she dialed went to voicemail, the next two were answered. "Whose idea was the cross? Yours or Harold's?" she asked.

The first to answer said: *"Lady, you have the wrong number."*

The second: *"No Harold here."*

The next produced a recording telling her the number she'd reached was no longer in service and that there was no further information available about the number. As did the listing that followed.

And all she got on the last two was an automated *"Please leave your message at the tone."*

As Moira said nothing and ended the call, she felt the heated surge of adrenalin ignite an intense longing for the man, which, sadly for her, went unfulfilled.

CHAPTER SIXTY-SIX

Inside Starbucks, sitting in the lotus position on a wooden chair, was Moira indulging in her 'nirvana moment'.

The dark Belgian chocolate that fueled her latte was intoxicating. Adding to her euphoria, k.d. lang's sultry voice was echoing her favorite tune, *Constant Craving*. Moira, addicted to both chocolate and coffee, found that this particular Starbucks, in her favorite seat beside the window, provided her with a perfect shooting gallery for her chosen elixir. While floating in her caffeinated netherworld, her gaze fixed on the passersby frantically crossing the intersection of Astoria Boulevard and 82nd Street, a rapidly moving band of uniformed parochial school children caught her attention. They were chattering like pixies. Mindful of her mischievous days at Mount Saint Ursula, she was tempted to join them in their monkey business.

Were her eyes deceiving her or did the gentleman who had stopped to check his reflection in the window resemble Pee-wee Herman? *My God! Could that be him?* She stared at what was left of her latte. *Or am I hallucinating?* Having once had an odd reaction to an Ethiopian Arabica, she brought the drink to her nose. There he was again. *Jesus Christ, the guy's coming in! Oh, my God, he waddles!* The rush of adrenalin that flooded her with trepidation was paled by the intensity of her sexual arousal.

"We meet again," he said, taking a seat beside her.

"You're the volunteer from the hospital. Your scarred face is gone, but you're him."

Tilting his head, Tilden eyed her as though she were a lab specimen.

"How did you find me?"

"I've been keeping tabs on you since you left the hospital. I know where you live. I know where you work. I know all your haunts," Tilden said, his odd gaze becoming an intimidating stare.

Moira bolted upright, her eyes widening as dread overshadowed her desire.

"Sit back down," he growled in a hushed tone.

Moira did as she was told as terror etched her face.

"I want you to loudly announce the following," Tilden quietly said: "'You're always full of surprises, Amedeo. That's what I love about you.' Then, get up, entwine your arm in mine and accompany me out of the shop."

"And if I don't?"

"You don't want to know the answer to that," he muttered, his eyes becoming slits.

"You're always full of surprises, Amedeo. That's what I love about you," Moira stammered as the horror of her plight gripped her.

"Now stand," Tilden ordered.

Frightened eyes stared at him.

"Stand, I said."

"You're always full of surprises, Amedeo. That's what I love about you," Moira shouted, sitting defiantly in her chair. Then shouted it again and again and again.

Her shrieking didn't stop. Not when several customers stood and stared. Not when the barista hollered he was calling the police. Not when the shop's manager raced over. Not when Tilden was long gone. And not when the EMTs strapped Moira to a medical stretcher and loaded her into the ambulance.

CHAPTER SIXTY-SEVEN

As the Lieutenant was sorting through the avalanche of paper that had amassed on his desk while he was out sick, his cell phone rang. Though he didn't recognize the caller's number, he answered it.

"Driscoll, here."

"Lieutenant, this is Doctor Hannah Adelman, Moira's therapist. I have some alarming news concerning Moira."

Oh, dear Lord, say it isn't so, his inner voice echoed, fearing she was dead. "What is it?" he asked, his heart racing.

"She's suffered what appeared to be a psychotic episode and was taken to Elmhurst Hospital Center by ambulance. The Psychiatric Emergency Room admitting nurse called me after seeing my name listed as a contact on her phone's Medical ID app. They've admitted her."

Driscoll fumbled through the pile of paper on his desk in search of his notepad to jot down what he was being told.

"Did the nurse say why she was brought in by ambulance?"

"The police were called to a Starbucks in East Elmhurst. Moira was reportedly shouting something odd and wouldn't, or couldn't stop. 'You're always full of surprises, Amedeo. That's what I love about you,' was what she kept hollering over and over again."

Driscoll's mind raced, scuttling through every bit of information he recalled about Moira. A name like Amedeo was one he'd surely remember, but he was drawing a blank.

"Was she with anyone?" Driscoll asked.

"When the police arrived she was alone. The officer's report indicates there was a man with her shortly before the outburst. Customers in the shop stated he left as soon as she started yelling. One patron told the police he looked older but no one could adequately describe him as everyone's focus was on Moira."

"You've been treating her for years, Doctor. Has the name Amedeo ever come up?"

"Never."

"OK. Thank you. I appreciate you calling me. Please keep me informed."

"I will."

When Driscoll ended the call he had more questions than answers. But his thoughts were interrupted when Thomlinson rushed into his office, grinning.

"I know that look. Wha'd'ya got?"

"Good news and bad. Which do you wanna hear first?" the detective said, spinning a hardwood chair around and straddled it, seating himself facing its back.

"Surprise me."

"The prints on the book and the church bulletin our guy gave to Margaret at the hospital produced no hits."

Driscoll's expression said he wasn't surprised. "And the good news?"

"The tip line's delivered," the detective said with a smile. "We got a call from Heathersville. A small town in Rockland County, an hour up on the Palisades Interstate Parkway. There's a diner up there. Our caller, Arnie Krieger, owns it. Claims one of his waitresses reported seeing a guy transporting a huge cross. He used an old Cadillac flower car to haul it. Like the ones used by funeral directors."

Driscoll, always in awe of Cedric's delivery, smiled. "A cross. A funeral director. It certainly has possibility written all over it." Driscoll said.

"According to the caller, the guy comes in for breakfast once in a while. Not much of a talker. He points to items on the menu. A waitress there, Loretta, says he's spooky as hell. And, get this, he waddles when he walks."

"Now, you've really got my attention."

"While pulling out of their parking lot, a tarp he'd used to cover his cargo was upended by the wind, exposing the cross, which the waitress spotted."

"She get a plate?"

"Yes sir. Not sure it'll help though."

"Why's that?"

"The tag matched a registration for a '62 Rambler that'd been crushed at a salvage yard outside of Oneida 20 years ago. The last registrant died two years before that."

"Dead end."

A smile erupted on the detective's face.

"That grin says you've saved the best for last."

"The waitress said the guy resembled her granddaughter's favorite TV character."

"Which one?"

"Pee-wee Herman."

CHAPTER SIXTY-EIGHT

Driscoll selected the Diana Krall station on the Chevy's SiriusXM Radio, figuring her soulful voice would be a soothing escape from the challenges presented by a madman. But before the jazz pianist's recording of *The Look Of Love* began to play, the vehicle's MyLink touch screen indicated Doctor Adelman was calling.

"Good afternoon, Doctor Adelman," the Lieutenant said by way of the vehicle's voice command system. "I've been anxiously awaiting your call. How's Moira doing?"

"To sum it up in one word, 'better'. The man who she was seen with before her outburst was the killer you're after. She hadn't arranged the meeting. He appeared 'out of nowhere'. Her words, not mine. We spoke at length about the encounter and because of confidentiality, I'm not going to go into detail about our conversation. I will say this, he scared the bejesus out of her. So much so that her fear was more powerful than her desire for the man."

"That sounds like a breakthrough," said Driscoll.

"An incredible one. She's agreed to stay at Elmhurst Hospital. They've recently opened a re-hab center and she's made the commitment to spend four weeks delving into her addiction. You should be proud of yourself, Lieutenant. I know I am."

Driscoll was flattered but had no clue why the therapist was lauding such praise.

"What is it I've done to warrant such a compliment, Doctor?"

"Many addicts must hit bottom before they begin their journey back up. This man represents that bottom for Moira. Had it not been for you seeking her assistance her addiction would have undoubtedly gone on untreated."

The Lieutenant was blown away. "Thank you, Doctor. I've been laden with a ton of guilt when it comes to Moira. I'm so…."

"Lieutenant," Adelman quickly interrupted. "It's time you let it go. Rejoice in her future and not dwell on her past."

After ending the call Driscoll glanced in the rear view mirror and smiled before continuing on.

After exiting the upper level of the George Washington Bridge, traffic slowed to a stop on the Interstate. His police scanner blamed a multi-car pile-up at Exit 19. Turning the volume up, he reached inside the Impala's glove box, retrieved a pack of Lucky Strikes and fired one. Inhaling deeply, he let his scarred noggin fall back on the car's headrest. Images from his past filled the panorama of his mind. Colette by his side, he had traveled this lackluster roadway to attend a wedding on a hillside inside Bear Mountain. It was the second go 'round for a pair of '60's leftovers intent on exchanging vows in a natural setting where they had first surrendered to their passion while playing hooky from nearby Peekskill High School.

The blast from the horn of a battered Town & Country minivan startled him. It was being driven by a black-clothed Hassidic, whose face, as viewed in the rear view mirror, wasn't a happy one. Traffic was moving while Driscoll was at a full stop in the middle lane of an Interstate. His thoughts had him stuck in the past. When the guy let loose a loud expletive in Yiddish, the Lieutenant put the cruiser in 'Drive'. "Alright, already," he groaned, catching up with the flow of traffic.

Heathersville, a small hamlet at the foot of the Catskill Mountains, was easy to find thanks to his Chevy's MyLink navigation system. Veering right onto Front Street, he spotted the triangle of gravel that served as the parking lot for Arnie's Diner and pulled in. Once out from behind the wheel, the fragrant mountain air reaffirmed he was no longer in downtown Manhattan. After his monotonous trek up the cheerless Palisades, Driscoll's hunger had kicked in. Hoping for a rustic menu flaunting local delicacies, he opened the eatery's screen door and stepped inside.

"Lieutenant Driscoll?" Arnie Krieger asked.

"That'd be me."

Krieger was a rotund man. His blue eyes, set back above reddened cheeks, were accented by thick white brows. He reminded Driscoll of a teacher he'd admired in high school, who always sported a Santa Claus outfit the day before Christmas break.

"How was your ride up," the cheerful proprietor asked, offering a welcoming hand.

"Uneventful. Something smells good."

"Hope you brought an appetite."

"Wha're'ya cooking?" Driscoll asked.

The man's eyebrows did a little dance as a smile creased his jovial face.

"Onion steak on a skillet," he boasted.

"Sounds good to me."

"Great. How do you like your steak?"

"Medium rare."

Arnie gave the Lieutenant a thumbs up before disappearing into the kitchen.

Driscoll scanned the restaurant. Eight cherry red Naugahyde swivel stools lined a parrot green Formica topped counter. Two patrons, wearing overalls advertizing Squeaky Clean Septic Tank Maintenance, were chomping on super sized sandwiches that dripped strands of melted cheese.

My arteries are clogging just watching those guys. Please Lord, let my steak be a mini, Driscoll prayed. "Arnie, hold the cheese," he hollered, with desperation in his voice.

One of the super-sized-with-cheese enthusiasts seemed to take issue with Driscoll's remark. "You a got a beef with cheddar, Mister?" he asked.

"I'm watching my cholesterol," Driscoll managed.

"Is that so?"

"Doctor's orders."

"Then you need a new doctor," the man said, nudging his cohort who chuckled.

Driscoll chose a corner table, putting distance between himself and the two patrons. As soon as he was seated, Arnie reappeared.

"Arnie, what's with the new guy? He doesn't like cheese," remarked one of the swivel stool patrons, as Krieger passed by, steaming cast iron fry pan in an oven mitted hand.

"City folk. What can I tell ya?" Arnie said to the regular, shooting Driscoll a friendly wink.

Driscoll was glad to see his steak was small and not garnished with Cheddar.

"Taste the onions. Tell me what ya' think," Arnie said, transferring the rib eye to a plate.

Their taste was rich and velvety with a flavor the Lieutenant had never experienced before. "You got a winner, there," he said.

"I fry them in B&B."

"Bénédictine & Brandy?"

"Bourbon and butter. This here's a diner. Not Lutèce."

Driscoll smiled. "Your secret's safe with me."

"Loretta's on her way in," Arnie said, taking a seat across from the Lieutenant. When he pulled the tab on a can of Michelob Light, its effervescent foam spilled onto the table forming a puddle which flowed toward Driscoll. "She works the morning shift. 5 to 11," Arnie explained, using his apron to soak up the beer. "We don't get much of a crowd in the afternoon."

"You said on the phone she waited on the guy. And she's the one who spotted the cross, right?" Driscoll asked, keeping his voice low.

"She often sees things. Like danger where it ain't. But, when some lunatic crucified a woman just a few miles from here, I figured I'd better call it in."

"I'm glad you did. By the way, I'm waiting on a police sketch artist out of Yorktown PD. I thought she'd be here by now."

"I hope she likes my onion steak."

"Who wouldn't?" Driscoll said, lifting another forkful to his mouth.

"They said on Eyewitness News the killer has an axe to grind with you," Arnie said.

"It's one of the perks of being a homicide commander."

"You're a funny guy, Lieutenant."

Driscoll's eyes were diverted toward the taller of the two Squeaky Clean employees who was lumbering toward his table. It was the one who'd taken issue with the Lieutenant's request for no cheese.

"Up from the city, are ya'? I'll bet you're here asking questions about that killing on the cross, no?"

Driscoll stared at the man without answering.

"I seen the guy," he said.

"What guy?" Driscoll asked.

"Not sayin' I seen him do it. But, I seen the guy who had the cross loaded onto his Caddy. I thought I was watching a Stephen King movie."

Driscoll's scoped the man. Was he an upstart who'd become a possible witness? "Where'd you see him?" he asked.

"At the church."

"What church?"

"Saint Peter's."

"Saint Peter's been shuttered for years, Lester. Whad'ya talkin' about?" Arnie protested.

"Didn't say I seen him in the church. But I seen him."

Zeke, the other patron sporting overalls boasting Squeaky Clean Septic Tank Maintenance moseyed over, a smudge of cheddar cheese on his upper lip. "Tell 'em what he was doing," he said, encouraging his work buddy.

"I'm riding my bike," Lester said. "Like I do every morning."

"Yeah, and God help those tires. Face it, Lester, your battle with the bulge ain't workin'!"

The heavyset laborer shot his co-worker a look of disdain before continuing. "Anyway, I'm comin' up Tombs Road and I see the top of the church's cross swaying back and forth. There used to be a clay Christ nailed to it but some hoodlum ripped it off. Seein' the cross movin' got me thinkin' 'what the fuck'? So I peddled like my legs were on fire and veered into the churchyard. He'd gotten the cross out of the ground. He must be a strong dude. That sucker was a twenty-five footer. And the guy did by himself. He was loadin' it onto an old black Caddy. One of those flower cars they used at funerals."

"Did you call the cops?" Arnie asked

"No," the man said, sheepishly.

"Lester's got shit for brains," his co-worker grunted. "I'd'a called the police."

"So would I," said Arnie. "The guy's stealing from a church!"

"He see you?" Driscoll asked.

"No. I was hidden behind the tall weeds."

"You get a look at his face?"

"Nope."

"Can you tell anything about the guy?"

"He kinda wobbled when he walked."

The door opened and Loretta strutted in, puffing on a cigarette. She had the face of someone who ate all the wrong things and washed it down with boxed wine.

"I thought you quit smokin'," said Arnie.

"That was last year," Loretta said with a smirk. "It's a new year so I switched to filters."

"Loretta, the guy wobbles, right?" Lester asked.

Loretta looked puzzled. She stared at Lester. "Who ya talking about? she asked.

"The man who was cartin' the big cross."

"Yeah, he wobbled, alright. And he's a bad tipper," she said, pulling up a chair to join Driscoll. "After scoffing down three eggs and two sleeves of bacon, he crumples a one dollar bill and tosses it on the counter. A real gem!"

"I'm glad you got a good look at his face," said the Lieutenant. "I've arranged for a sketch artist from the Yorktown Police Department to join us. You're going to help her draw his face. In fact, I thought she'd be here by now."

"She?" asked Lester.

"Sergeant Darlene Cavanaugh," said the Lieutenant.

"Imagine that? A sketch artist right here at Arnie's. Loretta, you're gonna end up on *Forensic Files*," Zeke said, grinning, exposing a sizeable gap between his front teeth.

"Like hell I am. I look like I just got out of bed."

"Loretta, while we wait for the Sergeant, how 'bout you tell me about the guy?" Driscoll asked.

Using an ashtray from the table adjacent to theirs, Loretta extinguished her cigarette "The dude made my skin crawl. His eyes. They looked dead," she said.

"He come in often?"

"I've seen him, maybe, twice. He's not a local."

"Loretta says he looks like Paul Reubens. You know, the guy. He plays Pee-wee Herman," said Arnie.

"Reubens? There's a sandwich with that name, ain't there?" Zeke asked.

"Zeke's got food on his mind 24/7," said Lester.

"He did sorta' look like Pee-wee," said Loretta.

"The two times he was in. You speak to him?" Driscoll asked.

"Only to ask what he'd have. Both times he ordered eggs up with bacon.

"Did he pay with a credit card?"

Muted laughter erupted.

"This here's Heathersville, Lieutenant. It's a cash town," Arnie said.

"He ever chat it up with anyone, Loretta?"

"Nope. Comes in alone. Eats alone. Leaves alone."

All eyes turned to the entrance door. Then to the high heels. A brunette sporting a suede leather jacket and a diminutive skirt smiled at the group.

Arnie was bowled over. He'd never seen such a beautiful patron inside his diner.

"Hi, I'm Sergeant Darlene Cavanaugh," she said, joining the group.

"Can I get you a meat loaf sandwich? Alamode?" Arnie stammered.

"Men," Loretta muttered, shaking her head. "Ice cream on meat loaf? Earth to Arnie. Earth to Arnie."

"Um… um…" Arnie looked flustered.

"He meant to say 'a meat loaf sandwich on the house'," Loretta said, prompting her boss to smile.

"Thank you. I'd love a meatloaf sandwich. Traffic on Route 35 was brutal," Cavanaugh said, smiling at the restaurateur.

"You got it!" Arnie sprinting toward the kitchen.

"I'm supposing Lieutenant Talmadge brought you up to speed on the case. Am I right?" Driscoll asked the newcomer.

"She did."

"Good. Loretta, here, saw the suspect."

Unconsciously, the waitress fiddled with her hair.

"OK, Loretta, if we were in my office, I'd likely go high tech with a computerized sketch, but some say my old school charcoal is better. That work for you?"

Loretta nodded.

"Good. I'll be asking questions about the man you saw and based on what you tell me I'll draw a nondescript face. After I have a semblance of him, you and I will modify the features until my sketch depicts what he looks like. You ready?"

"Fire away," Loretta said.

Darlene Cavanaugh opened her sketch pad and using a Wolff's carbon pencil, she drew a circle. "A white man? Black? Hispanic?"

"He was white."

"How old was he?"

"I'd say 35 to 40."

"Tell me about his hair. Short? Long? Wavy? Curly? "

"There was none. His head was shaved."

"His forehead. What'd that look like?"

Loretta looked to the chorus of men that surrounded her. After studying their foreheads, she shrugged. "It looked like a regular forehead. What else can I say?"

"Wrinkled? Flat? Blemished?"

"It looked pasty. And he had no eyebrows. I'm guessing he shaved them, too."

"His eyes? Big? Small? Round? Oval? Recessed? Something like this?" she asked, showing Loretta her initial depiction.

"Sorta' like that. Maybe further apart. His eyes were intense. Spooky intense. I remember that about him."

"What color were they?"

"Icy blue. When he looked at you, you felt something?"

"What'd you feel?" Driscoll asked.

"A chill. The guy had mean eyes."

"The nose? Wide? Narrow? Long? Short?"

"Like the nose on a Pug," Loretta said.

"How 'bout his lips? Wide? Thin?"

"It was almost like he had none."

"Thin it is," said Cavanaugh, trimming down the sketch.

"Any significant features on his face? A cleft chin? Any piercings? Blemishes? Scars? Tattoos?"

"None, that I can remember." Loretta's gaze widened. She inhaled quickly. It looked as though she'd seen a ghost.

"What is it?" Driscoll asked.

"The top portion of his right ear was missing. I can't believe I just remembered that. It looked as though it'd been chewed off."

CHAPTER SIXTY-NINE

Driscoll, seated behind the wheel of the cruiser, studied the sketch that Darlene Cavanaugh had prepared. "Who are you," he asked aloud, examining the features of the charcoal composite. Unpocketing his iPhone, he pulled up the hospital security video that Thomlinson had shared with him. In it, the suspect's hair was brown, unkempt, and covered the tops of both ears. *He likely added a hairpiece as part of his disguise. It would cover up that mutilated ear,* Driscoll reasoned, hitting speed dial his phone.

"Yes, John," Margaret said, answering the call.

"We got a face. Yorktown PD will be forwarding the sketch to you. Run it through the department's Photo Manager. Although it's a drawing, we may get lucky with facial recognition. I also want it to hit every newspaper in the tri-state area. Be sure the networks and the local channels run it at 6 and again at 11. Yorktown will send it out to every police agency in a three hundred mile radius. I have a hunch that face has been seen in the vicinity of Heathersville. Make sure the tip line is well manned."

"Will do."

"In the sketch, his head is shaven. And the top portion of his right ear is missing."

"The guy peddling magazines at the hospital had lots of hair. I couldn't see much of either ear. With a deformity like that, he'd surely wear a hair piece."

"That's my thinking, as well. OK. I'm leaving Heathersville. I've got a stop to make at a church outside of town. Could be where he secured the cross used in the crucifixion. They've had a lot of rain. I doubt they'll be any trace evidence. But, I'll check it out, just the same."

An ominous roll of thunder ripped though the rustic silence as Driscoll pulled to the curb alongside the deserted churchyard. As he stepped out of the cruiser, rain began to fall. It troubled him that a crazed killer had defiled these hallowed grounds. It troubled him more that God's creation, wondrous nature, had erased all evidence of his trespass.

CHAPTER SEVENTY

"Fuck you! You're off your mark, Michelangelo. I've looked better with a hangover," Tilden growled, throwing a half eaten slice of pizza at the 56 inch TV screen that featured the sketch Driscoll had circulated. "You like faces? You and me ought to get together. I'll show you a face!" He stared menacingly at the newscaster who was alerting his viewers to be on the lookout for a crazed killer.

Palpating his scarred ear, Tilden forcefully pressed the 'OFF' button on the TV's remote, and watched his likeness fade to black. "Time to check on my captive," he muttered. Creeping down the steps to the cellar, he turned the key in the lock and pushed the door open. The hooker's body was as he'd left it, shackled at the ankle to the boiler, face up in the center of the cot. He tip-toed toward her to make sure she was breathing. God forbid, he'd injected an improper dosage of sodium thiopental. It was imperative she remained alive. Unconscious. But alive.

He had picked her up working the corner of Birch Street and Second Avenue in Fairmont, a seedy area just west of the run down Amtrak station. She had the same emaciated look as Valerie. Which was precisely what he was looking for. The quizzical look on the harlot's face when asked if she knew was into pegging, made him smile.

"I ain't never had a guy ask me that," she'd said.

"You know what it is, right?"

"Sure. But I'm not into toys. Except when I'm alone."

After coming to terms on price, the hooker had opened the passenger door on Tilden's van and slid in.

Eyeing his unconscious captive, his mind raced. It'd only be a matter of time before someone in the area called the police. Although Driscoll's sketch wasn't an exact likeness, it was close enough. And since it clearly depicted his mangled ear, time was not on Tilden's side.

"Your cleansing's on hold, bitch. You and I are out of here," he muttered to his sleeping fille de joie.

CHAPTER SEVENTY-ONE

Under threatening skies Tilden towered over the unmarked grave. Six feet below a mix of sand and clay, the mortal remains of Valerie were being eaten away by an armada of earth worms. He toyed with the idea of exhuming her decayed flesh, but, pressed for time, he shooed away the notion.

A flash of lightning cleaved the ominous sky. As a rumble of thunder sounded, the rain intensified, savagely pelting his head. "Fuck this," Tilden muttered, sprinting for the van. Before fastening his seat belt, he turned to make sure his quarry was securely immobilized. Her gaping mouth and the lethargic roll of her eyes told him she was adequately sedated. Shooting her a wink, he took hold of her cell phone. "Time to touch base with that centurion in blue," he announced.

After tipping the restaurant's delivery boy, Driscoll walked to the kitchen and emptied the contents of the Fold Pak container onto a plate. Moo Goo Gai Pan from the Oriental Palace on Court Street would be tonight's dinner. Since Zagat's had high praise for the culinary delights prepared at this Brooklyn restaurant, the Lieutenant figured he'd give it a try. After adding a blend of gourmet soy and pungent Szechuan spices to the steaming dish, he used a pair of chop sticks to bring a slice of lotus root to his mouth. The mixture of the sauces and the ambient ginger gravy jump started his palette. That's when his iPhone rang.

"Hello?" Driscoll's voice echoed through the cabin of the Econoline van.

"Hello, Lieutenant," Tilden mumbled.

"Who is this?"

"Wish I had time to chat," Tilden whispered.

"Who the hell is this?"

"Frank Abagnale, Jr.," came the reply, followed by laughter.

"Listen, pal, whoever the hell you are I've got no time for you."

"Oh, you'll make time for me. How's Moira holding up?" Tilden asked before ending the call and turning off the cell phone.

Releasing the foot brake on the Ford Econoline, he exited the driveway and eased onto the road. Watching his childhood home grow smaller in the vehicle's side view mirror, he used an incisor to rip the cellophane from an Atkins bar. Chewing loudly on the protein-infused caramel and chocolate nut roll, he began to laugh. "Frank Abagnale, Jr., Lieutenant. Chew on that for a while," he intoned.

His laughter became a howl as he floored the gas pedal and raced toward the Interstate.

CHAPTER SEVENTY-TWO

Driscoll summoned Margaret and Thomlinson to his Brooklyn co-op. Both looked visibly concerned by the grave look on the Lieutenant's face.

"The son-of-a-bitch called me while I was eating dinner," the Lieutenant said.

"Called you? How?" Margaret asked.

"I had programmed my office phone to forward all calls to my cell. He told me his name was Frank Abagnale, Jr. Then laughed."

Margaret and Thomlinson exchanged looks. Their expressions indicated they had no clue who Frank Abagnale, Jr. was.

The Lieutenant pushed aside his plate of Moo Goo Gai Pan. "The name puzzled me as well until I Googled it," Driscoll said. "Abagnale was a con man who'd amassed millions of dollars by forging checks. Leonardo DiCaprio portrayed him in the Steven Spielberg movie *Catch Me If You Can.*"

"Cute," Margaret said, disdain in her voice.

"He's thrown down the gauntlet," said Thomlinson.

"I fear it's more than a challenge to try and catch him," Margaret said, anxiously. "He was intent on killing you when he came to the hospital. Fortunately, his plan failed. It's not likely he's given up on seeing you dead. I suspect his call was a lure to draw you closer to him."

"And raising the risk of him being caught?" Thomlinson asked.

"He's hell-bent on seeing me dead, Cedric. That rage throws his caution to the wind. With the sketch of his mug out there he knows it's just a matter of time. To him, the game's afoot. Thanks for the concern, though. I know it's heartfelt."

Thomlinson and Margaret nodded.

"OK, back to business. Verizon lists the owner of the cell phone he used as Brianne Lindstrum of Fairmont, New York. She's known to Fairmont PD as a prostitute," said Driscoll.

"No surprise there," said Margaret. "Has she become another victim or his captive? That's the question."

"Verizon lists the incoming call originating inside a wooded area near Tallman Mountain State Park in the coastal town of Piermont. That's Rockland County," Driscoll said. "It's within fifteen miles of Arnie's diner."

Thomlinson opened the Maps app on his phone and typed in 'Tallman Mountain State Park'. "It's likely he's seen his face on the News," Thomlinson reasoned.

"I'm certain of it. His challenge to catch him if I can says he's on the run. He's a bold son of a bitch. We need to focus on tracking him down," said Driscoll.

Thomlinson held up his cell phone for Margaret and Driscoll to view the area in question. "A call from inside this wooded area near Tallman Mountain State Park covers a wide stretch of land. Can Verizon be a bit more specific?" he asked.

"According to them, their cell towers up there are too far apart to have them pinpoint a more precise location. The best they can offer is that the call originated within a ten mile radius of Piermont."

"That's a start," said Margaret.

Driscoll's iPhone vibrated in his pocket. *Was the madman calling again?* he wondered.

"Good evening, Lieutenant," the voice sounded. "This is Melanie Anderson from Mercer Hospital. I hope you remember me."

Driscoll raised a finger. Both Thomlinson and Aligante read that as meaning the call was significant.

"Of course, I remember you, Melanie. We discussed an article you'd written about one of your patients. An Adrian Strayer, as I recall."

"That's right. You've got a good memory. I'm calling because something happened earlier this evening involving Adrian that I thought you should be made aware of."

Driscoll looked to his two investigators and shrugged. "What happened with Adrian?" he asked Doctor Anderson.

"Quite a bit, and I'm not sure what to make of it. After dinner, Adrian made his way to the Communal Area where he routinely sits alone and stares at the TV. It seems to soothe him. But tonight he was anything but soothed. ABC6 News was on. When the sketch of the man you're pursuing hit the screen Adrian panicked."

The Lieutenant gave his team a thumbs up, though his focus remained on the call. "What do you mean by panicked?" he asked.

"His anxiety level skyrocketed. After curling himself into a ball under a table he pointed to the TV and shouted: "'I'm sorry. I'm sorry. I didn't mean to do it. Please go away! Please go away! I didn't mean to do it. I didn't!'"

"'That face on the screen. It scares you?' I asked him.

'It's Tilden. Make him go away. Make him go away,' he hollered.

"To calm him down, I turned off the television."

Tilden? Hadn't Moira spotted that name on Harold MacKillop's phone? Driscoll pondered. "Melanie, I'd like to speak with Adrian in person. Would that be possible?"

"Yes, it would. It's best to speak with him with me present. Tomorrow after lunch
would work. Say, 2 o'clock?"

"That'd be perfect. I'll see you then," Driscoll said, ending the call.

The Lieutenant looked to Margaret and Thomlinson. Having heard only half the conversation their faces depicted a mix of curiosity and confusion. Without explaining, he picked up the phone, and called the therapist back.

"Doctor Anderson speaking."

"Melanie, it's me, again. Has Adrian ever used the name Tilden before tonight?"

"Not to me."

"What do you make of it?"

"I'm not sure. There's no record of the name in his file which lists everyone he's had contact with while he's been here. For him to blurt out the name, I suspect Tilden is real. Not imagined. And is someone he knows. Or knew."

"You told me he's been confined to the hospital for over twenty years, correct?

"That's right."

"The face in the sketch we believe is of a man in his forties. If Adrian had seen him in real life, it would have been when the man was in his late teens or early twenties. How could Adrian recognize him in the sketch if he hadn't seen him in over twenty years?"

"Something about the sketch transcended those years, Lieutenant. He was in panic mode."

"He said he was sorry to the face in the sketch featured on the TV, right?"

"Yes."

"OK. Got it. See you tomorrow," Driscoll said, ending the call.

Driscoll raised an eyebrow to his two associates, and bit into a chunk of his Moo Goo Gai Pan. Staring at the bite mark in the white meat of the chicken he smiled, knowingly. "Son of a bitch," he said. "It had to have been Adrian who chewed off our killer's ear."

CHAPTER SEVENTY-THREE

Tilden was tired. He'd driven for most of the night and only caught a few hours sleep at the Interstate's rest stop. With his female cargo adequately sedated again, he was sitting Buddha style on the deserted beach that served as the roadway's shoulder, watching a manic sandpiper extract lunch from the sand which had been moistened by the receding tide. The miniature crab, trapped in the bird's beak, was frantically jerking its legs in a struggle to alter its fate. Without regard for the crustacean's predicament, the piper gulped it down.

The macabre spectacle prompted Tilden to recall a televised news report out of Germany. Its subject: Armin Meiwes, 'The Master Butcher of Rotenburg'. Meiwes, a computer repair technician, had posted an ad on the internet. He was seeking a willing participant who'd agree to be eaten. Bernd Jürgen Brandes volunteered to be the entrée. Tilden remembered something about Brandes' raw penis being too chewy for Armin's taste, prompting him to fry it in a pan with a chunk of Bernd's belly fat. Tilden had been awestruck by Meiwes' confession where he claimed he had consumed Brandes to acquire a new identity. To prove his point, Meiwes argued at trial that his English improved greatly after eating Brandes, who was fluent in that language.

Watching the piper devour another crab, Tilden wondered if the bird had acquired the crab's identity. Or was that only a human phenomena? *Hmmmm....,* he pondered, giving it more thought. *Had JFK nibbled on the unctuous body of Marilyn Monroe after her titillating rendition of 'Happy Birthday, Mister President', would we have had the first transgender in the Oval Office? More importantly, would I become female if I feasted on my captive's breasts?*

Raising his hands over his head, like Moses parting the Red Sea, Tilden rushed the incoming waves. With a beatific smile distorting his pursed lips, he hollered: "Behold all ye children of men. I shall be born again!"

CHAPTER SEVENTY-FOUR

"Adrian, today's your lucky day," Doctor Melanie Anderson said as she entered her patient's room with Driscoll.

Though it was the middle of the day the shades were pulled down, tightly. The only light in the room came through the open door from the hall.

"Is it my birthday?" Adrian asked, from his seated position on the bed.

"No. Better."

"What could be better than my birthday?" Adrian asked, looking baffled. "Is it Christmas?"

"No. It's just Tuesday. But a special Tuesday for you."

A curious stare was Adrian's reply.

"This gentleman here knows you had a bad night and has come to make you feel safe," the therapist explained.

Adrian's eyes studied the Lieutenant from head to foot. "How ya gonna make me feel safe?" he asked, staring into the Lieutenant's eyes.

Though Driscoll was in the presence of a full grown man, Adrian's extremely forlorn look depicted him as the child he was.

"I lock up bad people, Adrian. That's how I can make you feel safe," the Lieutenant explained.

"Policemen lock up bad people. Are you a policeman?" the man-child asked, rocking to and fro in the center of the mattress.

Driscoll nodded and flashed his Department ID and his Lieutenant's shield.

The action halted Adrian's rocking motion. "L I E U T E N A N T," Adrian recited, dabbing each letter emblazoned on Driscoll's badge. "Did you pick those letters?" he asked, his head tilted.

"I did."

"You must be the boss if they let you pick your own letters. You got a gun?"

"I do."

"Can I see it?"

"Sure. But no touching." Driscoll pulled back the right side of his jacket revealing his holstered Glock 26 pistol.

"Wow! How many bullets in that?"

"Eleven."

"Holy moly. That's a lot o' bangs."

"Adrian, like I said before, I brought Lieutenant Driscoll here to make you feel safe," Melanie Anderson reiterated, taking a seat on the bed beside her patient.

"Really?

"Yes. He's after Tilden," she added, hoping the mention of the suspect's name wouldn't reignite his trauma.

"Holy cow. He was just on TV. Did you see him, Lieutenant?"

The therapist let loose a sigh of relief.

"I did see him," Driscoll said. "That's why I'm here. I'm hoping you can help me catch him."

"I can try. He's after me, 'cause I bit off his ear."

"You did? Why?

"'cause he took my bubblegum."

"He's got some nerve," Driscoll said.

"I know. It wasn't his bubblegum."

"What did you do with his ear?"

"His ear?"

"Yes, Tilden's ear?"

"I swallowed it."

CHAPTER SEVENTY-FIVE

Karl Lindstrum held tightly to his young daughter's hand as the two made their way to the African Alley exhibit inside the Utica Zoo where they could view the lions in a naturalistic setting.

"That big one looks dead, Daddy. Did a hunter shoot him?"

"No, sweetheart, Leo's fear of being shot by a hunter is far behind him. He's just taking a nap."

"How do you know his name is Leo?"

Lindstrum, who was an adjunct professor at Cazenovia College, stifled a laugh. Instead of boring Brianne by explaining the origin of the big cat's etymological name, Panthera leo, he opted, instead, on an explanation a six-year-old would grasp.

"Leo is the lion you see at the beginning of The Wizard of Oz," he said, referencing MGM's famed mascot whose animated growl introduced the film.

"Daddy, you're fibbing."

"Me? Tell a fib? Never." Karl Lindstrum rubbed Brianne's nose with his.

"You must be thinking of another movie, Daddy. In The Wizard of Oz you don't meet the lion until he growls at Dorothy on the yellow brick road. And his name's not Leo."

"Oh, Leo's there, alright. At the very beginning. I'll point him out the next time we watch it."

"Can we watch it tonight?"

"Sure we can, little girl. C'mon, it's time to visit the monkeys."

Brianne stopped dead in her tracks.

"What's wrong?" Lindstrum asked.

"These monkeys don't fly, do they?"

"No, Brianne, monkeys only fly in the movies."

Relieved, Brianne took hold of her father's hand. Just outside the big cats exhibit she heard a clattering sound. Distinctly metal on metal. Turning her head, she eyed the lion. He was no longer asleep, but upright, clawing at a metal gate that secured the enclosure.

"Daddy! Leo's trying to break out!" she screamed, the clattering sound growing louder. "Daddy. Daddy. Please save me," she hollered, instantly waking from her dream.

"Never gonna happen," Tilden sneered, yanking open the rusted door of the van and reaching for his captive. "We're here," he muttered. "Welcome to Saint Barnabas Academy."

CHAPTER SEVENTY-SIX

After Driscoll's illuminating chat with Adrian, he accompanied Doctor Anderson back to her office where the Lieutenant's eyes were drawn, once again, to the drawings she had Scotch taped to the wall.

"A mental patient's art is often revealing," she said, watching him scan the collage.

"How so?"

"They unknowingly leave traces of their inner self. Take for example that one," she said, pointing to a charcoal sketch near the top of the kaleidoscope of pastels. "That's 'Adrian's Masterpiece'."

Driscoll studied the drawing for a full minute, then shook his head. "Hard to tell what he drew."

"When he presented it to me I had no clue what he'd drawn. So I asked him what it was.

He told me they were his coffins."

The therapist studied Driscoll's reaction which was to study the sketch again, this time from every angle.

"Coffins? I still don't see it," Driscoll said, shaking his head. "He's got the mind of an eight-year-old, right?"

"That's correct."

"When I was eight I had a collection of toy soldiers," said Driscoll, squinting his eyes to focus on the man-child's 'masterpiece' one last time. "A collection of coffins, huh? I still don't see it and probably never will. It would make sense, though, considering the blood-letting drawing you referenced in your article I believe to be a crude embalming. Children draw what they see, right?"

"Many do."

"After witnessing Adrian's fear of retribution from someone he attacked for stealing his bubblegum I'm convinced Tilden is his brother. Could their parents have been in the funeral business?"

"We have no way of knowing."

"That's unfortunate," Driscoll said.

"What's unusual about that particular sketch is that I didn't ask him to draw anything specific. It came out of nowhere. That's why I called it his masterpiece. An unsolicited look inside his mind."

"What do you make of it?

"Only that he found inspiration in his memory."

"Could you get him to delve more into that memory?"

"I'm not sure. That one was spontaneous. But, I'll certainly try."

CHAPTER SEVENTY-SEVEN

With Brianne secured by zip ties to the radiator inside the shadowy and shuttered school dormitory he'd once called home, Tilden made his way across the grassy Commons toward the Boniface Building which housed the cafeteria. Using the pry bar end of the Econoline's lug wrench, he tore back the weathered plywood exposing the entrance. The door's rusted deadbolt quickly gave way under his forceful boot. Fanning away cob webs, he ducked inside.

The din of boisterous children stampeding down the circular staircase was merely a memory. Soothed by the eerie silence, he hurried down the steps. Hurrying past several rows of pine dining tables, he pushed open the aluminum doors and entered the boarding school's kitchen. A smirk disfigured his face as he opened the doors of the massive cabinets that lined the wall.

"They left them," he grinned, his eyes examining the arsenal of blackened cast iron pots and pans. "Ahhh, and the knives too."

CHAPTER SEVENTY-EIGHT

Adrian Strayer woke up trembling. His pajamas were drenched in sour sweat and urine. Maniacally hammering the nurse call button, he rocked to and fro on his stained bed sheets until Melissa McHale, a psychiatric nurse, entered his room.

"What's wrong?" she asked, prying the medical call pendant from his clawing grip.

"He's inside my head," he screamed.

"Who is?"

"Him," Adrian whined, still rocking.

"Him?"

"Yes. Please make him leave."

"I will, Adrian. But first I need to clean you up. I'll be right back."

"Where're you going?"

"I need to change the sheets. They're wet."

"I didn't wet the bed. Really, I didn't."

The nurse did an about face and left.

Who the hell was that? Adrian wondered.

When Melissa returned she was holding clean sheets and a laundered hospital gown.

"Adrian. I'd like you to slip into this while I change the bed sheets. Can you do that for me?"

"I can," he said, his eyes following her every move as he let his soiled gown fall to the floor and knotted the ties on the clean one.

Melissa stripped her patient's bed, rolled the soiled sheets and his stained gown into a ball and placed it on the floor near the door. After making the bed, she retrieved it, ducked into the hall, opened the door to the maintenance closet and dropped the soiled sheets and gown into a bin for contaminated linen.

When she returned she found Tilden sitting in the lotus position in the center of the freshly made bed. "You're not a friend of his, are you?" he asked.

"I'm not, Adrian. I'd like you to lie back on your pillow. Can you do that for me?"

Adrian Strayer did as he was instructed. "Who are you, really?" he asked.

"I'm Melissa."

"Melissa?"

"Melissa McHale. See?" She showed him her hospital ID.

"I'm Adrian," he muttered, his finger underlining her embossed name.

The nurse smiled, and helped Adrian maneuver his body under the top sheet. That task completed, she covered him with a blanket. "You just had a bad dream, Adrian. That's all it was. How are you feeling now?"

"Still scared. But I got a plan." Adrian narrowed his eyes and scanned the room. "Can you keep a secret?"

"Absolutely."

"I got a friend who's a cop," he announced, his voice booming.

"No way."

"He's a got a gun too. With eleven bullets!"

"Wow," the nurse said, lowering the temperature on the room's thermostat, forcing the air conditioning to kick in. The circulated air would further sanitize the room.

"He's the boss. My cop friend," Adrian continued. "They let him pick his own letters."

"Letters?"

"On his badge. L I E U T E N A N T."

"So what's the plan?" she asked, sliding a second pillow under his head.

"Plan?"

"You said you had a plan."

"I don't really. I just said I did so he'd hear me," he whispered.

"He's still here?"

Adrian exhaled deeply and nodded.

"How 'bout I sit with you, Adrian? Would you like that?"

"Yeah."

"Then that's what I'll do," Melissa McHale said, positioning a chair beside the bed and taking hold of Adrian Strayer's hand.

CHAPTER SEVENTY-NINE

"Melissa told me you had a bad dream last night," Doctor Melanie Andersen said, stroking Adrian's arm as he crouched like a twisted embryo under a mountain of sheets.

"It was no dream."

"Oh, I thought it was a dream."

Adrian's eyes darted around the room. His hands were shaking and it looked as though he were about to cry.

"I'm not gonna sleep ever again. And, I'm gonna keep the lights on."

"Why would you not sleep? You need your rest."

"He doesn't sleep either."

"Him, again, huh?"

"Yeah. He never liked the light."

The therapist raised the shades, letting sunlight fill the room. "It's noon now, Adrian. It's when the sun is brightest. If he doesn't like light this may scare him off."

Adrian nodded in agreement. His hands stopped trembling.

"I have a surprise for you," Melanie Andersen said, studying his eyes.

"New LEGOs?"

"Better than LEGOs. Lieutenant Driscoll's here," she told him.

"Really?" In an instant, his expression went from tearful to astonished.

"Yep. He told you he was looking to catch the man whose face was featured on TV, right?"

"That's right. He's after Tilden."

"He's the one who scared you in your dream. Right, Adrian?"

Adrian didn't respond. *Tilden could be hiding under the bed,* he reasoned.

"He's the one, right?" Andersen whispered.

"Yes," he silently mouthed. Head down. Chin to his chest.

"That's why you had the nightmare. You're starting to remember him." Andersen took hold of her patient's hands, a gesture that would let him know he's not alone as he faced the trauma that often accompanied remembering.

Adrian raised his head. "I'm remembering everything."

"I thought you might. I called Lieutenant Driscoll and told him you had another bad night. He dropped everything and drove down from New York to make sure you're ok."

"Really?"

A smile creased the man-child's face.

"He's parking his car now. Should be joining us in a minute or two," she said, squeezing his hands tightly.

"It's time he knows about Mother and what she did."

Adrian was still whispering. His eyes began scanning the room again.

"Whose mother?" Adelman asked.

"Mine," he said, his blank stare now on his therapist. "You got any bubblegum?"

"I'm all out."

"Me too. Tilden stole it." Adrian eyed Driscoll as he entered the room. "I hope you brought gum," he told the Lieutenant..

"Maybe. Let me check." Driscoll rummaged through his pockets. "No gum. How 'bout a Life Saver?"

"Only if it's red?"

"Yep, but I've got only one of those."

"You're out of luck, Melanie," said Adrian, breaking free from his therapist's grip to catch the Life Saver Driscoll had tossed him.

"I'll survive," Andersen said, conscious of what the Lieutenant's tossing of a life saver to someone in need of rescue symbolized.

"I hear you had a tough night, Adrian?" Driscoll said, placing the back of a chair against Adrian's bed and straddling it. Another action the therapist read as him building a fortress around her patient. She wondered if the Lieutenant was aware of his unspoken and subtle protectiveness.

"Mother was in my dream too," he announced solemnly. "She's afraid I'll tell."

"Tell what?"

"Everything."

Doctor Melanie Andersen glanced at Driscoll, then emptied a carton of soft pastels onto the small pine table adjacent to Adrian's bed. "There's plenty of paper, here, Adrian. We'll protect you from Mother and Tilden. How 'bout you draw?"

Tentatively, Adrian picked up a soft pastel. Then froze. After staring for close to a minute at the blank sheet of canvas paper, a few strokes appeared on its whitewashed surface. A contour was forming. It became a face with dreamy eyes and a delicate mouth.

"This portrait is beautiful. Who is this?" the Lieutenant asked.

"Mother."

"She has beautiful eyes."

"Not anymore. I hope she's burning in hell." Adrian shivered as if a gust of chilled air had enveloped him.

"How 'bout you draw Tilden now," the therapist urged.

"I can't..." Adrian moaned, his face distorted.

"Why? Why can't you?"

"He's right here. He's standing over me," he whispered, his quivering hand with his thumb extended pointed over his right shoulder.

"I'm here to protect you," Driscoll said.

"Did you bring your gun?"

"I've got in my pocket. It's loaded and cocked. With a bullet in its chamber."

Adrian slid the pastel across a second sheet of canvas paper. A few strokes later a face emerged. Designing the ear, Adrian stopped. His body then froze like a corpse in full rigor.

"Adrian. Adrian," Melanie shouted grabbing hold of his shoulders. "Adrian. Come back. Come back."

"My God, have we lost him?" Driscoll asked, frantically.

"I don't know. He's gone into catatonic shock. He could stay that way for….."

"Tilden, you stole my bubblegum!" Adrian shouted.

"Tilden's your brother, isn't he?" Driscoll asked. "You lived with him, right?"

"Yeah. But not after Mother threw me out."

"Where did you and Tilden live?"

"He wants to know, Tilden. And I'm gonna tell. Then he's gonna find you," he hollered.

"May I ask you some questions?" the Lieutenant asked.

Adrian nodded.

"What do you…."

"Ssshhh… he's watching," Adrian whispered, cutting off the Lieutenant.

"Who's watching?"

"Him," Adrian said, pointing to an apparition seen by his eyes only.

"Tilden?" Driscoll asked.

Adrian stared straight ahead and said nothing.

"He knows I'm here to protect you, Adrian. It's Tilden, yes?"

The boy-man nodded. "He doesn't want me to tell."

"What doesn't he want you to tell?"

"Where the house is," he said, eyeing the apparition.

"Will Tilden see what you draw?" the therapist asked.

"Not if I hunch over it like this," Adrian whispered, as he began to sketch.

"He's drawing willow trees," the therapist said to Driscoll. "He's drawn them before."

"Those sure are beautiful willows," said the Lieutenant. "You certainly draw them well, Adrian. Are they your favorite?"

"Yes. Tilden never liked them," he answered in a hushed tone.

"Why not?"

"They touched the ground whenever it rained. They shouldn't touch the ground, Tilden said. They should stand up straight so the house wouldn't get wet. Tilden always said they're supposed to be umbrellas, not brooms."

Driscoll looked to the therapist.

"Yes, Adrian, trees are nature's umbrellas. But sometimes it's ok for houses to get wet. The rain washes the house," Adelman told him.

"There were lots of willow trees close to your house, weren't there, Adrian?" Driscoll asked.

Adrian nodded.

"What else can you tell me about the house?"

"I liked it when the trees leaned over. Yes, I did, Tilden," he hollered as though his unseen brother had objected.

"Why?"

"It was easier to see the bell. It reminded me to pray."

Driscoll looked puzzled. "A bell reminded you to pray?" he asked.

"Yes. The bell on the church."

"According to Adrian, there was a bell atop his church," the therapist explained. "He had drawn it for me once. I'd asked him if his circled 'x' in the center of the steeple was a cross. He shook his head. When I pushed a bit he'd said "it's not a cross, Melanie. The bell's cracked, that's what the 'x' means."

"Where was the church?" Driscoll asked.

Adrian's eyes widened. Fear marked his face.

"Tilden, stop scaring your brother. Let him talk," Driscoll ordered.

"He's got a gun, Tilden. And it's loaded," Adrian said, smiling.

"So, where was the church?"

"On Sycamore Street," Adrian said.

"Now we're getting somewhere," the Lieutenant said to the therapist. "Was that near your house?"

"Two blocks over. First Maple. Then Sycamore."

"I see," Driscoll said. "Sounds like they named the streets after trees."

"Willow Lane."

"Willow Lane, huh? Is that the street you lived on, Adrian."

"Yep."

Doctor Melanie Anderson was astounded.

"Stop, Tilden, stop it!" Adrian hollered, waving his arms in front of his face as if warding off an imagined assault.

Driscoll unpocketed his cellular. "Thomlinson, this is Lieutenant Driscoll," he shouted into his phone. "I need you to go and make an arrest. The suspect may be armed and dangerous. Any resistance. Shoot him."

"It would help if I had an address," Thomlinson said, not sure where the Lieutenant was going with this but wasn't about to ask.

"You'll hear it from the victim himself," Driscoll said handing Adrian the phone.

Adrian froze.

"I'll need an address," Thomlinson said.

"You have to tell him," Driscoll urged.

"An address, please," Thomlinson repeated.

"Go ahead, Adrian," Melanie pressed.

"42 Willow Lane," Adrian stammered.

"What town?"

"Piermont. Piermont, New York," he muttered.

"We're on it," the detective said, ending the call.

As Adrian collapsed on the bed, the Lieutenant placed his hand on his shoulder. "Back off, Tilden. Your brother's under my protection now!" he hollered at the invisible spectral presence in the room.

CHAPTER EIGHTY

Angry clusters of storm clouds were collecting in the distance. As Driscoll floored the accelerator on the Impala, jetting the police cruiser past the Ardsley exit on the New York State Thruway, a splintered streak of white light tore through the lackluster sky. An eerie silence followed until, without warning, torrents of rain pelted the metallic roof of the Department vehicle. Visibility instantly reduced, traffic slowed to a crawl in the hazy glow of brake lights.

"This is one helluva storm," Thomlinson muttered, nervously dragging on his Juul electronic cigarette.

"There enough nicotine in that sucking stick to keep you from getting all panicky on me?"

"Nicotine's my friend. She's got me through a lot. I'm just not a fan of sudden storms."

"Speaking of friends, how's your breakup with booze going? That acupuncturist helping you keep your distance?"

"In more ways than one," Thomlinson replied. "No more thirteen stepping for me."

Though Driscoll was familiar with what AA called the twelve step program he hadn't a clue what "thirteen stepping" meant. Pleased that Cedric was happy with his progress, he chose not to ask what the term stood for.

As quickly as the rain had started, it stopped.

Fifteen minutes later, when the Lieutenant veered the Chevy into the driveway of 42 Willow Lane, sunshine was raining down on a canopy of American sycamores that shaded the three-story Victorian. Alongside it, an army of local police personnel stood at the ready.

A uniformed officer sporting a biker's mustache approached Driscoll and Thomlinson as they stepped out of the cruiser. "Which one of you is Lieutenant Driscoll?" he asked.

"That'd be me. This is Detective Thomlinson."

"I'm Sergeant Claude Havermeyer. I head up the crime scene unit at Piermont PD. We were dispatched to lend a hand. There's been no incident recorded at this museum. What is it we're looking for?"

"Museum?" Driscoll asked, looking puzzled.

"Well, it hasn't functioned as one in several years. But, that's what it is."

"What type of museum?" Thomlinson asked, eyeing the century-old residential structure.

"The family that lived here ran it as a business. Quite lucrative from what I'm told. We're going back a good number of years. After the parents died, the one remaining son, Tilden Quinn, used his inheritance to convert the home to a funerary museum to showcase his family's decades-long service to the community. They were undertakers."

CHAPTER EIGHTY-ONE

The 18-Gauge stainless steel table was no match for Tilden's Victorian Era cold air ice casket with its adjustable headrest and nickel-finished Kant slip triceps clamps. He regretted having to leave that particular "workbench" behind. The industrial strength food preparation table and the duct tape he'd pilfered from the school janitor's supply closet would have to do. He wondered how Armin Meiwes, 'The Master Butcher of Rotenburg', had prepped Bernd Jürgen, his willing partner in cannibalism, before cooking him. Mindful of Meiwes' confession where he claimed he had consumed Brandes to acquire a new identity, Tilden stared down into Brianne's terrified eyes, then tightly fastened the grey tape around her lips, drawing blood from her pallid skin. Scoping her securely fastened form, he wondered what each segment of her body would taste like. The thought brought to mind a poster that hung inside a salumeria in downtown Piermont where Mother shopped. Whenever he, as a young boy, accompanied her, the shop owner would reward him with a slice of mortadella. He liked how the white fatty morsels inside the Italian sausage melted in his mouth. The poster featured an elementary drawing of a steer. The animal's body was sectioned, depicting the choicest cuts of beef. *Sirloin* and *top sirloin* where themed in red while lesser cuts, like *shank* and *chuck,* were highlighted in gray.

Tilden eyed the oversized wall oven. Opening it, he rubbed a finger across its blackened walls. Returning to his captive, he delineated her body with soot to replicate the sectioned steer. Satisfied with his handiwork, he palpated her calves, inner thighs and breasts, feeling exhilarated by the variety of textures her body offered. He sniffed her arm pits, inebriated by the scent of fear her sweat emitted. He inhaled the musty mineral aroma of her vulva; burrowing his nose deep inside her rosy-colored fissure.

"Such a thrill it will be to roast you," he whispered, before inserting his pointed tongue inside her ear, sampling the honey in its wax. "Let's begin," he panted, then quickly bolted upright as though he'd seen something he'd overlooked.

"My, oh my. That's some bush you've grown. Not a fan of shaving, eh? Well, I'm not into smoked jerky," he grunted, tugging on her pubic hair. "And look at that hair on your head. No. No. No. It's plucking time, Missy. And since, I'm without a razor. This will hafta'do," he said, brandishing a meat cleaver.

Running his fingers through her opulent main of auburn hair, Tilden became pensive. "It'd be a shame to discard these luxurious locks. Tell you what. I'll wear them as a wig in your memory," he said, beginning the tonsure.

While shaving her pudenda, he blew the brittle cuttings into the air, accidently inhaling some, irritating his trachea. Coughing spastically, he forced the tiny curls of hair out of his lungs.

"This is worse than mesothelioma. I'll bet you don't know what that is, do you, Missy? Hell, I may need a lawyer. I can see the headlines now. *Class Action Lawsuit Filed By Piermont Man For Exposure To Asbestos-like Pubic Hair.*"

"Alright, it's time to mix the spices. Oh. Wait. What kind of a chef am I?" he whined, taking hold of a paring knife to shear off Brianne's eyebrows. "Now, don't you blink. Those lashes have to go, too," he added, scraping them away.

Satisfied with his handiwork, he took hold of a humungous bowl and mixed the provisions he'd scattered across the butcher block, ingredients he'd procured an hour earlier at the Gourmet Specialty Shop in Saugerties.

The blend of paprika, nutmeg, cumin, dried garlic flakes, saffron, rosemary, Worcestershire sauce, Malabar black pepper, and sage was pungent, fragrantly lacing the air in the stale kitchen. Adding a cup of olive oil, soy sauce, and Dijon mustard he produced an awesome marinade.

"Time for your rub," he said, eyeing Brianne. "It may burn a bit, but, hey, I love the smell of napalm in the morning. Wait a minute. That's what's missing! Damn it! We need the soundtrack from Apocalypse Now!" Opening YouTube on his iPhone, he blasted the first chords of Wagner's Ride of the Valkyries. Spreading wide his arms, he welcomed the fluttering descent of those winged angels who would carry him to his promised Valhalla.

As the music stopped, Tilden's euphoria ended as well; delivering him back to his culinary prepping. "Yep, this rub is gonna deliver one helluva burn," he muttered, before using his fingers to knead the spices against her shamelessly protruding labia. Deaf to her muted screams, he pummeled her breasts and abdomen with the grainy spices. "This is a full service spa, young lady," he snickered, coating the soles of her feet with the coarse mix.

"Damn! Can you believe it? I forgot the stuffing. Now, don't you go anywhere. I'll be right back."

Brianne's scorched vulva throbbed, unleashing torrents of pain that defied description. Tilden reappeared holding a bigger mixing bowl. In his other hand was a syringe.

"I know this'll hurt like the dickens," he said. "So, I'm going to inject you with lidocaine. It'll numb you so you won't feel a thing. Wait! Why the hell would I do that? That'd interfere with the taste of the cumin. Brianne, you gotta tough it out. Let me tell you what's in the stuffing. It's got dried mushrooms, chopped onions, celery, and green pepper. With cherries. Pitted, of course. Damn! What else?" Tilden squinted his eyes. "Parsley!" he hollered. And, the pièce de fucking résistance? Lychees! Check this out," he said peeling back the lychee's course skin. "Look at that flesh, will ya. Man, that's white."

Holding the gleaming small fruit between two fingers, Tilden refocused his eyes on his captive. "Sweet to the sweet, my dear. Let the stuffing begin."

Tilden packed a flexible cloth pastry tube with his stuffing mix. Sliding his left hand between Brianne's legs, he lifted her torso just enough to enable him to insert the tip of the tube inside her rectum and give it a squeeze. "I wish I had thought of doing that to Valerie. It sure would have been fitting considering what she'd done to me," he muttered to the panic riddled woman. "Okey Dokee. That fills that one. Now on to the next hole. Oh, my. That's one helluva cave you've got there, Missy. You've been fucking a Clydesdale, haven't you? Gotta reload."

Brianne sobbed.

"And now for the other cavities," he said, inserting the nozzle into her left ear, and then the right. Both filled quickly. "We're almost done. One more to go," he sing-songed.

When he ripped off the duct tape, he encountered no resistance. The prostitute's lips were listless. Her eyes, glassy. Her mouth took the last of the stuffing.

"I'm going to shut off the lights and let you marinate. I've set the alarm for 7:00 a.m. That's roasting time."

CHAPTER EIGHTY-TWO

After Piermont PD's electronic detection system indicated 42 Willow Lane to be unoccupied, its deadbolt lock gave way under the heel of Cedric Thomlinson's boot. Its scarred entrance door then squeaked under its whining hinges, inviting Driscoll into the darkness.

"Where the fuck is the light switch?" Thomlinson groaned, his search coming up empty.

Using the Braille method, Driscoll's fingers located the misplaced control and clicked it on, forcing a timid bulb to flicker in the hallway's ceiling. He and Thomlinson moved cautiously under the hesitant light. Though on record at Piermont's Department of Buildings as a museum, the Lieutenant felt he'd stepped onto a movie set of some haunted house in a Hollywood paranormal flick.

The first floor could have passed for a residential home except for the sense of dread that permeated throughout. If this was a museum, it was of a sort Driscoll had never visited.

The living room was huge. An oversized sofa stretched the width of one wall. Driscoll noticed three depressions in the mauve texture of the fabric. Not long ago, three sitters had occupied that space, lingering long enough to affect the geography of the couch. The flooring was a hodgepodge of wooden planks. Heavily discolored and scuffed. A vast wall with a plethora of photographs caught the Lieutenant's eye. It would take an eternity to analyze the content of those vestigial images. The pictures looked archival, antique in their off-white hues. In one, an elderly man, sporting a Salvador Dali mustache, smiled sardonically. Another photo flaunted a woman with cascading hair and a glint in her eyes like that of a madam in a turn of the century New Orleans brothel. Alongside her, three boys, their identical faces ravaged by smallpox, held pear-shaped whirling tops. "*Who are these people?*" Driscoll wondered, staring at the human menagerie on display.

"Which one of you is Tilden?" Thomlinson asked the mute photo.

"Maybe he's one of these triplets," Driscoll replied.

Closed pocket doors made up the rear wall. Opening them, Driscoll and Thomlinson stepped into a formal dining room, where a large mahogany table with eight matching chairs crowded the space.

"The table's set for three. What's that about?" Driscoll pondered aloud.

The two lawmen, intent on a quick scan before the CSI team scoured the place, entered the kitchen to find three dishes in the sink. With forks and knives.

"Three on the couch. Three for lunch. Wha'd'ya make of that?" asked Thomlinson.

"Your guess is as good as mine," said Driscoll.

There was a winding staircase in the far corner that led to a backyard visible through the kitchen window. The Lieutenant watched as the team of Crime Scene Investigators set up next to a wooden shack. A pair of K9 German Shepherds were sniffing the tires on a vintage Cadillac flower car that was parked beside the shack.

"Our tip line caller mentioned an old Cadillac," Thomlinson said.

"Could be the flower car he used to transport the cross," Driscoll replied.

"The guy's hauling a cross and he stops for breakfast?"

"Bacon and eggs at Arnie's Diner. Our guy's no vegan. Here's another door," Driscoll said, opening it. "Those steps must lead to the cellar."

"That's Stephen King's territory. I hope we don't come across what they found in 'Salem's Lot," Thomlinson groaned. "You read that one?"

"I didn't. What'd they find?"

"Vampires. Asleep in coffins."

"You believe in vampires?"

"Damn right I do. I was married to one."

"The things you learn. Well, Cedric, I hope you packed a stake and a hammer 'cause we're going down."

The wood of the staircase whined under their weight as the uninvited visitors descended into the darkness. Dampness and the pungent stench of bleach assaulted their senses.

"Again with the hidden switches. Where's the one for the damn light?" Thomlinson growled, his fingers palpating the wall. "OK. I found it," he said, switching it on. A 20 watt incandescent bulb flickered, casting faint shadows on the blistered floor. "What the hell is that?" Cedric grunted, pointing at a rectangular box sitting atop a gurney.

"That's a casket."

"It'd better be empty."

"It is," Driscoll said, drawing near. It's a cold air ice casket."

"What the fuck is that?"

"I came across photos of them when I began my inquiry into embalming. In the 19th Century they used it to slow down the body's putrefaction during a viewing."

"You're saying they packed the corpse in ice."

"Exactly."

Thomlinson eyed a row of glass decanters lining a shelf. "They're filled with liquid. It's probably the embalming fluid he pumped into his victims."

"We're inside a museum, Cedric. Hell, everything about this guy is from another era. Vintage Cadillac. Years old mortuary equipment."

"Whoa! Did you hear that?" Thomlinson asked looking alarmed.

"I heard it. It's just thunder. Rain's on the way."

"Lieutenant, you'd better come out here," Sergeant Havermeyer, said grimly, poking his head inside the rear doorway.

They followed the CSI into the yard.

"The cadaver dogs led us to this," Havermeyer said, pointing to a corpse in a partially excavated grave.

"No casket," Thomlinson remarked.

Another roll of thunder warned of the incoming storm. Unpocketing his iPhone, Driscoll pulled up the local weather app. Clusters of green, yellow, and red patches signaled torrential rain was on the way.

"Sergeant, you've gotta preserve that body. There's a monsoon coming. In ten minutes this yard will be a flood zone."

"On it," said Havermeyer.

"Cedric, I can't shake the feeling we overlooked something on that wall of photos." Driscoll and Thomlinson ducked inside the house and approached the collection of pictures.

"Where do you wanna start?" Thomlinson asked.

"I haven't a clue. There's so many."

The crash of thunder directly above the town rattled the house, causing several photos to crash on the wooden floor, shattering their frames.

"I'll need a hand with these, Cedric. Watch out for the tiny slivers of glass," Driscoll warned.

Thomlinson crouched and carefully gathered the fallen photos, his eye zeroing in on one. "Wow, that's a small church. Not many parishioners would fit inside that one.

You think they built it for hobbits? Why's it surrounded by water?"

"That's gotta be the smallest church in America," Driscoll said, examining the tiny structure in the center of the photograph which featured two young boys seated on the small deck the church sat on.

"It might be the smallest church in the world," said Cedric.

"Let's ask Siri."

"You trust that talking Barbie?"

"That's a voice I'd marry."

"You're saying you'd have sex with a cyborg?"

"Mind your manners, boys," the synthetic voice responded.

"Ssshh. Once you mention her name, she hears all," Driscoll said.

"Ask her if she's got a sister."

"We need to ask her about the church. Siri?"

"How can I help you this afternoon?"

"What's the smallest church in the world?"

"OK, I found this on the web for 'What's the smallest church in the world?' Cross Island Chapel, the world's smallest church sits in the center of a pond in Oneida, New York. It's open to the public only by request. And is accessible by boat. It was built in 1989 on wooden pilings with a total floor area of just under twenty-nine square feet. There's a wooden cross embedded in a pile of rocks nearby. This non-denominational church has room for only 2 people and a minister."

"Siri, may I have a visual."

"I'll be happy to help you with that."

Within seconds, an image of a tiny white-walled chapel glimmered in the center of a lake on the Lieutenant's phone.

"Son of a gun. She's on the money." Thomlinson said, visibly impressed.

"The question is who are the kids in this framed photo?" Driscoll asked, eyeing the two pre-teen boys sitting on the pilings, their feet dangling in the water. "They're wearing matching polos. Is that a school insignia?"

"Could be. Hard to read what it says."

"Havermeyer will have the tools to ID the logo. Have him come in."

"Will do," said Thomlinson.

Driscoll removed the photo from its frame. "Damn!" he yelled as a sliver of undetected glass lacerated his finger. "Son of a bitch, you found a way to lash out at me, didn't you?" he griped, catching the icy stare from one of the boys in the photograph. "Admit it," he added, pointing his bleeding finger at the kid with the pale eyes. Flipping the picture over, he read two scribbled lines:

To my adoring sons, Tilden and Adrian...
And throughout all eternity I forgive you, you forgive me.

Driscoll recognized William Blake's verse. *What was the mystery behind these lines? And what type of parent would make such a pact?* he pondered.

"I understand you need my help," Sergeant Havermeyer said, entering the room with Thomlinson.

"Can you blow up the area of this photo with the polo shirts? I'd like to be able to read the logo," Driscoll said.

Havermeyer examined the picture. "A school insignia, would be my guess. I've got some equipment on the truck that may help. If it doesn't, I'll bring it to the lab."

Another clap of thunder shook the house, unhooking several more photos that tumbled to the floor.

"These special effects are getting to me," said Thomlinson, visibly spooked.

"Hang in there, Cedric. They're working in our favor," said Driscoll.

"The tent we'd set up over the grave was no match for the windswept rain, Lieutenant. We moved the corpse into the shed," said Havermeyer. "We're ready to move inside and turn this place inside out. Highway reports they'll be shutting down parts of 9W in fear of flooding. Were you planning on staying on site?"

"Not if we'll be stuck here indefinitely. Can you arrange to have the body transferred to NYPD's Office of the Chief Medical Examiner?"

"Will do."

"Cedric, you got your wish. We're out'a here."

CHAPTER EIGHTY-THREE

Margaret and Thomlinson exchanged looks as the Lieutenant, his desk phone's headset to his ear, was listening intently to Havermeyer's report.

"Thank you, Sergeant. Be sure to extend my appreciation to your Crime Scene team," Driscoll said ending the call.

"Well, what'd he say?" Margaret asked, motioning to the notes Driscoll had hastily jotted down.

"They removed the plumbing trap under the embalming table in the cellar. Lots of blood. Likely from those he embalmed. We'll have to await DNA analysis, but it'll likely place the victims Larry Pearsol autopsied inside that cellar. Along with the excavated body in his yard. Havermeyer's team took apart every framed photograph. Someone had scribbled a few lines of poetry on the flip side of three more photos, each addressed to Adrian and Tilden, though the pictures depicted only landscape."

Margaret was startled by the sudden change in Driscoll's facial expression. "What is it, John?"

"Luminol revealed evidence of fresh blood in a second floor bathroom at 42 Willow. Female. Between the age of eighteen and thirty," Driscoll said.

"Likely to be another victim," Thomlinson groaned.

"Or a captive. And if she's still alive, she's in the clutches of a murderous embalmer."

Driscoll's eyes narrowed as a silence settled between the three dedicated police officers. It lasted for just under a minute.

"Havermeyer had his lab run an analysis on the blood," Driscoll continued, checking his notes. "Her cortisol level is through the roof. That's indicates stress. Her magnesium level at 1.38 borders on hypomagnesemia which is minutes away from a heart attack. And if that doesn't get her, she'll die from kidney failure 'cause they're shutting down. Her blood sugar is off the charts. Her hemoglobin levels and her red cell distribution point to one thing. He's starving her. If she's still alive, she won't be for long."

"Jesus, Mary and Joseph," Margaret growled.

Driscoll's cell phone sounded. He listened. Shutting it down, he turned to his team. "That was the graphics lab where Havermeyer sent the photo of the tiny chapel. We've got a lead. The insignia on the polo the two boys were wearing reads S B A. They ran the letters through a data base of schools, summer camps, gyms, and martial art centers in and around the area. Our best bet is Saint Barnabas Academy as it's within ten miles of the small church. Margaret, check ViCAP for Henrietta Strauss, the woman who was crucified. She was a former nun charged with child abuse and manslaughter. I'm betting Tilden crossed paths with her as a young boy. The FBI data base will tell us where those crimes took place."

"Looking at it now," Margaret replied. "Strauss…. Henrietta…. Sister Agathon…. Yep. Place of occurrence…. Saint Barnabas Academy. Sconondoa, New York."

"I wanna know more about Saint Barnabas," Driscoll ordered.

"Checking…. Saint Barnabas Academy. Private school. All boys. Shuttered in 1998."

"Cedric, you still have that connection at 'Cyber Central'?"

"I do."

"Have her do a deep dive. We need it now."

Thomlinson unpocketed his phone and called Leticia in Computer Crimes. He frantically scribbled as their conversation crackled. After thanking her, he smiled at Driscoll. "DMV lists a van in the name of Tilden Quinn at the address we have for him in Piermont. A 2001 Ford Econoline. Two days ago E-Zpass placed him on Interstate 90, exiting onto Route 13, toward Sconondoa. It's a small town north-east of Oneida. And former home to Saint Barnabas Academy."

"Let's go," said Driscoll.

CHAPTER EIGHTY-FOUR

Driscoll hated heights. He was earthbound, terrestrial. Like the mythological giant Antaeus, he found strength with every step he took. Did he know his severe acrophobia likely stemmed from having witnessed his mother's leap into the path of the oncoming 10:39 from Penn Station? With a woman's life hanging by a thread three hundred miles away he shunned his fear and squeezed himself into the narrow seat of the Bell 429 twin engine helicopter. As soon as he was buckled in, the chopper's massive blades whirled, slicing the air like the rotating steel of a colossal food processor. The proximity of Thomlinson up front and Margaret at his side offered little solace against the waves of anxiety that began their assault.

"You'll be alright," Margaret whispered, placing her hand over his. "I've got an iPod in my purse. The earbuds won't drown out these noisy rotors but some Coltrane at maximum volume may be soothing."

"I'll be alright, Margaret. But, thank you," Driscoll said.

"How long will we be in the air," Margaret yelled to the pilot in the seat ahead of her.

"Ninety minutes," came the reply.

"Any chance of cutting that down?"

"The wind's not in our favor."

An hour and a half later, clusters of light poked through the dusk as the copter began its bumpy descent.

"What the hell is that?" Thomlinson hollered, eyes fixed on a raging inferno.

"It's half past five. A little early for a bonfire," Margaret reasoned.

"You've got that right, Sergeant," yelled the pilot. "That's our destination. Saint Barnabas Academy. It's on fire."

CHAPTER EIGHTY-FIVE

Acrid smoke singed Driscoll's sinuses as he climbed out of the helicopter the pilot had set down on the Academy's abandoned football field. Using the collar of his Burberry overcoat, he shielded his face against the twister of dust and smoke the chopper's rotors had set in motion. Hunched below the gyrating blades, he sprinted clear of the vortex.

A scene of sound and fury greeted the Lieutenant as he and his team approached the roaring blaze, where youthful volunteer firefighters were directing high velocity water on the scorched and collapsing walls of a fully engulfed building.

"What happened here?" Driscoll shouted to the battalion chief who looked like he might still be in high school.

"Who the hell knows. We got the call thirty minutes ago," the young man responded.

A man with a generous paunch and a graying handlebar mustache nonchalantly approached. "Lieutenant Driscoll, right?"

"That'd be me."

"I'm Sheriff Garrison. I was dispatched from County to meet and assist. Who knew we'd be staring down a fire?"

"Any idea how it started?"

"Too early to say. Come with me. There's something you'll need to see," he said, leading the NYPD threesome toward his cruiser.

"Where's he taking us?" Margaret whispered.

"To clarity, I hope," said Driscoll.

With a click of his key fob, Garrison opened his Crown Victoria's trunk, exposing an electronic device the size of a hand drill. It featured a viewing screen. "This here's a thermal imaging sensor, Lieutenant. It sees through walls. I imagine FDNY uses a unit like this to search for survivors. Up in these parts, the volunteer units depend on us, the police on scene. We got a look inside that building. Lemme play it back for ya'. See. That's a kitchen in the basement. With one hell of an oven. And that, my friend, is a body. Inside that oven."

"Whoa!" Thomlinson cried out.

"Jesus Christ! Who stuffs a body in an oven?" Margaret shouted. "You sure that sensor's working right?"

"'fraid so."

The youthful battalion chief approached. "Fire's out, Sheriff. The fire marshal's going in."

"Tell him he'll have company," Driscoll said.

CHAPTER EIGHTY-SIX

They weren't Prada, but Margaret's pumps cost her three-hundred dollars, on sale, and she wasn't about to stain them traipsing through the sooty marsh that now carpeted the oak flooring of the shuttered school for boys. Shooting the freckle-faced firefighter a smile, she slid her manicured toes inside his Wolverine Raider boots. "Christian Louboutin wouldn't approve of these, so we'll keep it our secret. OK?"

"You're dating a Frenchman?"

"No. He's a fashion designer."

"Yeah, but you're rockin' those Wolverine boots like Paul Newman."

"Paul Newman, the actor?"

"You didn't see him as Governor Earl K. Long in the movie, Blaze?"

"I missed that one."

"He never climbed into bed without his boots on. You wanna know why?" he asked, grinning.

"Yes and no. But, not today." Avoiding the glint in his eye, she feigned a smile as he draped her body in his bulky Lakeland fire protective turnout coat.

"Gloves?" he asked.

"Will they fit me?"

"One size fits all."

"Then, yes."

They didn't. Margaret shot the young fire fighter a glare, her hands swimming inside the oversized mitts.

Kicking off their dress shoes, Driscoll and Thomlinson also stepped into borrowed boots and gear.

Looking like they'd been cast in a remake of *The Towering Inferno,* Driscoll and his team adjusted the straps on their compressed air breathing apparatuses and followed Sheriff Garrison, the fire marshal, and three firefighters into the charred remains of the smoking edifice.

As he trudged across the water logged ground floor, the Lieutenant felt as though he were crossing a marshland in a black and white movie as everything was covered in dark gray ash. Acidic smoke hung in the air, and despite his breathing gear, his nasal passages burned.

The trek down the rusted circular staircase was risky. Though it was made of iron, it whined under the human weight of the investigators. Once inside the boarding school's kitchen, the three firefighters led the way, raking through layered ash, using handheld extinguishers to put out the still glowing embers.

"Gas service to this building's been shut down for years," said the fire marshal, using the toe of his boot to stir the burnt debris below the wall oven. "I'd say this is where the fire started. You see that?" he asked, pointing to the charred remains of a large metal canister.

"Looks like a propane tank," the Lieutenant remarked.

"Correct. Someone tried to jimmy rig it to the natural gas line at the base of the oven. And that went sideways in a hurry."

Driscoll had a pretty good idea who that someone was and wondered if he was injured in the fire.

His thought was cut short, eclipsed by horror. Sheriff Garrison had pried open the oven's door.

CHAPTER EIGHTY-SEVEN

The whiskey inside his glass was the focus of Driscoll's attention. The Lieutenant had selected the Black Hawk Inn, a tavern of great solemnity and calm where he and Margaret could escape the horror of their find.

Two torchieres cast a soft light on the pub's mahogany paneling, highlighting the iridescence of a simple landscape painting. The booth, illuminated by the glow of a candle, provided an intimate privacy for their bereavement.

"For God's sake. What kind of soul would entertain the broiling of another human?" Margaret asked, her eyes lost in a haze.

"Right there is evidence that demons walk this earth," Driscoll said.

"And we're the demon slayers?"

"You're damn right we are."

"Was she to be his dinner," Margaret asked, incredulously.

"He stuffed her like a Thanksgiving turkey. I'd say that was the plan."

"We should be grateful for the fire, then. But, why feast on another human being?"

"I have an answer but you're not gonna like it," said Driscoll.

"Like it or not, I'm listening," said Margaret, downing what was left in her glass.

"I recall a class in Primitive Anthropology in college. Our teacher had us read this essay detailing the field work of a team of social scientists in the Trobriand Islands, off the coast of New Guinea. The natives, pressured to give up their primitive customs, reluctantly accepted the white man's way of life. Shortly after their conversion, though, a tribal chief complained about having to bury his daughter. 'The worms will eat her. That's not right. It'd be better if I ate her. That way she'd live on inside me,' he argued."

"Well, that's a morsel of information I could've done without." Margaret tapped her glass to catch the waiter's eye. "Just bring the bottle," she said.

"It makes you wonder who's right, Margaret. The natives or us."

"You're not defending our killer, are ya'?"

"Hell no. Just entertaining a possible motive that may help us catch the bastard."

CHAPTER EIGHTY-EIGHT

No sooner had Sister Antonia Fielding used her hands-free cell phone to alert the authorities to what she had figured was an expansive brush fire twenty yards off the road she was on, was she forced to slam on the brakes of the school bus to avoid striking the man illuminated by its headlights. He was running in the center of the road looking like a human torch.

"We gotta do something! He's on fire!" an adolescent girl screamed just as Tilden dashed off the paved roadway and into the woods.

When the nun veered to a stop on the road's shoulder, a dozen students from Saint Stanislaus Academy for Girls spilled out of the bus and began running after the candle on the run.

"He's heading for the pond," one of the girls hollered.

Seconds later, Tilden dove into the shallow water, extinguishing the flames. Emerging from the pond, he was stunned to find he had an audience. There stood a nun, dressed in religious garb, alongside a dozen of girls clad in Catholic School uniforms. They all looked frightened.

"Are you OK, Mister?" one of the girls cried out.

"I am now. Thank you. Am I in heaven? You girls look like angels. And you, Sister. Are you a saint?"

"I'm just one of the brides of Christ," she answered.

"Sister, I think we witnessed a miracle," said one of the girls.

"God gives us miracles every day."

"Amen to that," Tilden said wincing in pain, afraid to touch his scorched forehead.

"Oh my! That must hurt like the dickens," the nun said. "You'll need some aloe and maybe some bacitracin for that."

"You're probably right," Tilden said.

"My dad's pharmacy is about eight miles down the road. We could take him there, Sister. I'm sure my father would be happy to treat him," one of the girls offered prompting Tilden to shoot the cherubic-faced brunette a smile.

The students surrounded Tilden, embraced his water soaked body with loving arms and escorted him onto the bus. Never had Tilden experienced such tender care. From a group of females, no less. *Being a victim has its rewards,* he said to himself as he boarded. *Perhaps I'll play the victim from here on out.*

"It's a miracle you're alive," said Sister Antonia, as Tilden settled into his seat beside a blushing freckle-faced teen. "You wondered if you were in heaven. Well, this bus may not be paradise but you did just escape the fires of hell. Baptized in the holy water of that pond."

"Reborn am I," said Tilden. "Praise the Lord."

"Children, I think it's time for a prayer," the nun announced. "Bridgette, would you kindly lead us?"

The doe-eyed red-head lowered her childlike face and began: "Dear Lord in heaven above, we thank you for your blessings bestowed on this man. We thank you for soothing his wounds with the holy waters of your compassion and mercy. Amen."

"Amen," said Tilden.

Sister Antonia engaged the gears of the bus, and proceeded down the road. Ten minutes later, they arrived in Everley, a small rural town. The nun parked in front of a rustic looking shop, featuring a modest sign depicting a pharmaceutical pestle and mortar. The name 'Johnson's Pharmacy' was stenciled in gilded paint below the apothecary's insignia.

"I'll be right back," Charlotte Johnson announced as she rushed off the bus.

A few minutes later she returned with a pudgy man sporting an apron and a whitening beard.

"What have we here?" the jovial pharmacist asked.

"This poor man was burnt. And was saved. Can you tend to his wounds?" Sister Antonia asked.

"Let's have a look."

The pharmacologist approached Tilden. After gingerly examining his forehead he asked how it happened.

"Mother and I were preparing dinner when the oven sorta' backfired ," Tilden said, studying the druggist's face for any sign of suspicion.

"Oh, my! Was your mother hurt, too?"

"No. I threw myself over her."

"What a courageous thing to do," Sister Antonia said, smiling at Tilden.

"That's what good sons do, isn't it?" asked Tilden.

"It sure is," said the pharmacist. "I have the perfect ointment for your burnt forehead. Just give me a minute and I'll be back with the medicine."

Tilden feigned a smile as he watched the pharmacist step off the bus and hurry inside his store.

"Your mother is blessed to have a son like you," said the nun. "We never did get your name. What is it?"

"Innocent."

"Oh, my!" echoed an excited voice from the rear of the bus. "We were just studying Pope Innocent III."

"That's a holy name, son. Your parents christened you well," said Sister Antonia.

The pharmacist returned with the tube of ointment and snapped on a pair of latex gloves. "I'm sorry, this is gonna sting a bit," he said, before spreading the medication on Tilden's scorched skin.

"He's the anointed one now, Sister," Charlotte Johnson proudly announced.

"Just like the Pope he was named after," Sister Antonia proclaimed.

"I feel better already," said Tilden. "Such a compassionate group of girls you've got here, Sister. You've taught them well."

Tilden's gaze travelled the length of the bus, briefly staring into the eyes of each and every one of the girls.

"Yes, I'd like to think I taught them well. I'm the Lord's instrument," said the nun.

"You're much too modest, Sister. Take credit where credit is due. You're nothing like the nun I knew," Tilden growled as his eyes narrowed into slits like those of a viper.

Sister Antonia was thrown by his remark and sudden change in temperament. His distorted expression chilled her. Had she encountered one of Satin's minions in disguise? "Children. Let's pray."

"Who's turn is it to lead?" Charlotte Johnson asked.

Three hands went up.

"It's my turn," Tilden said, the pupils in his eyes glistening. "Lord, keep these children under your wings. Protect them from the evil that surrounds them. Watch over the watcher at all times, lest she goes astray," he muttered, his reptilian glare fixed on the nun.

Silence filled the bus.

"Amen," said the pharmacist, unnerved by the awkward quiet.

As the sinister silence resumed, Tilden stood, stared down the nun's frightened gaze and stepped off the bus.

CHAPTER EIGHTY-NINE

"My scalded noggin connects me to the fire. I sure as hell hope that stuffed filly was burned to a crisp," Tilden's inner voice said as he continued along the meandering country road in the dark. He was amazed how familiar he was with the terrain. The last time he wandered these woods he was a twelve-year-old student at Saint Barnabas.

Tilden was furious he'd lost the chance to take on a female likeness by consuming the hooker. And though he hated to admit it, someone would inevitably recognize him. Hell, someone aboard that bus may already have. It's best he find a place to hide. And quickly.

Detouring off the country road, Tilden trampled across the rotting leaves that carpeted the ground. A discordant symphony of sound clashed in his ears as the green mist of the forest embraced him. Behind the mask of innocence and serenity, a massacre was unfolding. It was dinner time for the beasts inhabiting these woodlands and the resonance of jaws lacerating living flesh thrilled him. Evidently, it was not God who'd created this botanical garden, but some demon, carnivorous and thirsty for blood. He wasn't fooled by the semblance of harmony the clusters of birches and oaks were meant to portray. Behind that façade, horror thrived, making him feel very much at home. Surrounded by tooth and claw, he identified with the forest's soullessness.

As an owl screeched, Brianne's face filled the panorama inside the hollow of his head. Her ghostly visit disturbed him.

It was a taunt, a reminder that he'd missed the opportunity to savor her feminine flesh. Filled with regret at his lost meal, he thought of the girls on the bus. His reflection triggered an olfactory reward: the scent of grilled pubescent meat.

Tilden was certain he'd been born in the wrong era. *Gone were the antique rites of blood, where, on thousands of smoky altars, young boys and girls were roasted for the gods,* he lamented.

Lost to his thoughts, Tilden stumbled face first into a prickly hedge. In his reverie, he hadn't seen the gnarled root protruding through the ground. There were yellow berries on the shrub. Instinctively, he picked a handful and shoved them in his mouth. Their tangy taste reminded him of the lemon drops he, as a child, stole at a nearby bodega. Growing hungry, he wondered if the village diner he'd frequented as a teenager was still on Cloverdale Road. The house special was to die for. Mama Bertha's liver, sautéed in onions, with a scoop of sour cream. It wasn't what he'd planned on eating but it'd be the closest he'd get to Brianne's raspberry-colored entrails.

Grabbing hold of a fallen branch, he righted himself, and with the help of his new walking stick, trekked down the uneven path that brought him to the edge of the woods. In the distance, the façade of the town's funeral home shimmered in the moonlight, an Eden beckoning its prodigal son with open arms.

CHAPTER NINETY

"Marjorie, I'm so proud of our daughter," the pharmacist slurred as his wobbly hands brought the crystal goblet to his lips.

"Which one?" his wife asked, using a handful of Bounty paper towels to sop up the Merlot her husband had spilled on the dining room table.

Marjorie Johnson was a chubby woman with an oddly shaped face. Her chin protruded forward and one side of her thin lips curled downward. She wore no makeup.

"Which one? Charlotte, of course," the pharmacist replied.

His wife glared at him. "Naturally. She's your favorite," she said, disdain in her voice.

"You're damn right," Henry Johnson stammered. "You know what she did?"

"Another extraordinary feat, I'm sure." His wife feigned excitement.

"She redirected a school bus to help save a burn victim."

"Yay! Daddy's Wonder Woman to the rescue." With a roll of her eyes, Marjorie Johnson corked the wine bottle and yanked it off the table.

"Whoa. Where ya' goin' with my wine?"

"You've had enough," she sneered, heading into the living room.

"Charlotte? Where are you?" Henry Johnson hollered.

"She won't hear you. She's out there saving the planet," his wife's voice echoed from the adjacent room.

"You're a pistol and a half, Marjorie," he fired back.

The front door flew open and a peel of laughter announced Charlotte was home. With a cell phone glued to her ear, the sixteen-year-old strolled into the dining room, smiled at 'Daddy', then shouted: "No way I'd go out with him!" into her phone.

"Can I fix you some dinner," her mom asked, ducking her head into the dining room.

The teen gave her mother an enthusiastic thumbs-up before ending the call and tossing her phone on the table.

With her mom in the kitchen, Charlotte shot her father a mischievous grin. "How 'bout a little wine for me, Daddy? We can call it a reward for saving that guy who was on fire."

"I got no problem with that but your mother put the bottle back in the cabinet in the living room."

The girl produced an exaggerated frown.

"Here, use this to get us some," he whispered, handing her his glass. "But, be quick. Gingema will be back any minute."

"Gingema?"

"The Wicked Witch of the East."

"Ain't that the truth," Charlotte groaned, grabbing hold of her father's goblet and rushing out of the room.

When she returned wearing a wine mustache, her father quickly downed what was left in the glass and used a napkin to scrub away the tell-tale signs of his daughter's transgression.

Using her butt to push open the double swinging door between the kitchen and the dining room, Mrs. Johnson returned with a steaming bowl of chili for Charlotte. "How was school?" she asked.

"Not so good," Charlotte replied.

"Why? What happened?"

"We were in the middle of Religion class going over the wedding feast of Cana when Sister Everista asked if anyone had any questions."

"And?"

"Well, I asked if Jesus was an alcoholic."

"Why the hell would you do that?" Marjorie Johnson glared at her husband who was laughing hysterically. "You think this is funny, Henry?"

The man grinned and gave his daughter a high-five.

"I also asked if Jesus ever went to rehab?" Charlotte added.

"Oh, my God! Tell me this is a joke," her mother pleaded.

"C'mon, Mom. You know how many references there are to wine in the bible? There's the marriage at Cana. The Last Supper. There's Tirosh this, and Shekhar that. They even dipped the sponge used during the crucifixion in wine, for Chrissake!"

Henry Johnson nodded approvingly at the teen.

"There was a high regard for wine culture during those times, Charlotte. Even today, during Shabbat, everyone drinks it," her mom said.

"Cheers!" said Henry Johnson. "Let's convert."

After shutting her husband down with a defiant stare, Marjorie Johnson turned to her daughter. "I understand you helped a burn victim?"

"The guy had an odd way of showing his thanks," Charlotte griped. "He sorta told everybody on the bus that we should be careful around Sister."

"Sister Antonia?" The mom looked astonished. "That woman's a saint."

"Pain changes people, it makes them trust less, over think more, and shut people out," Henry Johnson explained.

"Wow! That's insightful," said the wife, astounded by her husband's sudden burst of sobriety.

"Charlotte! You'll wanna see this!" a voice hollered from the adjacent room.

With her parents in tow, Charlotte Johnson hurried into the living room where her older brother was curled up on the couch. The TV was on, but the telecast was frozen.

"I rolled it back to the beginning," her brother said, depressing a button on the remote to replay the news bulletin.

As the sketch of Tilden filled the TV's screen, a reporter's voice sounded: "The police are seeking your help in locating this man. He's wanted for questioning about a fire that broke out earlier today that took the life of a young woman."

CHAPTER NINETY-ONE

Tilden found it odd that the funeral home's service entrance was unlocked. He knew residents of small town America often left their windows and doors unsecured. But this house was a business. Smiling at his good fortune, he very slowly opened the steel door, making certain the hinges didn't squeak. God forbid his entry was detected by an inhabitant. It was late and he was in no mood for hostility. Ducking inside the two-story Queen Anne, he closed the door, and stood in silence.

As his eyes grew accustomed to the darkness, he let his tactile senses take in his surroundings. His feet detected the decline of a sloping floor. It probably led to the mortuary and the embalming room. Though he'd never stepped foot inside this particular dead house, judging from the overall size of the residence, he figured there'd be a large refrigerated room where corpses would be stored before prepping. He imagined there'd be a couple of stainless steel embalming tables, supported by a hydraulic pump system. They'd coast smoothly on four wheels before being locked in place with a foot brake. In an adjoining room there'd likely be an arrangement of caskets on display so the bereaved would have a choice where the departed would spend eternity.

Funeral homes have a distinct scent and this place was no different. Closing his eyes, he breathed in traces of lavender, hints of pine, and a touch of citrus. That subtle blend of pleasing fragrances had undoubtedly been infused into the funeral parlor's air filtration system. A trick of the trade. Heaven forbid a mourner should inhale the natural aroma of human putrefaction.

His senses inebriated, Tilden smiled, feeling at home in his newfound Paradiso. That is, until he heard the pump-action slide of a shotgun.

CHAPTER NINETY-TWO

Driscoll felt as though he was back inside the pine-floored corridors of his elementary school as he walked down the echoing hallway of Saint Stanislaus Academy. It was Sister Antonia's call to the tip-line at the mobile command center that brought the Lieutenant to the girl's school. He was eager to hear about the exchange she and her students had with the man whose sketch was featured on TV.

Following the nun's instructions, he knocked on the door to Room 212 at precisely 10:25, five minutes before her Civics Class would end. In attendance were all the girls who'd raced off the bus to chase Tilden, the human torch, into the woods. The nun felt the teens would feel less intimidated inside their familiar classroom when the Lieutenant questioned them about their encounter.

"Class, this is Lieutenant Driscoll from the New York City Police Department," she announced, ushering him into the room. "In Civics we often discuss the responsibilities of being good citizens. Well, today, we're going to see that in action!"

"Good morning, Lieutenant Driscoll," the chorus of teens sing-songed.

"Yesterday, as many of you are aware, thanks to last night's news bulletin, we rescued a man the police wish to speak with about a fire in the area," Sister Antonia announced. "Anything we can do to assist that effort would be commendable."

Driscoll studied the mix of excitement, boredom, and apprehension etched on the girl's faces.

"OK. I'll turn it over now to the Lieutenant who has some questions?" the nun said.

"They said on the news that somebody died in that fire," a frightened-faced teen muttered.

"Sadly, a young woman did lose her life." Driscoll said.

Someone in the back of the room inhaled deeply while another voice whispered shouted: "Oh, my God!"

"Who was she?" a doe-eyed teen asked.

"We haven't been able to identify her," the Lieutenant replied.

"Sarah's been missing for two weeks!" a voice bellowed. "Could it be her?"

"We know the victim was in her twenties," said Driscoll.

"Thank God, then! It can't be Sarah. She's only sixteen," the girl who'd asked the question responded.

"Which one of you is Charlotte," Driscoll asked, scanning their faces.

Charlotte Johnson stood.

Driscoll was disorientated. *"That face. She's the reincarnation of Nicole,"* Driscoll inwardly stuttered. It took him what seemed like a full minute to reconcile the haunting reflection of his daughter. Snapping out of his momentary gap of consciousness, he approached the girl. The nuance of an upscale perfume flooded his sinuses. Recognizing the familiar fragrance, his detective instinct kicked in. How could this high school student afford Chanel N°5? Having purchased the eau de parfum spray several years ago for his wife, he figured today's cost would be about eighty bucks. *Was there a sugar daddy in town?* He pondered, feeling unhinged by the audacious thought. *Get ahold of yourself, John,* he reprimanded himself. *The nun told me this girl's father owns the town's pharmacy. Of course that's where she got it. Not from a sugar daddy but a sweet loving Daddy, a druggist.*

I'll bet she shoplifted it! Margaret's voice echoed inside his head.

"Chanel N°5, right?" asked Driscoll.

The girl's blush surprised the Lieutenant. She drew close.

"Daddy won't miss it. Please don't tell him," she whispered in his ear.

Driscoll detected the source of the scent. She had sprayed the tender spot behind her ear. *Was she anticipating a kiss? Was there a boyfriend in Charlotte's world? Would there've been a boyfriend in Nicole's world had she not been taken from him at such a tender age?*

You're damn right she's got a boyfriend, Margaret's voice echoed. *And I'm bettin' the cheapskate stole it from her father's store to give to her as a gift. Go ahead, John, ask her.*

"Charlotte, do you have a boyfriend?" he asked, immediately regretting he'd let her mystifying resemblance to his daughter affect his professionalism.

The girl's eyes darkened. Her face turned as red as a candied apple.

"I knew it. She's doin' Doug!" a voice shouted from the other side of the room.

"Shut up, Elizabeth. Or I'll tell everybody about you and Laura!" Charlotte yelled.

Peals of laughter erupted inside the crowded classroom.

"Lieutenant, you'll have to excuse my unruly students," Sister Antonia said, glaring at the bickering teens.

"Not to worry, Sister. They're being age appropriate."

"Charlotte, we'll discuss this later," the nun said, sharply. "And Elizabeth, you'll be part of that discussion."

"How may I help you, Lieutenant?" asked Charlotte, mustering a cherubic smile.

Driscoll, amused by the girl's chameleon-like prowess, stifled a laugh. "I understand it was you who arranged to have him treated for his injuries. That was a kind gesture. You should feel proud," he said.

"The guy was on fire."

"So I've been told. Sister tells me he left the bus right after being cared for. That put him right in front of the pharmacy in Everley, correct?"

"Yep, my dad's place."

"He said a prayer before leaving," said one of the students. "Well, it wasn't really a prayer."

"What'd he say?" Driscoll asked.

"I don't remember exactly."

"He told us we should be careful around Sister," Charlotte explained.

"On fire or not, it wasn't nice of him to say such an awful thing about Sister!" a voice from the rear of the room griped.

"That's a little unusual," said Driscoll, feigning surprise.

"It sure is. Everybody knows Sister's going right to heaven when she dies," Charlotte said.

"I gotta hand it to this kid. She knows how to score brownie points when she's under the gun," Driscoll thought.

"Let's not rush my ascension," the nun said, prompting an outburst of laughter.

"Have any of you girls ever seen this man before?" Driscoll asked.

Not one of them had.

"Where'd he go when he left the bus?"

"I watched his every move," said a freckle-faced teen. "I kinda got the feeling he knew the area. I'm not sure why. It just looked like he did. But the guy was spooky. Ya' know?"

"Spooky, how?"

"Well, he walked kinda weird."

"Like a wild turkey," another voice shouted.

"Wha'd'ya mean? You saying he waddled?" Driscoll asked.

"Yep."

"Where'd he go when he got off the bus?"

"He headed toward Maple Street."

Driscoll looked to the nun. "I'm not familiar with the area," he said. "Would that be north? South?"

"That'd be west, Lieutenant," said Sister Antonia.

"What's there?"

"The Post Office and a small coffee shop. And that's it."

"Whad'ya mean 'that's it'?"

"Well, there's nothing else there. Only the woods."

CHAPTER NINETY-THREE

Emergency Service Technicians Sean Fogarty and Patricia Nielson found Walter Harriman sprawled across the concrete floor inside the service corridor of the funeral home. The elderly undertaker's head was immersed in a pool of blood.

"Thank God you two got here," Harriman moaned, his hand still clutching the mobile phone he'd unpocketed to call 911.

"Lemme have a look at that head wound," Fogarty said, kneeling beside the victim and palpating his forehead with a gloved hand.

"The son of a bitch hit me with my own gun," Harriman griped as EMT Nielson manipulated the undertaker's arms and legs looking for fractures.

"You're lucky he didn't shoot you with it," said Fogarty, applying a sterile gauze wrap over the wound.

"I figured after staring down the barrel of a 12-gauge shotgun he'd have run. But, he didn't. He wrestled it from my grip and bludgeoned me with it."

"This guy was an intruder. I'd have just shot the bastard," Fogarty said.

"The shotgun wasn't loaded," Harriman told him. "I'm a man of God. A man of peace. I figured the sight of a Winchester aimed at his head would've made him shit his pants. It didn't. And now the bastard's got my father's heirloom."

"Does he know it isn't loaded?"

"Beats the hell out of me."

"You're a lucky man," said Patricia Nielson as she carefully lifted Harriman onto the transport stretcher.

"Don't I know it. That shotgun packed one helluva punch. Knocked me off my feet! I figured I was a goner. I was sure he was gonna kill me. He gave me the oddest look when I pleaded for my life. Then he said the strangest thing. He told me he too was an embalmer. One of the best. And that he'd never snuff out another master of mummification."

"Whoa!" EMT Nielson said, her eyes widening. "You ever find out why he broke in?"

Harriman shook his bandaged head from side to side.

The sound of a police siren grew louder. Then stopped. What followed was the sound of rapid footfalls.

"Fred, you alright?" asked a worried looking Deputy Sheriff Gil Hudson, who had raced through the service entrance.

"I am, Gil. Thankfully, the guy had a soft spot for people in my line of work. What are the odds? He told me he'd been in the undertaking business. Claimed he was an embalmer."

"What kind of drugs you give this guy?" Hudson asked the EMTs. "He sounds like he's tripping."

"He was a strange looking man," Harriman added

"Strange how?"

"He looked like he'd been in a fire. His forehead was singed. A sterile wrap covered part of it. And wet clothes clung to his body."

"Walter, you're one lucky son of a bitch," the Deputy Sheriff said, comprehension marking his face. "You came face to face with a serial killer."

"What the hell are you talking about?"

"Downstate cops just put out an APB on the guy you just described."

CHAPTER NINETY-FOUR

What started as a light drizzle had turned into a torrential downpour. Tilden, in his water logged clothes, cursed the unrelenting deluge. The sun had just set and he needed a place to hide and he needed now.

I shoulda' killed him, Tilden's voiced echoed inside his head. *Why on earth did I leave him lying there? But what if the old man wasn't alone? He coulda' had a wife. A son with another gun. Anyone of them coulda' set off an alarm. The odds were against me. I had to get outa' there fast.*

After shutting down the voice inside his head Tilden trudged forward through what was now an annoyingly active rainforest. He recalled a vehicular service road that ran through it. And hoped it still did. Drenched and tired, he found it. Falling to his knees, he stared through the downpour and prayed a vehicle would come his way. "Hallelujah!" he shouted, sighting the approaching glints of light. Was that a tractor? A combine? A car? Whatever it was, it was God sent.

Planting himself in the center of the narrow road, he targeted the undertaker's shotgun at the vehicle. The dazed driver's face grew larger as the rain swept truck came to an abrupt halt.

"Out! Now!" Tilden hollered, banging the Winchester Model 12 against the driver's door.

The frightened motorist, panic scaring his face, staggered out of the Chevy Silverado.

Tilden pressed the shotgun against his forehead.

"Please, Mister. I got two daughters."

"Hmmm..., I could use a female right now. Two might be better," Tilden said, bemoaning his screw up with Brianne.

"They're twins. One's mentally impaired. Under the spectrum. Ya gotta cut me some slack."

"Under the spectrum. What the hell does that mean?

"She's handicapped."

"She'll do."

"C'mon man. Have a heart."

"Time to say goodbye to your honeys," Tilden muttered, squeezing the trigger. "Fuck me," he growled, as the shotgun produced no flash. Grabbing the barrel of the Winchester, he raised it above the head of the trembling motorist. But, the distant glimmer of approaching headlights interrupted his murderous intent to repeatedly pummel the man with the rifle. "Oh, for Christ's sake," he groaned, smashing the butt of the shotgun once against the man's boney skull. "It's time to get the hell out of here," he grumbled, climbing behind the wheel of the Silverado, certain the approaching vehicle would bring trouble.

It didn't take long for him to realize his misfortune. The Chevy he'd carjacked was fully loaded. Cringing, he glared at the GPS indicator on the Silverado's electronic screen.

"You are 2.5 miles from your destination," a computerized voice sounded.

"Shut the fuck up!" he shouted.

After putting his fist through the truck's electronic screen, and brushing away shards of plastic, he yanked out the motherboard. Tossing it under the heel of his boot, he stomped on it.

Without warning, a man's voice, soft and inviting purred through the truck's radio. "Hello, sinners, this is WPLI, welcoming you to the Christian Hour. We're transmitting at 242 megahertz for those of you radio heads out there who appreciate the reach of God's message."

"What the . . .," Tilden muttered.

"Brethren, you've tuned into our Lord's broadcast. The Frequency of The Heart."

Tilden was puzzled. How had his fist of fury triggered the radio? *"I must be hallucinating?"* he reasoned. *"Too much time on the run."*

"This is Brother Justin, ushering you to the throne room of the Almighty with today's message from Saint Paul: To the church of God that is in Corinth, to those sanctified in Christ Jesus, called to be saints together with all those who in every place call upon the name of our Lord."

Hallucination or not, Saint Paul, his protector through life, had managed to get a message to him. "Halleluiah!" he shouted, for he knew now, where to find sanctuary.

"The church! Of course. The church!" he intoned.

CHAPTER NINETY-FIVE

Had the teenaged driver not swerved, he would've impaled the staggering man with the long plumbing pipe fastened to the roof of the mini pickup he was driving. "What the fuck," he hollered, stepping out into the rain.

"Some dude stole my truck! Ya' gotta help me," the stranded man begged.

"Sure! Hop in. We'll catch the bastard." The youthful driver said, kicking open the Dodge's passenger door.

"You got a phone?"

"We're in the woods. Reception sucks out here. But 911 might work." The teen handed over his Moto G Plus.

"It won't go through. It won't go through," the rain soaked victim groaned.

"Highway Patrol's got a station on I-90. We'll go there."

"Thanks a lot, man. I'm Dan. Dan Winters."

"Hector, here. Glad to help."

CHAPTER NINETY-SIX

Driscoll, inside the mobile command center, listened intently as Officer Blake Stratterly, a highway cop, detailed Dan Winter's harrowing ordeal. The other party on the three way call, Deputy Sheriff Gil Hudson, reported that a man, fitting Tilden's description, assaulted Walter Harriman, a local undertaker, at a funeral home three miles west of Everley.

Driscoll thanked the two lawmen and ended the call. He then turned his attention to Aligante and Thomlinson.

"He screwed up," the Lieutenant said, sporting an optimistic smile. "He broke into a funeral home and assaulted an undertaker. Then carjacked a Silverado."

"What year is the Silverado?" Margaret asked. "Anything after 2014 will have a GPS system."

The Lieutenant smiled.

"Ahhh, and this one had it," Thomlinson said, reading Driscoll's face.

"Score one for OnStar Navigation. Highway's recovered the truck. In a pond. Outside of Wampsville, New York. Cedric, tell me what's near that town," Driscoll ordered.

Thomlinson opened MapQuest on his iPhone. In less than a minute, he grinned "Lieutenant, you still keep that liter of Glenlivet in your travel bag."

"I do. Why?"

"Pop that cork. It's time we partied."

"Is your sponsor at AA going to be ok with that?"

"Hell, even Pete would knock one back on what I'm about to tell you."

CHAPTER NINETY-SEVEN

"Goddamn, this fucking rain!" Tilden hollered, as he labored on. He regretted leaving the Silverado half submerged in the pond. But, he was dead tired and couldn't push it in any further. He knew the GPS signal would bring that bloodhound of a Lieutenant to a dead end whether the truck was fully engulfed in mud or not. And he needed his leg muscles for one last errand as the shelter he sought was another four miles through the woodlands.

The leaves underfoot no longer crackled as he plodded through the soggy forest. The birches and oaks, poplars and ash, their foliage burdened by the incessant downpour, bent their trunks in surrender. The woods had become a marshland. He cursed at the vile puddles that pockmarked the ground, and the mud that'd infiltrated his boots, and the rain that had coated every inch of his body. He grabbed his testicles, checking to see if he still owned them. They had shrunk. Like plums to prunes, puny and decrepit. He swore loudly, blaspheming his scrawny balls, fighting the urge to gouge them out.

When he reached the edge of the forest, fog blinded his mudded eyes. Lumbering through the haze, he watched the silhouette of a diminutive structure take shape in the mist. With tears of relief flooding his penitent face, he approached the water's edge. A stone's throw in, the tiny church beckoned.

"God in heaven, I'm back," he said as he waded into the small pond.

With his arms draped over the shotgun braced across his shoulders, Tilden looked like an early Christian martyr wading through his own watery Via Dolorosa. He felt nothing when his knees crashed hard against the chapel's support column. Climbing atop the wooden deck, he knelt, his patellae making a crackling sound against the planks of weathered pine. His leaden eyes floated through the maze of names carved in the wood. Many were undecipherable, eroded beyond significance by years of cruel weather. Suddenly, three letters became crystal clear: **I L D** As memory surged, he smiled. Dragging his index finger across the markings, he thought of that scrawny ten-year-old boy who'd chiseled **T I L D E N** into the newly installed pine. Though the remainder of his name was lost to the harsh environment, his recollection of that day remained. He'd ducked out of school before the final bell on that sultry June afternoon, intent on being the first to cut his name into the newly refurbished deck. Not only had he succeeded, his remained the only inscription for nearly a week. In a way, he'd owned the sacred place.

As the thrill of the ten year old boy subsided, he righted himself, opened the weathered door, dragged his weary body inside, and allowed the darkness of the chapel to cloak him. Collapsing on the narrow pew, he sighed deeply. "I'm home. I'm home."

CHAPTER NINETY-EIGHT

Driscoll, having ended his call with Captain Cary Rawlins, the commanding officer at Oneida's Police Department, studied the faded black and white photo that he and Thomlinson had retrieved from Tilden's home.

The Lieutenant believed in the behavioral science of photo analysis. As did many forensic psychologists. Photographs were documents; archives that revealed much.

"There's no doubt in my mind I know where you are," Driscoll said, staring into the sullen face of the boy who'd become a monster seated alongside his brother on the wood pilings of the Cross Island Chapel.

"Local PD standing at the ready?" Margaret asked.

"And then some," said the Lieutenant. "The church sits fifty yards offshore. Oneida PD will dispatch a SWAT team to surround the lake. Once in place, it's show time."

"On your command?" Thomlinson asked.

"On my command."

CHAPTER NINETY-NINE

For a second time, Tilden crashed his knee into wood, this time by genuflecting on the hard oak planks of the chapel floor. The collision shot pain through the joint, unhinging the patella, straining ligaments. It was a throbbing he welcomed as part of his expiation. "I confess to Almighty God, to blessed Mary ever Virgin, to blessed Michael the Archangel, to blessed John the Baptist, to the holy Apostles Peter and Paul, to all the Saints, and to you, brethren, that I have sinned exceedingly in thought, word and deed: through my fault, through my fault, through my most grievous fault . . ."

His prayerful appeal was disrupted by a chopping sound that grew louder.

He didn't know what to make of the rattling crucifix nailed to the wall, nor of the tiny chapel's pillars when they began to quiver.

"What now?" he groaned.

As the rotors of the SWAT team's helicopter churned the night air and beams of fluorescent light seeped through the cracks in the rotting church's walls Tilden thought he may have somehow stepped onto the set of Spielberg's *Close Encounters of the Third Kind. "Was another UFO about to land in Oneida?"* he wondered.

In that moment Tilden had an out of body experience. It was surreal. It felt as though his soul was levitating. All links to his body were being severed.

"Tilden. It's over," the megaphone enhanced voice rumbled. "Step out now with your hands over your head."

"That was no alien," Tilden muttered, dispelling his nirvana.

"Come out, now. Or we're coming in," the voice boomed.

Tilden peered through a crack in the wall, spotting the black helmeted SWAT team pointing SIG Sauer assault rifles at his sanctuary. In the center was Driscoll, a man he despised. *"How the hell had he tracked me down?"* an astonished voice inside his head asked. "Son of a bitch!" he groaned.

Tilden was cornered. Literally boxed inside the small church. He wanted to comply with the policeman's last order but his legs refused his command. He needed them to get outside the chapel before the hail of bullets perforated the tiny edifice. If this was the end, and it appeared it was, he'd go out in a blast. With the butt of his shotgun, he smashed opened the door and willed his legs to carry him onto the deck incandescent with light.

Staring down the brigade of officers, he grinned. "Made it, Ma. Top o' the world!" he hollered, mimicking James Cagney in White Heat, before raising the unloaded shotgun and leveling it on the SWAT team.

Triggers were pressed. It crackled like the Fourth of July.

Tilden moaned as shards of metal bored holes through his lungs, ripped tears through his tendons, lacerated muscle, sliced through viscera, shattered bone. Yet he was still standing after the fusillade had stopped, leaving the air thick with smoke. An awkward silence had replaced the manmade thunder. And there stood Tilden, unmoving, petrified.

"Jesus Christ, with all of those hits, the guy's still standing? Looks like we've got another Freddy Krueger here," a SWAT marksman hollered, taking aim at Tilden's frontal lobe and pressing the trigger.

Tilden's head exploded like the crater of an erupting volcano. His body then slowly folded upon itself.

Though Tilden's takedown had ended Driscoll's long and arduous pursuit, the Lieutenant didn't experience the relief and satisfaction one in his position might have felt. He knew he'd be lionized by the Department and by the Press for having apprehended and terminated one of New York's most heinous killers. There would be radio and TV interviews. The City would honor him. The case would be marked closed, sealed, and buried in the archival vaults of criminal history. In the days and months to come, Driscoll's strategies would be the focus of lectures by professors at John Jay College of Criminal Justice. He'd be invited as guest of honor to many commencement exercises where he'd quote again and again 19th Century Detective Allan Pinkerton's adage, "Vice may triumph for a time, crime may flaunt its victories in the face of honest toilers, but in the end the law will follow the wrong-doer to a bitter fate."

The Lieutenant knew the public sighs of relief would be temporary because evil always metastases. So, closure eluded him. A lingering feeling of unfinished business will wake him often in the middle of the night.

Driscoll approached Tilden's remains which had been brought ashore in a small boat. His body had been mauled by a shower of bullets. A ferocious attack but not unlike the depravity he'd shown to his victims. The Lieutenant stared down at the murderer's pulverized remnants sensing an apathy which disturbed him. Here lied the bleeding body of the ghoul who had pierced the carotid artery of Sinthia Loomis to arterially embalm her while she was still alive, for Chrissake! Her only crime, perhaps, was to live a life outside the boundary of morality. But what empowered this organism to take on the role of judge, jury, and executioner? Had he felt even a tinge of compassion for the nameless Jane Doe he'd irrigated with formaldehyde before hammering 6 inch nails into her wrists and metatarsal bones and hanging her on a cross? Driscoll reflected on the sheer ferocity he'd lavished on Henrietta Strauss, the former nun who'd been charged with child abuse and manslaughter. *Had Tilden nailed her to the cross to lure me into his evil dominion?* Driscoll wondered. And Brianne Lindstrum of Fairmont, New York, who he'd garnished like a Thanksgiving fowl before shoving her inside an oven to be broiled. And who was the still unidentified female subject whose corpse was unearthed by Haverstraw and his CSI team? Why the hell was it left to decay in Tilden's backyard?

Driscoll felt he was walking amongst the dead. The deceased had a hold on him. He knew he would engage with them in interminable conversations. But first, he'd need to gain their trust, something which is built with familiarity. He would wait, knowing they would visit him in the weeks to come. For when the dead awaken they have much to say. Unannounced, at any time during the day or at night they would make their presence felt. They would ask questions. They would demand answers. They would challenge his professional conscience. Why hadn't he protected them from evil? They will feel betrayed, for as irrational as it was, he had not prevented their annihilation. Their charge would be abandonment. They will deride him, forcing him to feel the stabbing of his conscience time and time again. He'll apologize for what he hadn't done. For his delay. He'd agree with them and concede. And carry the weight of that anchor around his neck. He'd sometimes protest, claiming he did all that was humanly possible and had failed only because he'd confronted something that was not human.

Would he ever find reconciliation? He doubted he would.

For More News About Thomas O'Callaghan,
Signup For Our Newsletter:

http://wbp.bz/newsletter

Word-of-mouth is critical to an author's long-
term success. If you appreciated this book please
leave a review on the Amazon sales page:

http://wbp.bz/nowhysa

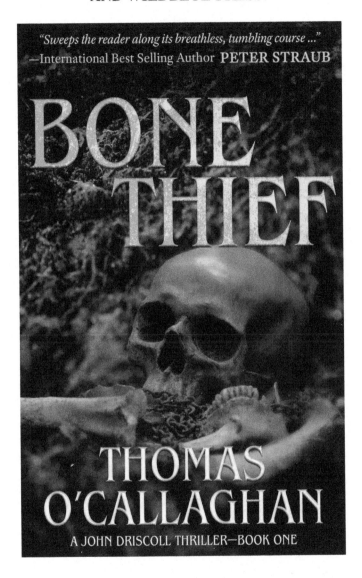

"*Sweeps the reader along its breathless, tumbling course ...*"
—International Best Selling Author **PETER STRAUB**

BONE THIEF

THOMAS O'CALLAGHAN

A JOHN DRISCOLL THRILLER—BOOK ONE

BONE THIEF by THOMAS O'CALLAGHAN

http://wbp.bz/bonethiefa

INTERNATIONAL BESTSELLING AUTHOR

JAMES BYRON
HUGGINS

DARK
VISIONS

DARK VISIONS by JAMES BYRON HUGGINS

http://wbp.bz/darkvisionsa

Thrillers and Mystery Boxsets
Available From WildBluePress

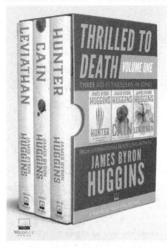

**Thrilled To Death: Volume One /
wbp.bz/thrilledtodeatha**

**Thrilled To Death: Volume Two /
wbp.bz/thrilledtodeath2a**

**Thrilled To Death: Volume Three /
wbp.bz/thrilledtodeath3a**

Murder Loves Company: Volume One / wbp.bz/mlca

See more fiction boxsets available from WildBlue Press:
wbp.bz/boxsets